FEATHER FALL

EVELYN ELLIOTT

DREAMSPINNER
PRESS

Published by
DREAMSPINNER PRESS

5032 Capital Circle SW, Suite 2, PMB# 279, Tallahassee, FL 32305-7886 USA
www.dreamspinnerpress.com

Feather Fall
© 2016 Evelyn Elliott.

Cover Art
© 2016 Christine Griffin.
alizarin_griffin@yahoo.com
http://christinegriffin.artworkfolio.com/
Cover content is for illustrative purposes only and any person depicted on the cover is a model.

ISBN: 978-1-63477-257-0
Digital ISBN: 978-1-63477-258-7
Library of Congress Control Number: 2016901413
Published April 2016
v. 1.0

Printed in the United States of America

This paper meets the requirements of
ANSI/NISO Z39.48-1992 (Permanence of Paper).

To every fan who loved Crow.

Acknowledgments

I AM amazed by the warmth and kindness of the romance community. Many people have helped me… listening to me chatter, giving me critique, or just lending me encouragement. Some of you were total strangers. Every improvement I have made, I have made because someone took me aside and offered me advice.

And thanks specifically to my wonderful betas: Anna, Lenore, and Azalea.

Chapter ONE
Kidnapped

THE MARKET was alive with color. The buildings in this part of the city were short, made of yellow sandstone, hung with banners. All the rich merchants gathered here to sell their most expensive wares. There was perfume and incense in the air. People jostled Crow as he walked, rudely pushing past him to look at market stalls.

Crow was grateful for the crowd. It made it easier to hide.

He followed his quarry carefully. He kept thirty feet away, close enough to keep track of the man but far enough back to avoid being seen.

Ahead of him, the man he was following—Regis—stopped at a market stall full of books. For a powerful sorcerer, he didn't look like much. If he put any care into his appearance at all, he would have been a remarkably attractive young man. Instead, his hair had knots and his fingers had ink stains. His shirt was half-tucked into his pants. He tied his messy hair out of his face, then rubbed his neck. He glanced in Crow's direction. His eyes were still the same steel-sharp gray that gave Crow shivers.

Crow ducked around a corner. His heart hammered.

He hadn't seen Regis in two long years. They'd parted on bad terms, and Crow didn't look forward to another confrontation. He needed a favor, though—a big favor—and he needed to talk to Regis. Soon. If he could only gather the courage.

He needed to time this perfectly. The center of Tyrigaine held a grand fountain made of an expensive man-made stone called cement. It would be the perfect place to approach him. The water cascading, the subtle mist….

Crow peeked around the corner just in time to see Regis walk into an alley. Crow followed, but when he looked into the alley, he found it empty. A street urchin sat halfway down it.

Crow bent beside him. "Excuse me. Did you see which way that redheaded man went?"

The street urchin met his eyes and said, "Got you, you weaselly son of a bitch."

An unseen force threw Crow back against the wall, pinning him there. With a flicker of silver magic, the urchin's body rippled and changed. His features became finer. His hair flushed ginger. His clothes straightened themselves.

"Regis," Crow gasped.

"I haven't quite gotten the hang of shape-shifting yet," Regis said, dusting himself off. "Tweaking my appearance is a nice trick, though. Any reason you're stalking me?"

Crow twisted. "Let me go."

"No. No, I don't think so. In fact, I have a better idea. You and I are going to find somewhere private, and then you're going to tell me where the hell you've been."

"I—"

"Don't want to? That's a pity, see, because I'm one of the most powerful sorcerers in Tyria. I could move you like a puppet. I could freeze your vocal cords. Is that what you want? You want me to drag you?"

The force released him. He fell, and Regis gripped his arm. The heartbroken nineteen-year-old boy who Crow had abandoned was long gone. Regis's mouth was an angry line. "Walk in front. If you run, I'll make you sorry. Go left from this alley, and then take a left at the fountain."

"Regis—"

"Shut up," Regis said. "We can talk once we're somewhere safe."

"SOMEWHERE SAFE" turned out to be a run-down boarding house near the gates.

An overgrown garden sprawled around it. *The Overlook*, the sign said. What did it overlook? The dirty forest, perhaps? Regis led him in, then motioned him through a door. They were alone in a large lodging room. Thick carpet, an enormous trunk, and a bed big enough for two people. Regis locked the door.

The room smelled like Regis. Old books and fresh ink. Crow shivered. "Why are we in a dusty old inn outside the city?"

Another door led outside to the garden. Regis opened it. "Chartreuse lives here."

A dragon slunk out from a grove of lilac bushes. She was roughly the size of a horse, lithe and powerful. Her yellow eyes fixed on him. Regis rubbed her behind the ears. "The innkeeper lets her stay in the garden, provided we pay double. She likes to catch animals and leave them on our doorstep. If you run, she'll catch you."

"Are you—are you threatening me?"

Regis shut the door as Chartreuse returned to her lilac bushes. "Me? Threaten you? Perish the thought. I'm just letting you know that if you decide to disappear on me again, you're going to have a hard time."

Crow had fantasized about their reunion for days. He'd pretended his old friend might be happy to see him. The truth was so much worse.

Despite the number of crimes his mother—the Flesh Witch—had committed, no one knew anything about him. There were no wanted posters with his face. There were no soldiers sent to find him. By all appearances, he did not exist. The truth was obvious: despite their nasty breakup, Regis hadn't breathed a word about him. Somewhere deep inside, Regis still cared. He had to.

Regis uncorked a bottle of wine. He poured a glass and offered it to Crow. Crow turned his head away. "Take it," Regis snapped.

Crow took it. He didn't drink.

Regis gestured. Blinds sank down from the windows. The latch turned in the door. With a wave of his hand, he lit a candle. He sank into an armchair. "Let me make this clear. I will have none of your manipulative bullshit. If you give me any trouble, I will hand you over to the authorities. You will answer my questions in a straightforward and honest manner. Got it?"

Crow shut his eyes. He nodded.

"Okay. First question. Are you in danger?"

"Yes."

"I don't mean from me," Regis said. "Are you in danger from anyone else?"

"Yes," Crow said hoarsely.

Regis drummed his fingers on the arm of the chair. "Your mother's been missing for quite a while now. No new attacks, no missing people. Is she planning some sort of attack soon?"

Crow shook his head. "I'm keeping her occupied as best I can."

"Why were you stalking me?"

"To talk to you. Please, I know you won't believe me, but—"

Regis gave him an icy look.

Crow shut his mouth.

"Okay," Regis said after a lengthy pause. "Next question. Does she know where you are?"

"No."

"She didn't send you, then?"

"I need your help," Crow said. "You're the only one I… you're the only person I can…."

He stopped there, about to admit something very dangerous.

Regis took a sharp breath. He pinched the bridge of his nose and leaned back in his chair. He looked torn. Then, seeming to come to a sudden decision, he swept to his feet, marched over, and hugged Crow awkwardly.

Crow buried his face in Regis's neck, inhaling the scent of him—clean cloth and dust, the rosemary oil he used to keep his hair in order. Had Crow been able to collapse, he would have. "Regis," he croaked. He spoke the name just to feel it in his mouth.

"I would prefer not to hurt you," Regis said quietly. "I want you to know that."

"Would prefer not to hurt me or won't hurt me?"

"Would prefer not to," Regis said after a long pause. "Where have you been? I've been looking high and low for you. You've avoided me for two years solid."

"Because my mother is dangerous!"

Regis shoved him. "No, because you've never trusted me. Not for one second. Because the moment I decided to stop being your fucktoy, you stopped caring about me at all." His voice cracked. "Crow, I thought—I thought maybe you were dead."

Crow averted his eyes. For once, he wasn't sure what to say, so he said nothing.

Regis sat down again. "I'm sorry it has to be like this."

"I'm sorry, too, sweet." Crow winced as he heard himself use a pet name. He didn't mean it. It just sort of came out. He averted his eyes. "I need your help."

"You said you were in danger?"

"Something is wrong with my mother. She's ill. The spell she used to make me is coming undone. I'm afraid that if she... if she dies...."

Regis bit his lip. "Well, good. She deserves to die."

"Regis. Please. I'm begging you. Her magic is the only thing keeping me going. You were her apprentice. You're the only one who had access to her research, her notes. You're the only one who could possibly keep me from dying with her." He sank to his knees. "I'll do whatever it takes. I'll go to prison. I'll spend the rest of my life feeding the poor. Please. Don't—don't let me die."

"How do you know the spell is breaking?"

Crow sat in the chair and lifted his shirt over his head. He could feel the feathers on his back, catching on the cloth and pulling. Cool fingertips rested on his shoulder blades, and he shuddered. "There's scales on my feet. My toenails have turned black, like talons. Some days I can't keep food down."

Regis traced the feathers and didn't say anything.

The touch sent prickles down Crow's spine. "Can you fix me?"

"I don't think you understand how difficult shape-shifting magic is. How rare you are. A living, breathing, fully functional human being created from an animal.... There's no one else like you in the world, Crow. Myra Belcane is a genius, and you were her only successful attempt. If I had her notes and some time to study them—yeah, I could fix you. Otherwise? No."

A bitter taste flooded his mouth. He turned to face Regis. "I'm dead, then."

Regis puffed up a little. "Actually, I ransacked her library the moment she disappeared. I can fix you."

"Regis!"

"Sorry. You were being a bit presumptuous, though. And I only took three of her journals. She had nearly a dozen." He fell into his armchair. "I just need to review some things."

"You've been studying her journals since...."

Regis rubbed his neck. "Since you disappeared, yes. All I have to do is recast the spell that made you. Then when Belcane dies, her spell will fade, and mine will remain. You'll become tied to me instead of her."

"How long have you been able to fix me?"

"About a year," Regis said. "You know, around the time I started searching everywhere for you."

The floorboards creaked as the lodging house began to settle in the cool afternoon.

Crow took a painful breath. "I'm sorry. I should have—"

"Come to me earlier? Yes, you should have. You idiot," Regis said, and he got up one last time to hug him. "I've missed you."

Sparks crackled as Regis worked his magic. Crow had an odd crawling sensation as the feathers on his back reformed into skin. "There," Regis said. "That should keep you human for a few days. Give me some time to look over my notes, and I'll have you right as rain in the morning." He turned his head. "We can talk about the rest of it once you're no longer dying."

A key turned in a lock. Jonathan swept into the room, shutting the door behind him. He was dressed for riding, his boots dusty, his sword at his hip. "Alain said you brought a black-haired man to the room," he said breathlessly.

Regis smirked. "I caught him. He was stalking me again. The shape-shifting trick we discussed worked." He kissed Jonathan on the cheek.

Jonathan wrapped an arm around Regis's waist. He glanced at Crow. His jaw flexed.

"White," Crow said.

"Belcane."

"Don't call me that."

"Did you get anything out of him?" Jonathan asked Regis.

"A few things. We should talk." He steered Jonathan toward the door.

Jonathan dug in his heels. He gripped Regis's wrist. "Do you really think we should leave him alone?"

"Chartreuse is outside. He won't try to leave. Crow, stay here. Put your shirt back on. All right?"

Crow ground his teeth. "Fine."

Jonathan stepped into the hall with Regis. They shut the door.

Crow sat heavily on the bed and put his head in his hands. Quietly, the voices of the men outside rose. Too faint to make out words, but the tone was low and hurried. Were they hugging? Kissing? Crow's heart twisted. He laced his fingers together, and he began to plot. If Regis could fix him, then maybe it was still possible to get a happy ending out of this. Maybe he could get Regis back.

But first, he needed to get rid of Jonathan.

REGIS PUSHED Crow and Jonathan out the door. "Neither of you are allowed to bother me," he called after them. "Jonathan, watch Crow. Crow, no plotting."

Crow headed downstairs into the common room. A dozen or so lodgers had returned for the evening, and they were eating and drinking noisily. He sidled up to a gaggle of drunk women and struck up a conversation. They were kind enough to sit with him, and he repaid them with jokes and flattery. After ten minutes, they paid for his meal, then bought him a drink.

He needed to get Regis alone again. He'd never put much stock in love or stupid promises, but if it meant getting Regis back, maybe it would be worth it. He needed to tell Regis how much he cared. What was so special about Jonathan, anyway?

As someone passed by, Crow heard them say, "Is the sorcerer alone?"

Crow glanced over. The speaker was a bald man. "Alone," said a second man beside him.

"Finally. And the dragon is gone as well?"

"Just left. Every evening, like clockwork."

One of his new friends noticed his confused look. She leaned over. "There's a dragon out back normally," she whispered loudly. "It goes hunting this time of night." Crow patted her arm and craned around to look. The bald man handed the innkeeper a purse, and the innkeeper passed back a key.

Huh.

Crow showed the women a knife trick, tossing it, rolling it over his hand, and catching it again. The men filed into the hallway. Something felt wrong. "Excuse me," Crow said, sheathing the knife. He laced between tables toward the hall. With each step his heart sped up.

Paranoia, Crow scolded himself. Who would want to hurt Regis? He hurried anyway. The men had vanished, and Regis's door was closed. He rattled the doorknob. Locked.

"Get your hand off the door," said a voice behind him. Crow whirled. Jonathan stood there, arms crossed.

"I want to check on something," Crow said. "You have a key, right?" Jonathan rolled his eyes and turned to go. "No, wait! Listen. I think some men went in there. Armed men."

"You're so full of shit," Jonathan said. "All you want to do is get him alone so you can weasel your way back into his pants. You don't care if it ruins him, do you?"

"Give me the fucking key."

Jonathan held up the key. He made a rude gesture, then turned to leave. Crow dove for it. He grabbed Jonathan's wrist, and Jonathan shoved him back.

Crow tackled him. They wrestled on the floor, hands in each other's clothing.

Jonathan grabbed Crow's arms, dragged him upright, and shoved him against the wall. He wrenched Crow's arms behind his back and pinned him there. "Let me make this clear," Jonathan breathed in his ear. "I've kept my mouth shut because Regis insists you're a decent person. But give me one reason, Belcane, one damned reason, and I will turn you over to the City Watch. I'll tell them everything. Maybe they'll lock you up. Maybe they'll turn you over to the queen. Maybe they'll give you to a sorcerer for experiments. Want to find out?"

"Fuck you."

A crash came from inside Regis's room.

Both of them tensed at the same time.

Jonathan dropped Crow, shoved the key in the lock, then threw the door open. Three armed men stood in the room. The largest had Regis forced against the wall, one hand holding his hands behind his back. He held an open vial beneath Regis's nose, and he had somehow gotten a collar around Regis's throat.

The man let go. Regis staggered, then fell to his knees. He looked at Crow, gaze focused on the middle distance. His eyes rolled up in his head, and he collapsed.

The largest man snatched Regis up and threw him over his shoulder. He unlatched the window and tossed Regis into the arms of another man waiting outside.

Crow reacted first. He shoved past the first man and darted after the second, vaulting over the sill and landing in the garden. His target was already two dozen feet away, throwing Regis over a horse.

Crow reached the man in seconds. He sank the knife into the man's thigh, but as he did, the man spurred the horse forward. The knife tore out. The man gasped and cursed as he rode away.

Crow tried to shift into a bird. Agony shot through him, and he staggered. Instead of his usual instantaneous change, the shifting was slow and painful. There was no time to force it. He let himself remain human.

Crow glanced around, then ran to a passerby atop a horse. He grabbed her arm. "Get off," he said, showing her the bloody knife. "Now."

She spat at him and slid off the horse. He swung his leg over and dug his heels in.

The kidnapper rode into the city gates. Crow's horse refused to follow his directions no matter how hard he tugged the reins. He slapped the horse's ass, then felt incredibly stupid when it did nothing. So he stumbled off the horse and ran. By the time he reached the gates, the kidnapper was gone. Was that him disappearing into an alley? Crow followed, but the alley forked.

Panic settled in. He spun in a circle. Was this some sick joke? Who would take Regis?

He wandered. Night fell, and the city's inhabitants began to trickle home. Two women passed him by on a street corner. "Slavers are at it again," said one. "I hear they grabbed that redheaded sorcerer."

Despite the warm summer night, Crow suddenly felt frozen.

In time, he found his way back to the inn. Guards surrounded the building. Crow slipped in, then stopped once he saw a familiar shock of blond hair resting on a table. Jonathan sat in a corner, tankard in hand.

Crow tapped him on the shoulder. Jonathan squinted up at him. "Crow? Where…." He surged upright, looking around.

"The rider got away. Who were those people?"

Jonathan's eyes narrowed. He looked at Crow with sheer hatred. "How should I know?"

"Are you suggesting I'm involved in this?"

"Real convenient, isn't it?"

"Convenient," Crow said. His anger boiled over. "*Convenient*. I need his help, and someone kidnaps him. Are you insane? He agreed to fix the spell on me. Everything was going to be fine. Everything was going to be fine! You think I've been avoiding you two for the past couple years? I've been following you. Through the countryside. Across rooftops. Making sure Regis is safe. If I wanted you dead, you'd be dead. If I wanted you separated, you'd be separated. You know what would be convenient for me? If my best friend wasn't fucking kidnapped!"

They stared at each other stonily. Jonathan's eyes were bloodshot.

Jonathan grimaced. "I've been sitting here for the past hour trying to figure out why you'd do this, and I can't think of a single reason that makes sense."

"Exactly," Crow said.

"You've never made any sense, though," Jonathan said.

Crow ignored that remark. He sat down. "We need a plan. If we act smart, work together, and move quickly, maybe…."

"Maybe what? Regis's body will still be warm when we find it?" Jonathan thunked his head back on the table. "Ancestors. Who did we piss off? I mean, I know Regis and I have enemies, but… I can't think of anyone who would do something like this."

"The two kidnappers I left with you," Crow said quietly. "Did you kill them?"

Jonathan started to answer, but then one of the guards—an officer— stopped by. "Can't do anything for you," the officer said. "Sorry, but there's no one left to interrogate. We've taken care of the man you killed. You won't be arrested. The state of your room and the loss of your partner makes it clear what happened here, Sir White."

"Slavers," Crow said suddenly. "I heard a passerby talking about—"

The officer ignored him and left.

Jonathan opened his eyes again. His irises were a sharp contrast against the reddened whites. "They're useless. They never deal with anything." He pushed himself off the table and staggered to his feet. "Fuck it. Come with me." He led Crow down the hall and unlocked the room. Instead of opening the door, though, he leaned back and peered around. There was no one in sight.

He opened the door and ushered Crow in. He locked the deadbolt.

The room had been superficially cleaned. Blood wiped but not scrubbed; bodies absent; furniture righted. Jonathan went to a large trunk in the corner and unlocked it. A man—thickly gagged, bleeding from the head, hands bound—lay inside.

Crow jerked back. "Good gods, White."

"They would've arrested him," Jonathan said. "Help me, will you?" Together, he and Crow hauled the man out and set him on the bed. "Can you write?" Jonathan asked the man.

The man nodded.

"Good. If you scream, we'll cut out your tongue." Jonathan slit through the gag. "He might know where Regis is," he said to Crow. "For all the good it does us."

"Us," Crow echoed. He walked to the bound man, footsteps impossibly loud. Distantly, he could hear the chatter of the street. "What do you think we should do?"

We.

Jonathan hunched his shoulders. "I'm not torturing anyone."

Crow thought of Regis, alone and terrified. Imprisoned. In pain. He took a breath to brace himself. "Give me a few minutes alone with him."

Jonathan's eyes met his. "A moment alone." He scrubbed a hand through his hair. "All right. Just don't kill him." He got up.

"Help me get him into that chair before you go."

Crow held a knife at the man's throat while Jonathan bound the man to the armchair. Once the man was secure—ankles tied to the legs, wrists tied to the arms—Jonathan left. Crow waited until his footsteps had faded, then pulled up the other chair. He sat back-to-front, facing the man. "What's your name?"

The man licked his lips. "Cl-Clyde."

"It's a pleasure to meet you, Clyde. Have you ever heard of a witch named Myra Belcane?" He smiled. "Of course you have. Terror of the kingdom. Vanished a while ago. I'm her son."

Clyde's face went white. "Her s-son?"

"In a manner of speaking, yes. She created me from magic, a bird, bits of her own blood and bone."

"But that's—"

"Impossible, yes, I know. It's amazing what a sorceress can do when her research isn't hindered by law. Alas, my poor mother is ill. Now the spell that created me is breaking apart. There's only one man skilled enough to fix me, and you snatched him from my fingers the moment I grew close." His voice lowered. "That man was my dearest childhood friend. Ask yourself this, Clyde: What do you think I'd do to get him back?"

Crow shifted partway. Just enough to make his face look monstrous. His nose flattened to nothing. His fingers curved like talons. His skin bleached white as paper. The whites of his eyes disappeared, leaving him with two black pits.

Clyde began to shake.

"They say you need to enjoy torture to be good at it," Crow said. "I disagree. My mother wasn't sadistic—merely practical. When she needed to know something, she always found out."

He drew a knife from his boot. One edge was serrated, perfect for sawing through things. "I hated her," he said. "You know what a conscience is, Clyde? Empathy? She took it from me. Slowly, I watched her take it from Regis as well. I wanted so desperately to save him that every night I would lie awake, plotting my mother's death. I became very inventive."

Clyde couldn't seem to speak. He stared into Crow's black eyes.

"For example," Crow said, "I know that if I tie tourniquets on your arms before I shave away your fingers, you will not die an easy death of blood loss. I know that if I gouge out your eyes, I should pour salt and vinegar in the wounds to prevent an infection that might otherwise take you from me. I know how to make you last, and while I am not a sadist, I *am* practical."

Clyde's jaw locked. He stared wide-eyed into the middle distance.

Crow shoved the torn gag back into Clyde's mouth. Then he drew a knife and sank it into Clyde's hand. The wide blade cleanly severed his smallest finger, and Clyde shrieked into the gag. Crow helped muffle it with his hand.

"Now," Crow said. "Tell me what your friend did with Regis, and you can keep the rest of your fingers."

The man seemed entirely incapable of speaking. Crow cinched a cloth around the little stump, tamping down on the blood flow.

The door creaked open, and Crow glanced back. Jonathan shut the door and locked it. He stopped when he saw the finger lying on the floor, then glanced at Crow. He grimaced but said nothing. He handed Crow a flask.

Crow untied the gag from Clyde's mouth. He offered the flask. "Dry mouth?"

"S-slavers," said the man.

"Slavers," Crow said. "What slavers?"

"The H-House of Red Silk. The boss tells us who to grab."

"Your boss. Who is he?"

The man's eyes darted to Jonathan, then back to Crow. "The bald-headed man. The, the one you killed, Sir White."

Crow sat back on the bed. "The House of Red Silk, hm?"

"They sell people," Jonathan said. "High-priced sex slaves, mostly, but sorcerers as well. Queen Isolde has been trying to tamp down on slavery, but the nobles are resistant. The wealthy are all in on it. The guards refuse to do anything."

"So, what, you started bothering these slavers? Tried to handle them yourself?"

"I asked around a little, yeah. You think this is my fault?"

Hesitantly, a voice spoke up. "Well, it's not anyone's fault. The boss said—he said this boy of yours was a strong one. Not a beauty, but nice to look at. He'll fetch a high price."

Crow and Jonathan looked at Clyde.

"Jus' sayin'," Clyde said.

Jonathan rose to his feet and clapped Clyde on the shoulder. "Come on, Clyde. Let's get you somewhere safe."

JONATHAN DRAGGED Clyde down the middle of the street, waltzed right up to the prison, and—after a polite chat with two City Watch thugs—walked right off again. "Did you tell them what happened?" Crow asked when Jonathan came back over.

Jonathan shrugged. "I said they missed one."

"And they believed you?"

"I'm a knight," Jonathan said, as if that explained everything.

They passed through the market district. Crow's eyes fell on a shelf full of round crystals the size of his thumb, carved to look like eyeballs. He reached out, and the merchant slapped his hand away. He gave the merchant an injured look.

"If we're going to get into this House of Red Silk place, you need to look more respectable," Jonathan said. "You know. Less like a thieving whore."

Crow glanced down at himself. He wore his favorite tunic—thin, purple, sleeveless. An unusual style he thought was quite dashing. The open design kept him cool, and the thin hood kept the sun from his eyes. "No," he said suddenly. "I have an idea. A fantastic idea."

Jonathan gave him a deeply suspicious look.

"Let's break in," Crow said. "We'll pretend to be slavers. One of us will play master, and the other his slave. We'll ask for a sorcerer—"

"I'm not pretending to be your slave."

Trust Jonathan to pick the position of obvious power. Slavery was the better choice. A slave could move unnoticed. Noticing that the merchant was fussing over another customer, Crow pocketed one of the eye-shaped crystals. He put a scowl on his face. "Fine," he said, "but you owe me."

Jonathan frowned at him.

"Look, if you don't want to do it, fine," Crow said. "But I'm not going to be your slave for free."

Jonathan pulled him into an alley. He pushed back Crow's hood, then tilted Crow's chin. Their faces were inches apart.

Crow flattened himself against the wall. He hadn't been this close to anyone in a very long time. Maybe he shouldn't have been so cruel to Jonathan. "What are you doing?"

"Your eyes. They've gone hazel."

"Hazel?" He took out a small mirror he kept tucked into his waist.

"You keep a mirror with you?" Jonathan said incredulously. Crow ignored him. Despite the shadowed alley, he could see that yes, his eyes had changed color. He tucked the mirror away, then rolled the crystal eye around in his pocket.

He offered the crystal to Jonathan. The moment Jonathan took it, his blue eyes turned brown. "Huh," Crow said. "Have mine turned black again?"

"Yeah. Mine changed color?"

"Yes."

Jonathan slipped the crystal into his pocket. "We need disguises. I do, at least. I have a small reputation. These slavers might recognize me, especially if they've been keeping tabs on Regis. And you... you need to look like a sex slave."

At a bathhouse, they paid a man to file the calluses off Jonathan's hands and soften them with lotion. They bought secondhand boots, soft brown with branded designs. Three vests, none of which were quite the right size. Jonathan paid a seamstress a hefty fee to modify them overnight.

Slave clothing was easier to find. They bought what they could—another hooded tunic and some tight breeches, then two sheets of silk meant to tie around the hips. Jonathan's purse looked noticeably smaller, but he didn't seem to care.

Near the end of the day, they passed a shabby shop marked with an eye symbol. The sign said *Strange Solutions*. Crow motioned Jonathan in. "That scar on your mouth is too recognizable. We should get rid of it."

Jonathan grimaced. Some unknown thing seemed to hold him back. He ran his fingers over the ridge. After several moments, though, he grudgingly went into the shop.

The old sorceress inside was eager to take their money. Jonathan stood rigid as she touched his lips and faded the scar. "Could you grow his hair as well?" Crow asked.

"Oh, yes." The sorceress ran her fingers through Jonathan's hair, and the length grew three inches, giving Jonathan a total of four.

"Color it too," Jonathan said. "Dark brown."

Crow sighed and gave her two silver from his own purse. The sorceress brought out a pouch, then tossed it to Jonathan. "Magic really isn't the way to go with hair color," she said. "Dye is better."

CROW'S FEET ached. When they got back to the lodging house, he kicked off his boots, then ran a hand through his hair. He spied a comb by a mirror. He untangled his hair and swept it over one shoulder. Tried a smile. It didn't fit his mouth today. He pinned on his favorite sapphire earring.

A servant dragged in a wooden tub. A second servant followed with buckets of steaming water. It took them several trips to fill the bath.

Jonathan leaned next to the door and crossed his arms. "Where did you get that?"

"The earring? It's mine."

"Regis used to wear one exactly like it. He lost it shortly after you disappeared," Jonathan said. Crow made a vague noise. Realization crossed Jonathan's face. "You stole it, didn't you?"

"I gave it to him," Crow said. "He didn't want it, so I took it back."

Jonathan gave him a sharp look. "You tracked us down, stole it, and then left? You could've used the time to tell him you were all right. That you weren't lying in a ditch somewhere."

"Shouldn't you be glad he cast me off?"

"First of all, he didn't cast you off. He stopped sleeping with you. You left. Secondly—" Crow opened his mouth to argue. "*Secondly*," Jonathan said, "if you gave it to him, then you had no right to take it back. No, I don't like your bizarre friendship with Regis, but I also don't like waking up in the middle of the night to find my partner is having night terrors because he's afraid his best friend is dead."

Crow winced. He'd stayed away because he had to, because it was better for everyone involved. There was no point in explaining that, though. So instead he said, "The bath is done."

"So it is."

Jonathan stripped off his shirt. He was a handsome creature, for sure. It was a pity that such symmetrical features were wasted on such a violent man. He sat on a stool next to the water and dunked in his head. "Give me that dye, will you?"

Crow took out the pouch. He took a handful, then—without thinking—he rubbed it into Jonathan's hair.

Jonathan went rigid.

Crow went rigid too.

He was faced with a decision: either stop and hand Jonathan the dye or pretend there was nothing weird about this. Crow began working his fingers again, moving in circles against Jonathan's scalp, and Jonathan let out a long breath, rolling his shoulders. "I… that feels good," Jonathan said helplessly.

"Mm." Crow carded his fingers through Jonathan's hair, scrubbing in the powder. A trail of dye seeped down Jonathan's neck. Crow quickly rinsed off his hands, coloring the water. "You should get in. The dye might take to your skin a little. Couldn't hurt."

Jonathan sighed. Gingerly, he sat up, then pulled off his breeches. Crow stepped around the partition before they came off completely. He collapsed on the bed and closed his eyes.

Maybe he should strip and join Jonathan. If he could prove to Regis that love was stupid and that Jonathan was unfaithful, then perhaps Regis would come back to him. Except Crow wasn't sure he wanted that. Not the heartbroken look on Regis's face—not the crying he'd do—not the way Regis would ignore him for… weeks, likely.

Besides, Jonathan would probably just punch him.

After a while, Jonathan stepped out from around the partition, toweling off his hair. "Did the dye take?" he asked, hanging the cloth over a chair. He picked up the crystal from where it lay on the bed with his clothes.

Jonathan was remade. The dark hair made his skin seem brown rather than tanned. With the crystal, his eyes were dark. Even his lips seemed like a new color. He no longer looked like the man who was Regis's lover. He looked like someone else entirely. Like a young nobleman. Like one of Crow's many meaningless sex partners. He jerked back. "You look—really different."

"No shit," Jonathan said.

Wordlessly, Crow gestured to the mirror.

Jonathan's lips parted as he looked. "The people of the North are of two kinds," he eventually said. "Pale-skinned *hvitr* and brown-skinned *kahad*. We're mostly mix blooded now. My father was white and my mother was dark." He studied himself. "The dark hair casts me in a new light. Makes me favor my mother's heritage."

"Your skin is naturally that color? I thought you were just tan."

"Not everyone is born snow-white like you."

The change was an illusion, Crow reminded himself. This was still the deadly vigilante who had nearly killed him.

Jonathan had stories about himself. Wild tales about how he'd beaten the Flesh Witch. How he'd fed an entire band of raiders to his dragon. How his dragon roasted his enemies alive. People liked melodrama. They were good stories, but Crow didn't want to become another piece of fiction. He shuddered. Crow Belcane, the shape-shifter who plucked the eyes from merchants and stole innocence from boys.

Jonathan rifled through their purchases. He selected one of Crow's sleeveless tunics and a pair of tight cotton breeches. It was the sort of outfit a sex slave would wear in public, loose and slinky but tight in the right places. He tossed them to Crow.

"Picking out my clothes for me?" Crow asked dryly.

Jonathan selected a red vest with gold buttons for himself. "Get used to it. We need to fit you with cuffs." He looked away. "We need to—mark you too."

Crow turned his back, unlacing his clothes and casting them aside. A tunic hit him in the head from behind, and he scowled, glancing back at Jonathan. Jonathan was already bossing him around, huh?

He could put it on, or he could leave it.

Reject Jonathan's choice or accept his control.

Crow tossed the tunic aside, then selected his own. He felt Jonathan watching him. He laced up his pants but remained barefoot. "Pull back your hair," Jonathan said. "It'll get in the way at the blacksmith."

It was a decent idea. Without acknowledging that Jonathan had spoken, Crow braided his hair loosely, pulling it over one shoulder. He tied the end with a golden thread.

Evening had come, and a breeze drifted from the open window. The flowers outside had bloomed, scenting the air with jasmine and magnolia. He remembered hugging Regis. The feel of him. The overwhelming rush of familiarity. "Where can we find cuffs?" he eventually asked.

JONATHAN TOOK him to the pleasure district. They stopped by a blacksmith, where a row of cuffs lay—some plain, some so intricate Crow doubted they could actually restrain anyone. Each had a single ring. An easy way for a master to chain his property.

Jonathan spoke to the blacksmith while Crow looked at the wares. The cuffs made of interlocked wire strands looked uncomfortable. The thick cuffs seemed boring. There, that bronze pair—they were medium weight, beaten from a single sheet of metal. Someone had cut designs into them. They were a lacework of metal.

They'd be heavy on his wrists. He'd have to get used to them... and get used to the idea of obeying Jonathan. The cuffs wouldn't have chains, normally, but they had rings that could easily fit chains. If he misbehaved, Jonathan might punish him by locking his wrists behind his back.

Jonathan wouldn't intentionally try to fuck with him, would he? Probably not. They were allies, now. But Crow might slip up, and then....

Then Jonathan might be forced to discipline him.

A weird thrill went through him at that idea. Crow chalked it up to nerves. When Jonathan returned, Crow only glanced up for a moment before staring at the cuffs again. "Those," Jonathan said to the blacksmith. "The ones he's looking at."

The blacksmith was a heavily muscled man with a soot-streaked beard. He nodded politely to Crow as Jonathan steered his new slave into the forge. A furnace lit the room. A metal table stood nearby.

"Down," Jonathan said. Crow hesitated, but, obediently, he bent over the table. Jonathan took Crow's arm, then extended it. Manacles fit around his forearms, bolting him to the metal. Crow shut his eyes as the slave cuff was put around his wrist, then beaten shut.

Permanent. For now.

"A pretty one," the blacksmith remarked. "Just got him, did you?"

Shifting footsteps behind him. "Do you do brands?"

Crow sucked in his breath. He glanced back, but couldn't see Jonathan, couldn't protest, couldn't move. "Yes," the blacksmith said. "If you want a personalized one, that'll take time, though. Or if you'd like, we have some simple shapes. People usually use those to form their own mark."

Jonathan ran his hands along a row of brands lying on a table not far away. He picked one up. "This will do." It was a simple shape, a spiral with a long straight end.

The blacksmith brought out a thick strip of leather, then offered it to Jonathan. Jonathan bent. The gag touched Crow's lips, and Crow's gaze flickered up. He opened his mouth, and Jonathan shoved it in. Crow bit. Jonathan fastened the ends behind Crow's head, and the leather pulled tight, catching in his hair.

Jonathan rested the brand over the fire.

A cold sweat broke out over Crow's body, and the truth of what was about to happen to him sank in. He hadn't protested when they had bolted him down, and he hadn't protested the gag, and now he was restrained like a dumb animal. The end of the brand began to glow. He took a breath around the leather, saliva leaking from the corner of his mouth. He wouldn't scream.

Jonathan's finger traced a pattern in the soot. Three swirls, each connected to a common center point. He picked up the brand. "Three times, I think," Jonathan said. "A triskele." He moved out of sight behind Crow.

A hand pressed into the small of Crow's back, holding him flat. The brand seared into him. He screamed.

Chapter TWO
Slave

As THEY walked to the House of Red Silk the next day, Crow winced as if the brand still stung. They had visited a healer to scar it over. He was probably faking, Jonathan decided. Crow was that sort of person.

"Maybe we should just break in," Crow muttered.

"We can try that later."

"You mean once we foul this up?"

"Yeah," Jonathan said. "You know. Like a backup plan."

The House of Red Silk stood at the end of the street, a tall sandstone building draped with banners. Incense wafted from the open entrance where two guards stood. Jonathan leaned to speak in Crow's ear. "Keep your head down and do as I say." He padded up the steps, barely glancing at the guards as he moved toward the doorway.

The right guard let him go. The left snatched at Jonathan's arm. "Where do you think you're going?"

"I think I'm going in," Jonathan said. "Unhand me."

"Only known patrons are allowed."

Jonathan motioned Crow over. "This is my—" His fucktoy? His slave? "My pet," he decided on. "Crow, show them."

Crow pulled back his sleeve. The cuff gleamed against his pale skin.

There was a beat of silence as the guard looked at the cuff, then at Crow.

The silence stretched on too long, and bit by bit, Jonathan's heartbeat picked up speed. This was a mistake. A huge mistake. Slaves were a luxury and were typically confined to their owner's estates, toiling in the back fields. Sex slaves rarely left their owner's bedroom. A slave would not be traveling alone with his master, unrestrained, in the midst of a great city.

Jonathan put on his best snobby face and stared the guard down. Calm. Stay calm. He could do this.

"Oh, Garlant! You silly man. Let them in," called a female voice. A woman sashayed through the door. Her heavy silk clothing shushed against the floor as she walked. "I'm so sorry. My guards are instructed to keep out strangers. Our products are outrageously valuable, you know." She circled around Crow. "What a lovely specimen! You're here to sell?"

"To buy," Jonathan said.

"He's not enough for you?"

Her voice was full of coy implication. Jonathan grimaced. He couldn't stop himself. Her expression immediately became curious. "You're not lovers?" she asked.

Crow slipped her a teasing smile. "I have many talents, my lady."

Her gaze shifted between them.

From an aesthetic standpoint, Jonathan could tell she was attractive. She had a small, perfect mouth, coated with lip-paint. Tyrians wore cosmetics—men and women alike—a practice that Jonathan thought was particularly weird. This one had caked her entire face in skin-colored powder. Why, he could not fathom. It didn't make her look more beautiful. It only made her look like she was wearing paint.

"I am Madam Karis, owner of this establishment," she said. "May I have your name?"

"Murtagh," Jonathan said. "Just Murtagh."

"Ah. Are you related to Jarl Murtagh?"

Damn. "You know Northern nobility?"

"Of course," she said. "I know everyone. How is your father?"

Jonathan racked his mind. The Murtaghs lived a thousand miles away in the mountains, which was to his advantage. The entire clan was a bunch of bigoted thugs, and none of them would be caught dead with a pretty boy like Crow. "Jarl Murtagh isn't my father. Only a cousin."

"It's good to meet you, Lord Murtagh." She motioned them in. They passed through the foyer and into an atrium lined with pillars. A mosaic of broken glass formed the ceiling, throwing colored light on the floor where the sun hit. Against the wall hung polished chains and empty manacles. Wrought-iron benches lined the room. Jonathan searched desperately for Regis.

"An empty room?" he said.

"It's for large exhibitions. What kind of slave are you looking for?"

"A sorcerer."

"We have a female that just came in."

"Male."

"Male," she echoed doubtfully. "Well, I'll see."

Jonathan felt his face flush angrily, and he opened his mouth to speak. Crow clasped his hand and squeezed sharply.

Sorcerers were valuable, and they rarely made their way into slavery. If Madam Karis was pretending she had no male sorcerers in stock, it was only so she could gouge them for coin later.

"Does appearance matter to you?" Karis said.

Jonathan bit the inside of his cheek. He could have described every individual freckle on Regis's body. "I prefer the practical over the ornamental," he said instead. "Someone powerful. Really powerful. Doesn't matter what he looks like."

"And yet this is your pet." Karis looked at Crow with cool consideration, like one might examine a morsel of dessert.

Crow smiled shyly, as if embarrassed. "Well… my master is human. Anyone can be moved by a pretty face."

They emerged into a second, smaller room. The incense was thicker here. Karis guided them to a low couch. "Wait here," she said, and left.

Jonathan watched from the corners of his eyes as Crow arranged himself on the couch. Crow wore cosmetics as well, but more subtly. Powder dusted his skin, hiding imperfections. A golden necklace, thin as a thread, drew attention to his fine neck. Soft gray framed his eyes.

Jonathan had never particularly liked vain men. They took too much work. Crow was exceptionally good at looking pretty, and yet he was the most dangerous criminal Jonathan had ever met. Maybe that's why Jonathan disliked cosmetics so much. Properly applied, they could hide a predator.

Crow leaned over. His lips touched Jonathan's ear, and Jonathan's skin prickled. "One of the guards grabbed my ass as we walked in," Crow murmured.

Jonathan swallowed. From an outsider's perspective, the whispered conversation probably looked like a heart-to-heart between lovers. "So?"

"So he did it when you weren't looking. Isn't that creepy?"

"You can handle yourself."

Crow's voice was a breathy whisper, now. "We need a plan. What happens when she brings out our dear friend?"

"I'm figuring this out as we go."

One of the guards kept staring at Crow. He wet his lips lasciviously, raking his eyes up and down Crow's body. Jonathan sort of pitied him. The poor idiot didn't know he was eye-fucking the son of the Flesh Witch.

Crow settled closer. "I'm going on an errand. To get you a goblet of wine, or… something."

"And where are you really going?"

"Exploring."

Crow's jewelry made little noise as he slipped away. The creepy guard followed him a moment later. Crow's jangling footfalls faded, and so did the guard's boot steps. Jonathan leaned back on the couch. He drummed his fingers on the armrest. Yeah, the guard was definitely after Crow.

Poor guard, Jonathan decided. Crow was a viper. Any idiot stupid enough to threaten him would be bitten.

Except Crow couldn't defend himself right now. Crow was pretending to be a slave. Jonathan grimaced, thinking over his options.

Then he rose to his feet and followed.

The door led to an empty hallway. At the end, it intersected with another hall. Voices came from around the bend. One of them was the guard's. The other was Crow's. Jonathan pressed himself against the wall, inching nearer. "My master expects me back soon," said Crow's voice.

Crow sounded—

Frightened?

"Come on, now," said the guard. "You got a few minutes."

"Get out of my way."

"Where you going, pretty?"

A scuffle. "Let go of—"

"I could throw you out."

Sudden silence.

"We're customers," Crow said.

"You're a slave. You don't wanna cause trouble, do you? Your master will be pissed if there's a commotion. The madam will be angry too. Could tell her you caused me trouble. Could tell her I caught you sneaking around. It might ruin the sale. Come on. I'll be quick. It'll be easier if you give in." And Crow was quiet for a moment, a long moment, and Jonathan knew he was considering it.

"My master—" Crow said.

"He doesn't even like you, does he? He sat on the other side of the couch. I bet you need a good fuck."

Jonathan stepped loudly around the corner.

The guard had Crow by the wrist and by the hair. Crow's face was white beneath the powder. Cold fury took hold of Jonathan. He hated Crow, true, but the idea of laying hands on someone who was defenseless—

He didn't have a weapon with him. He scanned the room, then briefly decided on beating the man senseless with his bare hands. It was the only option. He glanced at the guard, and their eyes met.

The guard's wide smile slowly faded, and he took a step back, still holding on to Crow. Crow twisted. "Let go of me, damn you."

"In a moment," the guard growled.

Crow's expression was impossible to read. His eyes flickered from Jonathan to the guard. "Master, please go enjoy yourself with Madam Karis. I'm sure she has more slaves for you to see. I have this under control. We don't need to cause a commotion."

Jonathan ignored Crow. To the guard, he said, "Let go of my property."

The guard glared at him stonily.

"Let go of my property, or I'll break your jaw," Jonathan said.

The guard let go of Crow, shoved him forward, and Crow stumbled. Jonathan steadied him.

Crow's arm felt nothing like Regis's: no boniness, just lean muscle. He dropped it as if he'd touched something unpleasant. Then, because they were being watched, he put a hand in the small of Crow's back, turning and guiding him back down the hall.

The guard sneered. "You ain't fucking him. It's a waste. You need to learn t'be hospitable."

Jonathan whirled, and the man backed away. "No one *fucks him* but me."

The guard, grumbling, left. Jonathan and Crow held there, still touching, until at last his footsteps faded to nothing. They stepped away from one another.

Crow smoothed his clothes. "Thank you," he muttered.

They slipped back into the lounge. Jonathan sat against one armrest. Crow paused. He had an odd expression on his face. Consideration and… something else.

Jonathan pulled him into his lap.

Crow tensed. Then, forcefully, his entire body relaxed, pressing against Jonathan. Jonathan pushed him so that they were sprawled on the couch, Crow lying against his chest. He was calm. He was in control. He carded his fingers through Crow's hair.

Crow coiled an arm around Jonathan's neck. He leaned up. "Put your hand on my thigh," he said in Jonathan's ear.

The incense thickened. The smell made Jonathan dizzy. Was it laced with something? A servant passed through, offering wine. When he waved her away, she gave Crow a jealous look.

Jonathan shut his eyes. He thought of Regis. Regis was a surprisingly uncomplicated lover. He had no odd fetishes or kinks. He was highly motivated by orgasms and knew exactly how he liked them best: on Jonathan's lap, controlling the pace, biting his lip as he jerked himself off.

That strategy backfired on Jonathan immediately. Arousal shot through him, and he shifted. He was half-hard in moments. Crow didn't react. Had he noticed?

Crow didn't look the same as he had two years ago. Before, he'd moved with a careless grace. Now every movement was calculated. He watched the room like a cornered animal; he had an aura of wariness, even during relaxed moments. What had his mother done to him?

"That guard is staring again," Crow murmured.

Jonathan wrapped an arm around Crow's waist. He could barely tolerate being this close to him. It reminded him of the time Crow knocked him unconscious, tied him up, and threatened to skin him. He shoved aside those feelings. He stared the guard down.

What if the guard suspected the truth? Apparently he wasn't doing a good enough job of pretending Crow was his lover. Gods. Jonathan began to calculate the risks of what they were doing. If Madam Karis had the power to kidnap sorcerers and sell them—sorcerers, who were often in the public eye, who were dangerous—then he and Crow were in a great deal of danger right now. They were standing in her base of operations, after all. With a wave of her hand, she could have them dragged away and chained with the rest of the slaves. No one would come after them. She would sell them to some rich master miles away, and he would never see Regis again.

Karis swept into the room alone. Scuffling noises came from the door behind her. "You asked for the strongest," Karis said. "Behold. The newest addition to my flock. Magic more powerful than any you've ever seen."

Jonathan twisted around. He had left his sword back at the inn, but it didn't matter. He didn't care. If this were Regis, he would fight them all bare-handed. All he had to do was get the collar off Regis, and then Regis could more or less rescue himself.

The woman motioned toward the door, and two guards dragged the slave in.

Jonathan's heart nearly stopped. Ginger hair. Bony frame.

Then the slave stood upright, and Jonathan's heart sank back down. The slave wasn't Regis. It was a young woman. Her eyes were puffy and her cheeks were red. She balked.

Jonathan felt sick. Karis nudged the slave forward. "Introduce yourself."

The woman clasped her hands in front of her. "Athea. Sir."

She looked a great deal like Regis. Her eyes were blue, nearly gray. Her hair fell well past her shoulders. Karis pulled back the curls from Athea's neck, showing off the collar. Gilded, Jonathan noted. The opals were real, but the gold paint was cracked in some places. She looked at Crow, skimming his body. She seemed relieved. Probably because Crow looked like a healthy, clean, well-kept slave.

"You asked for a strong sorceress, yes?" Karis said. "Athea is unbroken."

"Male," Jonathan said. "I asked for a male sorcerer."

Karis inclined her head. "Perhaps if you explained what you want this slave for, I would better be able to serve you."

The slave had been beaten recently. Bruises covered her shoulders, and her throat bled as if she'd been dragged by her collar. She stared at him with a kind of helpless desperation that made Jonathan ill. The words were behind his lips. *We'll take her.*

"My master is speechless with rage," Crow said quickly. "How dare you? It's none of your business why he wants a male slave. He simply does. Do you always pry in your client's personal affairs?"

Karis blinked. "But... I...."

Jonathan pulled Crow closer to him. "Calm down, pet," he murmured. He smiled apologetically at Karis. "I give him too much free rein." He squeezed the arm around Crow's waist. "So, Karis. Is there some kind of price difference between males and females?"

He couldn't worry about the other slaves right now. He couldn't risk raising suspicions. Jonathan wasn't particularly worried about himself; frankly, he didn't care whether he lived or died and hadn't cared in a long time. But if he and Crow were caught, there would be no one left to rescue Regis. Regis needed looking after.

Karis shrugged. "Females are more valuable, yes. They live longer."

"Are you trying to bilk me? Show me a male. Now."

Athea shifted from foot to foot. Her eyes darted toward the door. She bolted.

One of the guards—the one who had cornered Crow—seized her almost immediately. It was like watching a wolf run down a rabbit. He dragged her back into the room by her hair. She scrabbled at the guard's face with her free hand.

He let go long enough to clout her across the head. She staggered, and blood dripped from her nose. Karis stepped forward, footsteps echoing in the suddenly quiet room.

She slapped the guard.

The guard nearly swore but stopped himself just in time. "We do not strike our products in anger," Karis said quietly. "We correct misbehavior, Garlant." She cupped his cheek. "We hit like a mother. Yes?"

"Yes, Madam."

Karis waved her hand. "Give her a whipping." She turned back to Jonathan. "Forgive me. I think you will be very pleased with our broken slaves."

Blood dripped from Athea's face. The guard dragged her through a door, out of eyesight. A servant passed by, holding a bowl of water and a sponge. Efficiently, the blood was wiped away. Spotless.

In the other room, sounds arose—a crack, then a shriek. The second scream was muffled. She had been gagged. Karis shut the door, and the sounds disappeared entirely.

Jonathan thought about Regis in their hands—he thought of a gag pressed between thin lips, hair stained, throat collared, wrists bruised from fighting restraints—he thought of Regis lashed to a post and beaten.

He shoved himself off the couch. "If you don't have what I want, I'm leaving."

She clung to his arm. "My good sir! I'm so sorry. I thought she was more pliable, I swear. I'll show you some nice broken slaves."

"A powerful male sorcerer," Jonathan said through gritted teeth. "Do you have one or don't you?"

"There will be an exhibition tomorrow. I'll show you every slave you could ever dream of. There will be dinner, drinking…." She hung off his arm. "Please."

An exhibition. He unfolded his options in his head. There would be nobles and wealthy merchants at the party. People he'd worked for—people who might recognize him. On the other hand, he needed an opportunity to search for Regis. If she had him, she might show him off at the party. Especially if there were lots of wealthy buyers around. Jonathan nodded curtly. It was worth the risk.

"Thank you for your patronage," Karis said. "I look forward to tomorrow evening, Lord Murtagh." She waved to one of the guards. "Show his lordship out."

The hulking guard trudged ahead of them. When they reached the front door, Jonathan took a breath of fresh air. He wanted that foul place out of his lungs. He and Crow hurried out of the city, watching for anyone who followed them.

Chapter THREE
Exhibition

CROW FOLLOWED Jonathan to the lodging house. Jonathan looked like he was going to explode with rage the entire walk home. Crow prayed they didn't come across anyone looking for a fight.

When they strode in, the woman at the counter scowled. "Your boy's only been gone two days," she said to Jonathan. "Already bringing whores home?"

Jonathan waved her away. "He's a friend, Marta."

"Friend," she muttered. "Yeah, all right." She sniffed. "Long as you send him on his way when you're done with him. Don't want him harassing my patrons." She bustled down the hall. Crow stared after her in shock.

"She thought you were a prostitute," Jonathan said helpfully. He opened the door, then locked it behind Crow. Immediately, he went to the back door and swept it open. In the garden, he hugged Chartreuse. His grip was white around her neck, and his entire body was rigid. "Fucking slavers," he muttered. "Fucking disgusting."

Crow leaned against the doorway, arms folded. "Why did the innkeeper think I was a prostitute? Do you often pick up whores?"

Chartreuse snorted. *Jonathan? No. But Regis does.*

Crow stared at her in shock, then began to laugh. "Regis buys prostitutes? What happened to flowers and poetry and perfect monogamy, White? What's the matter—can't satisfy him?"

Chartreuse sniffed. *Jonathan is very good at satisfying his mate. Jonathan is an alpha human, a proper male, and he is far better than you. You are a beta, a lesser male, feminine. No. Regis buys whores to talk to, not to sleep with.*

"To talk to," Crow said. "Honey, I don't think that's how it works."

"He really does," Jonathan said. "I'm not kidding. He pays them to listen to him talk about his work. I refuse to listen to him lecture about bodily functions for an hour straight, so he started outsourcing."

Crow couldn't stop himself from grinning. "Yeah, that sounds like him. Regis likes to think out loud."

Regis should learn to think with his mouth shut.

Jonathan relaxed a little, then went back inside with Crow. He shut the door. His fingers rested on the knob. "So," he said.

"So," Crow said.

Jonathan didn't look at him. His hands clenched. "I need a favor."

"A favor?"

"Will you teach me how to—" Jonathan grimaced. "How to be charming."

"What?"

"Charming," Jonathan said, like his teeth were being pulled. "It's just this—this thing you do. I mean, let's be honest with each other for a moment. You're a terrible person, and yet every single person that meets you wants to suck your dick. How do you do that? Show me. I need to get better at this whole 'acting' thing."

Crow didn't particularly want to teach Jonathan anything. They were working together, though, and if Jonathan messed up, they would both be in danger. "Sure," Crow said, sitting on the bed. "C'mere."

Jonathan circled the bed like a wary animal. He sat far away from Crow. "Okay," Crow said. "First lesson. Body language."

"What? Why does that matter?"

"You need to relax. People respond to social cues. If you're on guard, everyone else will be too."

"I don't feel relaxed," Jonathan groaned.

"You don't have to feel relaxed. You have to *look* relaxed." Crow leaned against the headboard and splayed his legs. "See? Like this."

"I can't do that. I can't fake it like you can." Jonathan popped his fingers, then cracked his neck. He stretched his legs out, then touched his toes. Finally, he rolled his shoulders and let out a breath. He did seem a little less tense now.

"Good," Crow said. He began musing to himself. "You already have the confidence bit down. I can't teach you to be funny, so we should skip that part."

"I can be funny," Jonathan said.

"I mean intentionally."

"You're a dick."

Crow flashed a smile. "That's part of the appeal. Look. Just be nice. Observe people. Listen to them talk. Make compliments. Social skills are difficult, but listening is an easy way to get people to like you."

"Really?"

"Yeah. It's that easy. I mean, that's what I did the night I met you."

And the room became weirdly silent.

The night they'd met. Right. The night Crow had waltzed in, spent a few minutes talking to Jonathan, and then stripped his pants off. Crow winced. It was probably a raw wound for Jonathan, considering the fact Crow had—at the time—been part of a plot to kill him. He shifted to the middle of the bed. He crossed his legs. "Look at me."

"What?"

"I want to teach you about sexual tension. It's important. We need to investigate the House of Red Silk as long as possible, but if we stall too long, Karis might realize we're up to no good. You must keep her attention. If she becomes impatient, pretend to be interested in a slave."

"Interested? How do I do that?"

"Like this." Crow leaned in. He lowered his eyelashes and tilted his head a little. His gaze slowly went from Jonathan's hands, to his chest, then—ever so slowly—he met Jonathan's eyes and held them. The air between them felt thin as paper, as though if he moved one inch closer, the barrier between them would tear.

Jonathan jerked back.

His face was unreadable, but his eyes were wide, pupils blown. Crow put his hand on Jonathan's arm, and Jonathan jerked. "Tension is a sense of anticipation," Crow said. "Stretch out that moment. Make it clear you want him."

Jonathan skirted away to the edge of the bed. "Oh, come on," Crow said. "If you can't do it with me, how are you going to do it with a stranger?"

"I keep thinking about that time you threatened to skin me," Jonathan snapped.

"That happened once."

33

The light outside had faded. Twilight lit the garden. Crow felt exhausted from his façade. He got up to draw the curtains.

"No, wait," Jonathan said. "I...."

Crow glanced back.

Jonathan had a painfully awkward look on his face. He blew out his breath. "Sorry. You're right." He got up. He rubbed his face. When his hand moved away, his expression was cool again. He scanned Crow's face, then—hesitantly—touched Crow's jaw, then his collarbone. He crowded Crow against the wall. Their chests didn't touch, not quite. Heat flickered through Crow's body, and he was aware, powerfully aware, of how long it had been since he'd trusted someone to touch him.

He shuddered. Ever since Regis had dumped him, Crow had lost all interest in fucking random strangers. The last person he'd slept with had, technically, been Jonathan.

Then Jonathan slid away. "Like that?"

"Yeah," Crow said. "Like that." He rubbed his forehead. "Look at the slave like you're undressing him. Like you're already planning how to fuck him. Don't stare at his ass—that's crude. Everyone has some special feature, so look for it. A lovely mouth. Beautiful eyes. Fine collarbones. Once you find that spot... linger." He looked at the place where Jonathan's scar once was. He couldn't help it.

"I can do that," Jonathan said.

"Good. Just don't do something stupid, like grab his ass."

"What? Why not?"

"Restraint creates tension. Hold back. Remember that night in the tavern? You know, when I touched you on the arm right before I kissed you? Try that."

"Why?"

"I don't know. But it works. See?" Crow rested a hand on Jonathan's arm.

Jonathan jerked. "Don't do that."

"Why not?"

"It feels weirdly personal."

"Yes. Exactly."

It was nightfall. They could share the bed. The hay-stuffed mattress was wide enough that they wouldn't even have to touch. Crow pictured

Regis bent over the edge of the bed, getting fucked hard and fast. The idea made him uncomfortable for some reason.

He swept up a pile of blankets and dumped them on the floor by the wall. "There's a bed, you know," Jonathan said dryly.

"I'm not sleeping with you."

"You Tyrians think everything is about sex. It's just a bed. You slept with family when you were a kid, didn't you?"

"No." When Regis was little, he used to crawl into bed with Crow, but those visits had stopped around puberty. Then abruptly started up again a few years later.

Jonathan shut up and went to bed. He lay fully clothed on the mattress, ignoring the last blanket. Crow burrowed into his little nest and closed his eyes. He didn't sleep. Where was Regis? Locked in a cage somewhere? Sold?

THE NEXT day, the exhibition began before sunset. When Crow and Jonathan arrived, many patrons stood on the terrace outside the House of Red Silk, and laughter and voices could be heard within. Crow counted two dozen nobles—minor and high alike—as well as other privileged members of Tyrian society, such as scholars and merchants.

The slaves were practically naked; they wore clothing, sure, but only to tease and entice. They were meant to be undressed. One man wore a wrap tied below his hipbones, dipping so low that Crow could see he'd been shaved. A touch, and the knot would come undone.

Crow, in his loose vest and tight pants, suddenly felt quite overdressed.

To be sexualized was to be disempowered. The lords and ladies were covered in cloth from chin to ankle. The women wore tight-laced dresses with high collars, and the lords wore austere jackets and high boots.

Jonathan looked like royalty. A sleeveless red vest over a crisp white shirt. Black gloves. Tall boots.

Crow had discovered a row of holes in Jonathan's right ear. When pressed, Jonathan had admitted that in the North, it was tradition for a jarl's children to wear a full set of gold earrings. The more bands, the higher the rank. Jonathan's went all the way up, leaving only a single gap at the top. Crow had bought eight thin gold bands and worked them into the scarred-over holes. If Karis knew Northern nobleman, she'd know what it meant, and doubtless it would intrigue her. A wealthy Northern nobleman promising her riches yet claiming to be only a lesser cousin, interested in a powerful slave.

The servants belonging to the House wore plain scarlet tunics. One bowed before Jonathan. "Please allow me to escort you, sir," he said.

He guided Jonathan away. Another took Crow's arm and steered him in the opposite direction. "Where are we going?" Crow asked.

"To be prepared."

Prepared? The servant guided him to a large bath where other slaves and servants worked. Some of the slaves were chained, but most were not. His appointed servant was a short, strong woman with a no-nonsense expression. She brandished a sponge menacingly, and Crow held up his palms, then slowly got into the bath.

She scrubbed him clean, then helped him out of the water as if he were some sort of delicate flower.

Crow rather liked it.

He lay down on a towel next to the water. A deep massage left him pleasantly aching. She had powerful hands.

His enjoyment didn't last long. Another servant, this one a burly man, appeared, and he set a bowl of oil down next to Crow. The woman dipped her fingers in oil, then reached around behind him.

Crow tensed, making a small sound of shock. The burly servant held him down. Too surprised to do much, Crow focused on the floor-tiles. Despite the oil, he could feel every ridge of the woman's fingers. They were soft and impossibly smooth, very unlike a man's.

He'd only been penetrated twice before. The first was Regis. Regis had wanted to try fucking him. A pretty mediocre experience: one finger, two fingers, three fingers, dick. It hadn't been right for them. Bossy as Regis was, he loved the sensation of getting fucked. And Crow had never really been able to surrender control.

And now Crow was naked, pretending to be a sex slave, obeying every order of the man who had stolen Regis from him. Getting worked open just in case his master wanted to use him later.

It was somewhat possible he'd made a miscalculation somewhere along the line. Several, in fact.

All of his decisions had been mistakes. All of them.

"There," the woman said. She wiped her fingers, then stroked Crow's neck, and Crow shut his eyes, a low, needy sound rising from his throat. The man snorted and hauled Crow to his feet.

"I hope your master's good to you," the woman said, sounding sympathetic. "He seems a bit cold. Does he not let you come?"

Crow blinked at her. "D-does he what?"

She mimed getting off. "Does he pleasure you? He seems like the type who takes without giving."

Crow shut his eyes. "I don't really know—" Shit. "No, he's good to me. He, uh, lets me take care of myself."

She gave him a deeply sympathetic look, then began to wipe him down with a soft cloth, leaving his skin silky smooth. Out came a long, thin blade. A razor. Crow made a choking noise and tried to squirm away. "You must hold still," the woman said.

"My master does not want me *hairless*."

"You will have hair," the woman said reasonably. "On your head."

And yet she acquiesced, for the most part. His chest she shaved entirely—not that there had been much there to begin with. She trimmed the hair of his armpits. She left his legs and arms alone. Then came his face, and Crow held as still as possible, watching his breath fog the blade as it passed.

Then she got to her knees and began to stroke him. Crow flinched. He wrenched his arms, but the man behind him held them still.

Panic bubbled up in his throat. He had thought he could do this. He had thought he could lie still and be branded and be chained and obey every word Jonathan said. Somehow this was different. "Stop," he said.

She frowned at him but let go. "It will be easier to shave you if you are hard."

"Trust me. As long as you're holding a blade against my privates, that's not going to work."

She sighed. Carefully, she began to trim around his soft cock. "What does he use you for, anyway? Public display?"

"No," Crow said weakly.

Blessedly, she didn't shave him bare. She left him trimmed. When she was done, she wrapped a golden chain around his hips. A panel of lavender silk covered his front, and another his ass. Overall, the effect was somewhat like a skirt, though of course his sides were uncovered.

"Here," she said, and guided him to a mirror. "Kneel." She gathered his hair and twisted it, artfully pinning it up. Loose strands trailed down his neck. Next she dabbed red dye from a small vial onto his lips, and she used kohl to darken his eyes. Crow blinked at himself in the mirror. The dark lines made his eyes seem slanted and sly. The red color flattered his skin.

"There," she said. "One beautiful, well-manicured slave. You'll please your master, indeed."

THEY LED him to the large exhibition room. There, piles of pillows had been arranged in between wrought-iron seats. A nearby brazier foamed smoke into the room. As Crow passed by it, the smell made him dizzy.

The female servant guided him to one of the larger pillows. He collapsed onto the soft velvet, closing his eyes. He opened them again, frowning, when she took his wrist and guided it above his head, then began to bind it with rope.

Soft cotton rope, dyed rich purple. She knitted it across his wrists and laced it down his arms, wrapping two cords of it around his neck; with a metal clip, she secured his bound wrists to a bolt on the wall. It was all very clinical. When he twisted his arms, the cords around his neck pulled taut, hands straining uselessly for the knot.

Jonathan emerged from a nearby doorway. He was frowning absently, as if working on some problem. He scanned the room, eyes passing over Crow. Then stopped. Went back. Focused.

He headed over, settling beside him. "You look comfortable."

"Mhm," Crow sighed. "They gave me a massage."

Jonathan ran a finger through the oil on Crow's chest. "And shaved you?"

"A little."

"Are you going to be able to help if… anything happens?" When he spoke, his hot breath teased Crow's ear and collected on his neck.

Crow jerked. Again, the rope on his throat tightened, cutting off his air. He shook his head.

He saw other slaves nearby, all in positions similar to him. Trussed-up, lying on pillows and furs. The art-like, lacy rope adorned them, a different color for each. For some, the rope was merely decorative, and those slaves knelt by their owners, serving food.

Crow, it seemed, was nothing more than a piece of furniture. One slave flitted by, pausing to coolly consider Crow. He left a metal platter on Crow's stomach, loaded with treats. Crow's mouth watered. He glanced up at Jonathan.

One corner of Jonathan's mouth turned up. He plucked a wafer with cheese off the tray, then held it a foot away. Crow couldn't lean forward, not without the tray falling over.

"I can't," Crow said.

"I know," Jonathan said. He grinned and popped it in his own mouth instead, licking his fingers with great relish.

"Prick."

"What?" said a startled voice.

Crow glanced up. One of the other patrons had passed by. She stared in confusion as Crow's face darkened. Jonathan tilted his head and regarded him. *Prick*, he had said. Like an enemy to a friend, or a recalcitrant slave to a patient master.

"What was that, pet?" Jonathan's tone was mild.

Crow's hands twisted instinctively as his master reached up and pinched one nipple—hard. He jerked, tray clattering, and it fell to the floor. The conversation in the room lulled as the patrons glanced over at Crow, frowning. Jonathan picked up the tray, then handed it away. "You," Crow said, then stopped.

In a corner, a dark-haired slave knelt between the legs of his mistress. He moved aside her dress. His lips parted, his hair sliding in the way as, rhythmically, his head began to move. The woman's fingers curled in his hair.

Jonathan tipped Crow's chin. "You need to work on your obedience." Heat coiled on Crow's gut. He twisted his wrists a third time, tugging. Jonathan leaned down, easing his thumb across the cords around Crow's throat. Jonathan's lips touched Crow's skin. "Behave."

Then, as if nothing had happened, Jonathan withdrew. He motioned over another slave, this one with yet another tray full of sweets, and took it, then placed it on Crow's upper chest, where it moved with every breath taken. Jonathan deliberated over the fruit, then held a grape to Crow's mouth.

Then stared, silent.

Until at last Crow moved, leaning forward the smallest amount he could. He bit. Juice burst in his mouth. Jonathan patted him, then turned his attention back to the nobles.

If he breathed too deeply, his side came in contact with Jonathan's, so he breathed shallowly and fast instead. Crow's entire world rested in Jonathan's hands. This was not who Jonathan really was, Crow reminded himself, heart beating a bit too quick. This was a game they were playing. This was a disguise. It was so easy to forget who Jonathan was when he looked so different. So easy to forget the awful things they'd done to each other.

It was the same tension that had existed between them the night they had met, except here Crow was not in control—was not toying with Jonathan for his own amusement, as he had been then—and yet again, Crow felt himself getting carried away. Jonathan knew who he was, now. Who they both were: vigilante and criminal. Hero and monster.

This was the man he'd bedded and fought and threatened.

Once, a patron came too close, and Jonathan put his hand on Crow's thigh, sliding upward. Crow shut his eyes tight, body shaking as he fought to hold perfectly still. Even breaths helped him control his body's reaction.

He wanted to be touched. A servant reached for him, but Jonathan warded her off with a cold look. Another servant sat next to him and reached to touch him, and Crow parted his legs, desperate for stimulation. Jonathan knocked the invading hand away. Crow thought he'd go insane.

A few of the slaves on display were getting serviced. Or teased. Or, in one case, jerked off. Pathetically, Crow realized that if Jonathan weren't "defending" him, there might be another slave sucking him off at this very moment.

A patron settled next to him. A noble, handsome in a plain sort of way. The man teased his hand up Crow's thigh, then began slowly stroking Crow's cock. The sensation was different with less hair down there. More sensitive. He was hard in moments. Jonathan noticed and moved to interfere.

"Please," Crow choked out. He pretended he was speaking to the patron.

Jonathan dropped his hand and turned away.

Crow bucked up into the noble's grip. The strokes were torturously slow, and he was desperate for more stimulation. As soon as he was close to orgasm, though, the man lost interest and left. None of the slaves were allowed to come, Crow realized. It would make a mess. They were objects put on display. He was left sweating and aching, hair mussed. Debauched.

Quite a few passersby stopped to admire him. Whenever he began to soften, someone would tease him back to hardness. A mouth on his nipples. Fingers on his cock. None of them gave him any real satisfaction. Jonathan, meanwhile, had stopped defending him and started ignoring him. Crow wasn't sure if this was heaven or hell. He swallowed. Maybe he should ask Jonathan not to let anyone else touch him. He was too proud to ask, though.

Why was he so hard? He was tied up and helpless. How could he be aroused? What was wrong with him?

The smoke, Crow realized in a blinding flash of light. *It's drugged.*

Jonathan plucked sweetmeats from the tray to eat, and occasionally, he gave one to Crow. Crow took the offerings gently, careful not to let his lips touch Jonathan's skin. "Jonathan," he murmured once when Jonathan came close. "The smoke is drugged. Hashish, I think." He didn't know of any drug that could incite desire—none that could be inhaled, at least—but hashish made sweet, relaxing smoke.

Karis had positioned them right next to the largest brazier. Jonathan got to his feet and leaned against the pillar awhile, and then—when guards escorted in the first slave to be exhibited—he tipped his cup of wine into the coal. A hiss, and the smoke all but stopped.

By then it was too late. Jonathan swayed a bit, and he sat too quickly, as though his muscles were weak. His face was slack, and his pupils were blown wide.

Servants blew out selected candles. The light dimmed. In the middle of the room, the first slave began to dance.

Crow lost his appetite immediately. The dancer was a boy, maybe fifteen. Seven veils fluttered around his body, and as he danced, he released one, then another, then a third. A drum began to beat, then a second. Bells. The more veils the boy dropped, the faster the music became.

At last, the final veil fell, and the boy was naked. "A child?" Jonathan said, sounding startled. "He's so young. How is this legal?"

"It's a gray area. Slavery was illegal before the queen fell into her coma. Now it's not properly regulated, and there's nothing to protect slaves from being sold too young."

"They shouldn't be sold at all." The muscles in Jonathan's jaw flexed. "This is disgusting," he said under his breath.

"Yeah," Crow said. "It really is."

Jonathan blinked at him. "Really? I wouldn't expect—" He changed midsentence. "I mean, you don't seem like the sympathetic type."

"I know what it's like to be a slave," Crow said. "My mother allowed me little freedom." They needed to stop talking. What if someone overheard? "Keep ahold of yourself. Once we get Regis, we can worry about the rest."

Jonathan nodded, and they settled down to watch the exhibition.

The sorcerers and sorceresses were few and far between. The ginger-haired slave—Athea—was absent.

Weaker sorcerers were sometimes born to poor families. The parents, unable to afford a decent education, would sell the child. Children were easy to mold. But Regis was a strong-minded adult with a great deal of magic. He would take months to break. Years, even.

A sorcerer as powerful as Regis was too dangerous to ever be trusted off-leash. What would they do with him? Torture him for information? Had someone discovered his relation to Belcane? Maybe he'd simply been murdered and disposed of.

There were a lot of ways to break a man. Take away his food and make him beg for it. Deny him clothing. Make him freeze. Break his legs. How long would Regis last? He'd be unruly at first. Defiant. They couldn't kill him. But in time he might be too weak and addled to continue his rebellion. And then....

After weeks and months of being locked away, only given human contact when he was polite, getting treats and affection when he was good.... Regis was strong, and he'd spent ten years locked up with Belcane. But Crow had been with him then. Now Regis was truly alone and enslaved.

"Crow," Jonathan said quietly.

Crow jumped. Jonathan was watching him intently. "What?"

"Are you okay? You look ill."

"I—I need a breath of fresh air."

Jonathan unpinned the metal clasp, and Crow's wrists were freed, though still bound together. He helped Crow upright. Glass doors stood on the other side of the hall, leading outside. Crow cut across the back of the room. He emerged into a small courtyard.

His ears ached from the sudden quiet. Over the wall, the lights of the city winked at him. Candles. Lanterns. Fireplaces.

When his lungs felt clean and his head felt clear, he returned. Karis was sitting with Jonathan. Jonathan's eyes were at half-mast, and he sprawled on the giant pillow. He loosened his collar and tucked his gloves in his pocket. His cup had been refilled, then half-drunk. Damn it, and damn him. They were supposed to be keeping their wits.

Crow curled up next to him. "Master," he said seductively, "you've been drinking."

Karis gave her tinkling laugh. "Oh, poor Lord Murtagh! Don't blame him, pet, I brought him some wine from his homeland."

Across the way, a man sank down on his master's cock. The slave's back arched. He began to ride. He wore rope, too, and the master used one cord like a leash. All around them, slaves unlaced clothing. Hands explored bodies. Was this normal? Crow looked at Jonathan, heart pounding. Were they expected to have sex too? Here, in front of everyone?

Jonathan put an arm around Crow's waist. The pillow was quite large, but not large enough for two full-grown men to sit side by side. Their legs tangled together, and Crow was suddenly sitting in Jonathan's lap.

Jonathan's body was relaxed. Loose. There was alcohol on his breath. His pupils were blown wide, black, and his fingers explored Crow's ribs. He smiled apologetically at Karis. "I think I'm drunk. Perhaps we should go, Crow."

"Stay," Karis said. "I insist." She motioned over a servant. "Markos, show the last sorcerer next."

The last sorcerer was the boy from earlier. The dancer. He knelt at the center of the room, in the sunburst tiles. Karis rose from her seat. She unlocked his collar. The patrons shifted nervously.

The boy spread his arms. Orange lightning crackled in the air. The sparks became golden dragonflies, and they fluttered around. One landed on Crow's arm. With a sharp sting, it disappeared. The boy raised his arms, and the dragonflies swarmed together. He threw this magic at the ceiling, and it burst, scattering into a thousand sparks that raced down the domed glass ceiling.

The patrons burst into applause. Their eyes were all on the boy, but Karis's eyes were on Jonathan. She took the boy's hand and led him to Jonathan's pillow, and immediately the boy sank to his knees, pressing his forehead to the tile. "This is Peter," Karis said.

"A bit young, isn't he?" Jonathan said.

"The young are malleable. What would you rather have: a hound you've raised from a pup, or an old dog from the street?"

"Is he strong?" Jonathan forced out.

"Powerful enough, and obedient." Crow doubted the child was nearly as strong as Regis, but a gifted and obedient sorcerer was worth his weight in gold. "Lord Murtagh, how are you planning to pay for this?"

Jonathan blinked at her foggily. "My father would give anything to buy—" His voice was a bit slurred. He stopped, his eyes widening, and he immediately changed what he had been about to say. "Jarl Murtagh has given me funds."

Crow bit the inside of his cheek to stop himself from grinning. Jonathan was apparently not nearly so drunk or high as he seemed. A man who claimed he wasn't related to the jarl, but wore the earrings of a firstborn son. Karis had to be dying of curiosity.

She sat next to Jonathan. "If you are someone of importance, you need not hide it," she murmured. "I am a woman who values discretion."

"Are you sure you don't have someone older? I don't need a broken sorcerer. Any will do."

"I am certain, my lord."

Jonathan narrowed his eyes. "All right," he said eventually. "Well, if you do get anyone new, let me know. For now, it's time I go home. I'd hate to make a drunken mistake."

Crow helped him upright. Jonathan staggered, and Crow steadied him. Despite Jonathan's performance, the imbalance felt real. Karis laughed. "Oh, you poor dear. Perhaps you should stay the night. What if someone accosts you on the way back to your inn?"

Jonathan opened his mouth, but Crow cut in. "Master, please, may we stay? I like it here." He smiled hopefully.

Jonathan met his eyes. *If we stay, we can look for Regis*, Crow thought.

Jonathan nodded. "You'll lend us a room, Madam Karis?"

"Of course. I'll send someone to show you the way."

A GUARD led the way by candlelight. After only a few feet, Jonathan began to lean on Crow. His weight was heavy, and he stumbled more and more often as they walked. Apparently the drunkenness hadn't been an act.

They arrived at a small door. The guard handed Crow a key, then left. "How much did you drink?" Crow hissed.

"Just a cup," Jonathan moaned. "She insisted. Don't know what it was. Something strong."

Crow fumbled to open the door. Once inside, he dropped Jonathan into an overstuffed chair.

The room was small but opulent. A chest of drawers had been squashed into one corner, a thick rug on the floor, embroidered with figures wrapped in chains. Not restrained and yet pulling—dancing, more like. Likely it was supposed to be erotic. Crow edged around it.

"I'm going to have a look around," he said. "Be good, will you?"

Jonathan reached out. He toppled out of the chair. "Wait," he said as he pushed himself up. "You, you're wearing sex stuff."

"I can't untie it. The knot is in the middle of my back."

Jonathan grabbed the ropes. He fought with them. "Maybe—" He sounded frustrated. "*There*." The knot between Crow's shoulder blades came undone, and the lacework rope harness sagged. Jonathan's hands flattened on Crow's back, palms on skin.

A bolt of shock and desire flooded through Crow. He had been teased all night, and his body was tightly wound. He snatched himself away, backing away until he hit a wall. Jonathan blinked at him, clearly confused. "I can do it," Crow said.

"Right," Jonathan said.

Crow unwound the rope. When he was done, he set it aside, then started to open the door. Something made him pause. He glanced back. "You did a good job tonight."

Jonathan closed his eyes. "Thanks." He sounded exhausted.

Crow closed the door behind him. He pressed a hand to his forehead, leaning against the wall, eyes shut tight.

What was wrong with him?

He hoped the smoke was all out of his lungs now. It was making him feel insane. He pressed a hand to his cock. He could take care of that little problem later. Tomorrow, maybe, when they got back to the inn. There was no time for it now. The hunger gnawed at him, and he moaned in frustration.

Hash always made him tired. His stomach was full; Jonathan had fed him quite a bit of finger food. He focused on that.

He had to explore. Quickly. Hopefully the nobles were still occupied at the exhibition. He walked briskly and kept a bored look on his face. No one he passed tried to stop him.

Once he picked a wrong door and wound up walking into a shabby room with four beds, all occupied. Crow backed out hastily. The servants lived here, it seemed. Doubtless they worked for room and board.

It seemed the guards did the same. Crow caught a glimpse of living quarters as a burly man left a similar room. The eventual rescue would have to be quick and quiet. If there were off-duty guards hanging around, Crow didn't want the alarm being raised.

He wandered like that for a while. How long, he wasn't sure. In time the exhibition let out, and drunk patrons left with their giggling pets. A few had nervous-looking new slaves still dressed in the House's colors. Crow made sure to move more cautiously after that.

He came across an empty hallway. A door opened, and Karis came out. She looked exhausted. There were ink stains on her fingers. She locked the door behind her.

Crow ducked back around a corner. An office. It had to be where she kept her records. All he had to do was break in and find out where Regis was being kept. He made his way back to Jonathan's room. He stole a bottle of wine from the exhibition room on his way.

WHEN HE returned, he found Jonathan half-naked. His shirt and boots were gone. Jonathan lifted up his head. "Why are you always scowling?" he moaned.

"Put your shirt back on. We have to sleep in the same bed."

"Sleep on the floor if it bothers you," Jonathan said, infinitely patient. He tipped his head back down. His eyes were dark. He didn't look like the controlled killer he was. The dark hair suited him.

"What?" Crow said.

"I can't stop thinking about you."

Crow set the bottle of wine well away from Jonathan.

"You were different when we met," Jonathan said. "That was all an act, wasn't it? The way you listened to me. A few polite compliments, a touch on the arm... you're good at that. You really are."

Crow shook his head. "It wasn't an act. I was curious. You caught my attention."

"We went three rounds that night," Jonathan said. "You could've fucked me. I'm kind of disappointed you didn't try."

Crow gaped at him.

"The real pity is that I found out who you were at all," Jonathan said. He closed his eyes. "I wish you'd just been a stranger, Crow."

An even longer silence this time. Jonathan was relaxed, sleepy-eyed, body loose. "I think I'm a bit too sober for this," Crow said.

"Don't worry," Jonathan said. "I will never, ever be drunk enough to ask you to fuck me." He laughed. "Mostly because I will never, ever be drunk enough to cross one of the most powerful flesh mages in Tyria." He got up and took the bottle of wine.

"You crossed my mother."

"I never fucked your mother." Jonathan wrestled with the cork. "The worst Myra Belcane could do to me is kill me. Regis.... Regis gets *creative*."

Definitely too sober for this. Crow took the bottle from him and worked the cork loose. He handed it back. Maybe if Jonathan passed out, they could stop talking.

Jonathan took a drink. "We got into a fight once. He ended up freezing my—my what did he call them? Vocal cords. He took my voice, I mean. Seemed pretty pissed off after that, kept talking to me and shooting me nasty looks during the silences. Turns out he forgot and thought I was ignoring him. Took him two days."

"What was the fight about?"

"Dunno," Jonathan said. "Wasn't important. Fights are never important. I miss him so much."

Crow collapsed onto the bed. "I miss him too."

"I forgot how lonely it was without him. How quiet. I have all these thoughts I used to tell him, and now I have no one to tell them to. There's never any bullshit with him."

Crow wasn't sure what to say to that. Sincerity made him break out in hives. So he said, "Once we find Regis, you should take down Karis. You know, as revenge. Burn down her house. Free the slaves."

Jonathan handed him the bottle. "That would be illegal."

"You're no fun." Crow took a long drink. The wine tasted foul, like unripe fruit.

Jonathan gave him a sly look. "I said illegal, not bad."

Crow laughed. "You want to?"

"If I had time, I would tie her ankles, hang her over a pot of boiling oil, and leave her there to cook."

"I bet her slaves would like to spend some time alone with her. We should chain her hands and toss her in with them. Let them take their revenge."

"We could tar and feather her."

"We could slather her in honey and bury her next to an ant hill."

Jonathan stared at him oddly. "What?" Crow said.

"I forgot that I liked you," Jonathan admitted.

Crow laughed. "You're drunk."

"You're drunk," Jonathan said.

"No, Jonathan. Factually, you are drunk and I am not."

"I thought about going to find you." Jonathan closed his eyes. "Before I knew who you were, I mean. I had it all planned out. I'd wake the queen, then disappear again. Find you and convince you to become a mercenary with me. Stupid, right? You were a total stranger, a one-night stand. Then Regis and I fell in love, and then I threw you into a bookcase, and then you threatened me, and now... here we are."

"Here we are," Crow said. He tipped the bottle at Jonathan, who stole it and drank the rest. Crow sat up. "How'd you get drunk off half a bottle of wine?"

His words slid together in his mouth. Belatedly, he realized he'd had too much. "Still drunk from earlier," Jonathan said. "Go over there." He nudged Crow toward the other side of the bed. "I gotta sleep on the outside. You get the inside, b'tween me and the wall."

"What? Why?"

"I always sleep on the outside. Regis sleeps against the wall. Safe spot. Little sorcerer. Need to protect."

Crow faced the wall. He closed his eyes. He thought about Regis. He should have come sooner. "I should have trusted Regis," he mumbled. He pressed his face to the pillow. "I should have trusted both of you."

His heart ached.

He should have told Regis the truth about what happened to Belcane while he had the chance.

Chapter FOUR
Housebreaking

JONATHAN AWOKE in a haze. His head ached, and his mouth was dry. He had the faint, muddled feeling he associated with being drunk. He would call it a hangover, except alcohol had never affected him enough for that before.

His eyes felt crusty, so he didn't open them. There was a familiar weight against his back. He sighed, rolling over. He pressed his face into the crook of his partner's neck. He squeezed the man's shoulder, then rubbed his arm, exploring his ribs with his fingers. Half-asleep, the man in his bed made a low noise, arching back and rolling his ass against Jonathan's hips. Jonathan opened his mouth against that lovely throat. Regis loved having his neck nibbled.

"Wha…?" the man muttered. His voice sounded strange.

Jonathan's eyes snapped open. Then focused. White skin. Black hair. Shit.

"Uh," Crow said, robbed of his usual wit. He paused, then said, "I'm not Regis."

"Right," Jonathan said.

"So. You should probably. Um."

"Right." He skirted away from Crow so quickly he fell right off the bed, tangled in a sheet.

Crow sat bolt upright. He held a fistful of covers over his crotch. He edged off the bed, maneuvering himself. "You know, I think I'll go grab us some breakfast." He fled.

Jonathan swallowed, because, fuck, he wasn't any less hard than before, only now he knew what Crow's neck tasted like. He crawled back into bed. His morning wood refused to go away. So he unlaced his pants, wrapped a hand around himself, and thought about Regis.

Last week, he and Regis had gone to watch the stars outside the city. He'd bought a bottle of wine, and they'd found a clearing in the forest. Divesting themselves of clothes had taken ages, as often they took breaks to drink and kiss. Just kiss, for a while.

Regis had freckles just about everywhere. Not like Crow's skin, lily-white, like he would bruise if touched too hard. Though, of course, Crow was tougher than he looked—

—and Jonathan was absolutely not going to get off thinking about Crow.

Except Jonathan couldn't really stop himself from thinking about him. Crow and Regis were lovers, once. What was that like? Regis was kind of a smartass, even between the sheets. Crow was talented, and pretty, and older than Regis, and....

Regis had admitted, once, that Crow was the only other man he had slept with. Crow must have taught him things. Like the swirling thing Regis did with his tongue. Did Crow do that first? He must've demonstrated. Long licks up the shaft, then suckling the head. Regis would have moaned, hands screwed up in the sheets as he came early— like it was the first time, because it had been the first time. Crow's mouth had been the very first on Regis's cock.

And then Jonathan thought of Crow, just Crow, bent over a metal table, hair curtaining his face. He thought of Crow tensing his back, his face flushed as the brand touched him—

No, not a brand. Neither of them had wanted that. No, his hand— Crow would arch as Jonathan's hand stroked his thigh—fingers moving farther up—a hand around Crow's cock, teasing as Crow bucked—

Jonathan's eyes screwed shut. He came.

HE LISTED awake again later, when Crow came in with a platter and a pitcher. Crow knocked the door shut with his foot and set the platter down. "Good morning," he said.

The rich scent of pastries filled the room. There were two redcurrant tarts and a plate of biscuits. A sheen of butter coated the biscuits. The tarts' filling began to crack as it cooled. Jonathan's mouth watered. "Good slave," he said groggily.

"They think I'm doting on you. I told them you wore me out last night. We're doing okay."

Jonathan bit into the tart. It crisped between his teeth, and when he swallowed, thick redcurrant jam coated his tongue. A gulp of wine washed it down.

Crow began to eat as well. "So. Regis must be locked away somewhere in the House. Shall we proceed to the next plan?"

"What plan?"

"We could have Chartreuse tear down the building."

"No," Jonathan said. "I have a better idea."

JONATHAN SPENT the day amusing himself. He made absolutely sure that Karis invested as much as possible in him. He asked for hashish, and she gave it to him in piles. At dinner, he drank too much wine. She steered him into negotiations for Peter. He insinuated, twice, that he wouldn't mind an unbroken sorcerer.

Karis smiled politely and shrugged each time.

Crow wandered. Where, Jonathan didn't know. Frankly, he was glad to get some space. Crow's needling remarks were irritating, and he often took control of the conversation even though he was a slave. Crow was…. Crow was….

Crow was kind of attractive. Jonathan didn't like feminine men—really, he didn't, honest—but Crow was lithe and exotic in a very appealing way. His black hair and white skin were very striking. Objectively speaking.

And for some reason, Jonathan couldn't stop thinking about Crow fucking Regis. It gave him a weird hot feeling. Initially he assumed this feeling was anger, but the more he examined it, the more he realized that maybe, (probably) *perhaps* he was kind of turned on.

So it made him hard. So he got off on the idea of Crow having sex with Regis. So what? He couldn't help it. He sort of liked Crow. Crow was one likable son of a bitch.

Ancestors. No one could know about this. Hopefully he'd see Regis again soon. He wanted to go back to having as much sex as he liked with the man he loved instead of playing an extremely confusing game of pretend with a man he was almost certain he hated.

Even after several years of living in this kingdom, Jonathan still wasn't quite sure he grasped how relationships worked here. The nobility never seemed to marry, only commoners. Tyrians were fiercely independent.

He and Regis were committed to each other, though. They slept in the same bed. They worked together. They loved each other. He'd asked Regis not to sleep around, and Regis had agreed without much discussion.

Jonathan didn't really believe in honor, but after all the shit he and Regis had been through—all the lies, the deceit, the murder—all they had left was trust. Trust that they would be honest with each other now and that they would not deliberately hurt each other.

So how was Regis going to feel about this? Outraged? Annoyed? Amused?

He passed Crow in the hall later. "Karis has given me one more night to decide," he murmured.

Crow eyed him. "Are you drunk again?"

"She thinks I am. Crow. Please tell me you found something. I keep hinting that I'd buy Regis if she presented him, but she's not taking the bait. Where are the slave quarters?"

A servant passed. Crow wrapped an arm around Jonathan's waist and pulled him close, and their hips pressed together. "To the south," he murmured. "The windows face the courtyard." He smelled like lavender. Jonathan shoved away as soon as the servant rounded the corner.

"Let's go somewhere private, shall we?" Crow said.

They went back to the room. As soon as the door was shut, Jonathan said, "If we can find him, all we have to do is get his collar off—"

Crow locked the door. "Do I disgust you?"

"What?"

"Stop pushing me away. You're uncomfortable. I get it. Really, I do. You and Regis are the perfect little couple. But every time you shove me away, you risk blowing everything to hell. I. Am. Your. Fucktoy," Crow said.

Jonathan swallowed. "I'll do a better job."

"See that you do."

Some rudimentary supplies lay on the bed. Doubtless Crow had gone to get them at some point. Crow began to unpack. The single bag contained two sets of clothing for both of them. Crow's knives were cleverly hidden in the folds of a jacket. "Your sword was too large to fit," Crow said.

"I get that a lot," Jonathan said with a straight face.

Slaves here wore such revealing clothing. Nothing obscene, but it pushed the bounds of good taste. Today Crow had chosen to wear a gold-trimmed vest and a form-fitting pair of breeches. A very discreet look, compared to what Jonathan had seen him in last night. Somehow this dressed-down version was more appealing. Less... blatant. Jonathan wanted to pull out the laces on Crow's pants. Wanted to feel the silky material. He'd slide his fingers up and down oh so slowly.

And then a thought slammed into Jonathan: *I've seen him naked before.* He gripped the table to steady himself.

"Did you drink too much?" Crow said, glancing back.

"No," Jonathan said thickly.

"Last night I saw Karis leaving a room with ink stains on her fingers. I bet you it's an office or a records room." Crow took a rolled-up cloth out of the bag. He unfolded it. A set of lock picks, a file, and a knife. "A lady like Karis must keep excellent records. Shall we take a look?"

"Sounds good to me."

They settled down to wait until nightfall. Crow had several practice locks in his bag, and he spent his time working them open. "How did you learn to do that?" Jonathan asked.

"Hm? Oh. It's just something I picked up when I was younger. Myra always sent me to spy on people for her."

"Why?"

"It was more efficient than killing them, I guess." Crow continued to fiddle with the lock. "She was a surprisingly practical woman. I don't think she ever really realized that what she was doing was wrong. She didn't think about it that way. She wanted power, so she went for it."

"I don't care what her motivations were, Crow. Evil is evil. Jam a sword into her and she dies."

Crow fumbled with the lock picks. He dropped one. "Is everything that simple for you?"

"Well... yeah."

"Is that your plan for me too, then? Jam a sword into me and I die?"

Jonathan winced. He hadn't realized he'd hit a sore spot. "You're not the same as her."

"She liked me, Jonathan. It bothers me, okay? She had me do all her little tasks for her. She enjoyed having me around. What does that say about me?"

"You're likable," Jonathan said. "Everyone likes you. It's not your fault."

Crow did relax a little at that. He popped the lock open with his picks, then closed it again. He set it aside and began working on another. "She laughed at me for befriending Regis. Youthful indiscretion, she called it. She kept telling me that infatuation was dangerous."

Jonathan sat upright. "Wait, what? Infatuation? You actually care about him?"

Through the single window, light had begun to fade, throwing shadows on Crow's skin. "Imagine having no one," Crow said. "No one except this scared little boy who looks up to you. Who needs you. Who admires you. And I suppose I—I wanted—" Crow lapsed into silence. "This is getting a little personal," he sighed, and he put away the lock.

"That's impressive," Jonathan said, nodding to the picks.

"Hm? Oh. Thanks. I'm not really sure what to do with myself. It's pretty easy to survive when you can fly into the windows of rich nobles and steal a jewel or two whenever you're low on funds. It's getting boring. It seems like I should be doing something, but I can't figure out what."

"I know the feeling."

Crow stood up. "It's late. Let's go."

Jonathan took two of Crow's knives and put one in each boot, then followed Crow out. There were guards patrolling here and there, but Crow avoided them expertly. Was that what he'd been doing all day? Memorizing patrol routes? Finally they arrived at a nondescript door. Crow knelt and took out his lock picks. Jonathan listened hard, keeping an eye out for guards.

At last, the lock clicked, and the door slid open. "Make it quick," Jonathan said. "I'll stand guard."

CROW WENT in alone. The room smelled fresh and clean, without the mood-altering incense in the rest of the building. A desk dominated the room. Against the left and right walls: bookcases full of identical brown books.

A shelf of black books behind the desk listed patrons. Names, addresses, preferences, personal details, secrets, wealth. The stacks of papers behind the desk were slave records. Each page listed one slave, their details, date acquired and date sold. Hands shaking, Crow found the most recent and began sorting through them. Regis's was among the newest.

He let out a shaky breath he hadn't known he was holding. He sank to the floor and began to read.

The page reduced Regis to a list of attributes. Ginger-haired. Gray-eyed. Five foot eight inches tall. Twenty-one years of age. Undamaged, literate.

There were detailed notes as well. *Erratic and violent behavior*, one read. *Bit off part of a man's finger for touching him.*

Crow's throat tightened unbearably. He bit the inside of his cheek to choke back either a laugh or a sob, maybe both. Regis was Regis, even in captivity. No doubt he'd given his captors hell.

And suffered dearly for it. Had they punished Regis the same way they'd punished that ginger-haired slave? Gods above. Crow had to find him as quickly as possible. He skimmed the paper. Regis had been sold the same day he had been acquired. He'd gone for a high price, nearly three times what normal sorcerers were worth. He'd been sold to—to....

The place where the buyer's name should have been was blank.

Crow stared down at the paper. His hands began to shake.

A wave of sickness, outrage, and fear overcame him. Spiteful tears pricked at his eyes. Gently, he set the papers down. He curled into a ball, clasped his arms around his legs, and began to weep. He breathed hard through his nose, mouth shut tight. His entire body shook. He made no noise.

He allowed himself sixty seconds of devastation. Then he sank his fingernails into his own wrist, took a steadying breath, and shook his head. No time for emotional nonsense. He pulled a folded piece of paper from his pocket, then began to scribble down everything the ledger listed about Regis.

He'd find and free Regis, and then Regis would fix him. Then the three of them together would slaughter every last slaver bastard in Tyria. Simple as that.

EVERY LITTLE noise set Jonathan on edge. There—were those footsteps in the distance? He opened the door. "Crow," he hissed.

Crow stood over a table, scribbling a note. Blearily, he looked up. Dim light from the hallway reflected on his face. Jonathan was taken aback. "Are you cry—?" He stopped in the middle of his sentence. "Never mind. Come on. Someone's coming."

Crow slipped a roll of paper back into its tube, then put it back with the rest. Jonathan motioned him down the hall. They moved as quickly as they could without breaking into a run. Loud footsteps would give them away.

When they reached the next corridor, Jonathan skidded to a halt. Footsteps approached from both directions. They were closed in. He and Crow looked at each other, frozen.

A door stood between them. It was mostly closed, but a wooden wedge kept it propped open an inch or so. They went inside, and Jonathan gently closed the door, leaving it propped open like before. The room was black as pitch. Jonathan felt his way to a wall, bumping into what felt like furniture on the way. A storeroom with one window and one door.

"Lovely," Crow said.

"Do you always have a sarcastic remark?" Jonathan hissed.

"Regis doesn't?"

"Regis just… swears a lot."

Crow stifled a laugh.

The footsteps were right outside. They looked at each other, vague shapes in the dark. Then—to Jonathan's utter shock—Crow shoved him against the wall.

"Play along," Crow hissed.

He tore open the buttons of Jonathan's shirt, unlacing Jonathan's pants, hand squirming inside to yank the cloth down. Jonathan jerked. He made a small sound of shock. "That's good," Crow whispered. "Moan for me. Louder."

Then Crow ground against him, pressing his face to Jonathan's neck. And Jonathan…. Jonathan could feel Crow's cock pressed against him, warm and a little bit hard. Crow's pulse beat a rhythm against Jonathan's nose, and his skin tasted like salt. Jonathan knew, because his mouth touched Crow's neck and he wet his lips after.

Jonathan said, "What the fuck—"

And that's when the door opened.

Crow kissed him.

Crow smelled a little like incense and a lot like a man. It was not a kiss so much as a squashing together of flesh, mostly because Jonathan couldn't quite get a grip on what *play along* meant. It probably looked like a kiss, though, to a guard who had just come from a brightly lit hallway.

And then Jonathan realized what Crow was doing.

He moaned loudly. He ground against Crow, opening his mouth. Crow's breath hitched, and he jerked a little, as if startled. Then he kissed back more fervently, unbuttoning Jonathan's clothing as if they were about to fuck then and there.

The guard made a choking noise.

Crow twisted around, putting a surprised look on his face. Jonathan did the same. "Oh, gods!" said the guard. "Lord Murtagh. I'm so sorry. Enjoy your—sorry!" And he backed out of the room, slamming the door shut behind him.

They stood there quietly as the footsteps retreated.

"Well," Crow said.

The heat of their bodies bled into each other. Jonathan could feel Crow's cock against him.

Getting hard was natural, Jonathan reminded himself, heart beating too quick. It didn't mean Crow was actually turned on, did it? It's just that there had been some half-naked grinding, and quite a bit of moaning, and getting hard was sort of a natural reaction men had sometimes.

And. Ancestors. Jonathan was hard too.

Crow leapt back and picked up his shirt. Jonathan leaned back against one of the shelves. He kept as far from Crow as the small room would allow. It sounded as if there was a second pair of footsteps, somewhere. "Sorry," Crow said, but Jonathan put a hand over his mouth. They stood in silence.

And, bizarrely, Jonathan lost focus. Started paying attention, instead, to the shape of Crow's lips beneath his hand. Finally, Jonathan let go. "I thought I heard someone coming back," he said, feeling foolish.

Jonathan went to open the door. The handle wouldn't move. He jiggled it, but it wouldn't open. "Uh."

"Don't tell me."

The handle was broken. Oh. That's why the door had been propped open. And now the guard had—without thinking—closed the door. Leaving them trapped inside until someone found them.

He shoved against the door with his shoulder. Not hard, just to make it shudder. "Heavy. Damn."

"It's really broken, then?"

Jonathan slumped against the door. "You said not to tell you." His entire body pounded with the desire to fuck something. Anything. The impromptu frottage had stopped, but his body hadn't gotten the message, and he wanted nothing more than to be touched. He thought about swordplay to calm himself down. Defensive patterns. The differences between various types of swords. Bastard sword techniques versus rapier duels. He took deep breaths.

Crow knelt by the door. Jonathan couldn't quite see what he was doing, but there were small metallic noises as he fiddled with the lock. "I can't pick it," he said after a few minutes. "It's good and stuck. Do you have a knife I could use? I think maybe I can get the hinges out."

Jonathan drew the knife Crow had given him from his boot. He handed it over. "Karis might notice if we start dismantling her doors. I thought the idea was to get away cleanly. If we take the door apart, she'll notice we were here, and the guard will be more likely to confess that he found us fucking in her closet."

Crow sighed. He rose to his feet. "Maybe I can fit through the window instead."

"The window? That window?" It was less than a foot wide.

Jonathan couldn't see his expression, but he could sense something was wrong. "If I can shift," Crow forced out. He put his palms flat on the wall. "Once I'm out, I'll come open the door for you."

Jonathan studied him.

Crow's face was unreadable in the dark. "I swear I won't leave you. I need your help, and you need mine."

"I know."

"Then why are you looking at me like that?"

"You threw me off a building," Jonathan said.

"That was two years ago. Stop holding a grudge."

"You *threw me* off a *building*," Jonathan said.

Watching Crow shift was always a bit weird. His body would shrink, reform, and grow feathers. His clothes changed with him. Normally it took only a second for Crow to go from fully human to fully animal, but this time it took longer, and it looked like it hurt him. He grimaced, doubling over. His body collapsed onto itself. Jonathan knelt, and the bird hopped on his arm. He helped the bird out the window.

Jonathan settled down to wait.

CROW SLIPPED out the window. The night air was cool on his feet, and his feathers rustled. It felt good to stretch his wings again. He flew in a circle outside, then landed on the ground.

Being a bird was different than being human. He was still the same person, essentially, but it was harder to focus. In a distant way, he remembered he was Crow, one of the giant fleshy creatures who walked on the ground. But his thoughts were like liquid: formless, quick, and hard to hold onto.

Bugs in the dirt. City smells. People nearby.

His bird self was uncomfortable knowing he was inside a city, and it didn't like being on the ground. But it felt really good to be a bird again. This was how he was meant to be, wasn't it? Maybe he should just fly away into the forest.

Distantly, the human part of him felt alarm. His bird self was much stronger than usual, and it was impossible to hold on. He felt his human side rapidly slipping away. It wasn't supposed to be like this. The spell was so weak now.

He was going to get stuck.

Panic stirred inside him. He tried to grasp the spell that made him human. He fought to change back, but it was like shoving on a locked door.

He should've been frightened, but it was so hard to hold on. He was supposed to be doing something important. He fought to remember what he was trying to do, why he'd shifted into a bird—

Human smells. Scary city smells. Get up somewhere high.

He managed one moment of clarity. He was trying to get Jonathan out of a locked room. He needed Jonathan's help so they could save Regis together.

Regis.

Bright hair and sharp eyes. Gentle hands and sweet kisses. He remembered Regis more clearly than he remembered himself, and he clung to that memory like a drowning man clutching a piece of driftwood. He fought to change back into a human. The dying magic inside him began to work.

His body crumpled and collapsed on the ground. He writhed as, slowly, agonizingly, he became human again. But the pain was too much, and darkness swallowed him up.

MINUTES CRAWLED by, and Crow still wasn't back. Twice Jonathan thought he heard footsteps, but they passed each time. He itched to escape. He couldn't imagine why Crow might abandon him, but then again, Crow had never been a predictable man.

Finally, Jonathan took the knife and knelt by the hinges. He fit the blade in the metal and began to pry. Crow would come back, Jonathan thought to himself. Surely Crow would come back.

But by the time the hinges were out, Crow was still gone. Jonathan put away the knife and carefully removed the door. He breathed clean air, then glanced back at the window.

A groan came from somewhere outside the window. Was that Crow? What the hell was going on?

A nearby door looked like it led outside. He snuck through it into an enclosed yard. It was a beautiful space. A gazebo with wrought-iron benches occupied one corner, and lush grass covered the ground. Against the wall stood several bloody posts.

There, on the ground against the wall—beneath the window—lay a body. Crow's body. He'd never even left.

Jonathan knelt and rolled it over, then recoiled. The face was deformed. He looked like an unfinished puppet. Crow's lashes fluttered. His eyes had gone completely black, and they slid shut again after only a moment.

"Ancestors defend me," Jonathan said shakily. He wasn't the superstitious sort, but he still drew a shield over his heart.

He hoisted Crow up bridal-style. He held his breath as footsteps echoed inside in the hall. If anyone saw and began to question things, he had no idea what he'd say. Crow groaned softly. Jonathan held him, heart pounding, as the guard passed. Then he carried Crow into the building and headed straight for their room.

Once there, he set Crow down on the bed. "Crow. Wake up, dammit! What's wrong with you?"

No good. Jonathan cursed.

He waited. What else was there to do? At last, he gave up. He had to help Crow somehow. He grabbed a cloak, then wrapped Crow in it. Crow seemed more awake now. His eyes were open, and he stared straight ahead. Jonathan helped him up, and Crow moved as if in a trance. "What did you do?" Jonathan said, and Crow acted as if he had not heard.

There came a knock on the door. Jonathan turned.

Karis opened the door. She wore a dressing gown, and she had her two hulking guards with her. "Master Murtagh," she said. Her voice was sickeningly sweet. "How has your stay been?"

Crow moaned.

Karis glanced at Crow. "Used up?"

"We've had a long night," Jonathan said weakly.

"If you need someone to watch you fuck your slave, I can arrange that," she said smoothly. "But please. Refrain from destroying my property."

"Er. I'll... I'll do that. I mean—I won't," Jonathan said. "We'll keep it in here."

Karis inclined her head. "That is all that I can ask." She spun on her heel and marched away.

Jonathan guided Crow out of the House. They stepped out onto the street. Crow wavered, and Jonathan kept him upright with a tight grip. A nighttime breeze stirred the hood of the cloak, revealing his lipless mouth. "Magic," Jonathan murmured. "Would magic help?"

HE WALKED toward the healer who had fixed his scar. The shop with the *Strange Solutions* sign was closed. Jonathan pounded on the door anyway. "Healer!" he hollered. At last, a window opened above, and the old lady stuck her head out. She held a chamber pot, and she began to tip it over.

Jonathan leapt out of the way just in time. "Wait! My friend is ill."

The healer disappeared back inside with the chamber pot. She reappeared down below a moment later. The door jangled as she opened it a crack, a chain across the front. "I don't do criminals," she said.

"We're not criminals."

"Like hell you aren't," she said. "Sick? In the middle of the night? What did you do, have a run-in with the guards?" She peered under Crow's hood. With a gasp, she slammed the door shut.

Jonathan continued banging.

The healer cracked open the door and peered at Crow. "Fine," she said grudgingly. She swept back the chain, then motioned them in. "Get in quick, before someone sees. Don't want people to know I'm consorting with—well, with finely dressed noblemen and mysterious cloaked strangers."

Jonathan guided Crow into a chair. He pulled back Crow's hood. The healer stayed back, shifting around this way and that to look at Crow. At last, she prowled closer to poke at him. "What did you do?" she asked finally.

"I'm not sure. He has this spell on him that lets him shape-shift, and I think it's gone wrong somehow. I've seen him do it before, but it hurt him this time. And when I found him, he was like this. He responds to commands, but he's not speaking. It's like he's lost his...." Jonathan struggled. There was a phrase for it in his own language, but he wasn't sure what it was in Tyrian. "It's like he's not behind his eyes," Jonathan said.

"Like his mind is gone?"

"That's it, yes. Can you fix him?"

The healer looked at Jonathan as if he were mad. "I don't know what kind of spell is on him. Or how it was cast."

"Can't you do anything?"

"I can try to break it."

A huge risk. What did the spell even do? It helped Crow shape-shift, he decided. Breaking the spell would make Crow completely human, right? But breaking a strong spell could damage the victim. Regis had told him that, once. But a half hour had passed since Crow had last turned into a bird, and he showed no signs of waking from his stupor.

"Do it," he said.

Chapter FIVE
Breakdown

THE HEALER knelt by Crow and put her hands on him. Her magic was much weaker than what Jonathan had seen before. When Regis worked large spells, his power weighed down the room like gravity. Hers could barely be felt. Her tiny sparks skittered across Crow and sank in.

Something was wrong. Crow immediately got worse. His nose flattened into nothing. His eyes became perfectly round, and he screamed. He seemed to come back to himself.

"Don't touch me," he shrieked.

His voice sounded wrong. Like air hissing through a bent pipe. The healer backed away, and Jonathan didn't dare touch Crow. Crow's eyes were shut, and he looked agonized. For a few frightening seconds, it looked as though the changes were still getting worse. Then Crow seemed to gain control, and his face became human. Gingerly, Jonathan unpinned the cloak. The feathers on Crow's shoulders absorbed back into his skin.

At last, Crow opened his eyes. "What—" A crack. He cleared his throat. "What did you have her do to me?"

"I told her to break the spell."

"You *what?*" Crow's face flushed with rage. He shoved Jonathan against the wall, hands fisted in Jonathan's clothes. "Do you have *any idea* what you almost did?"

He didn't. He knew better than to say so, though, so he just sort of stood there, flummoxed. "No," Crow said, suddenly calm. He let go. "No, that's stupid. You don't know what you did wrong. Of course not." He spun on his heel and left, slamming the door behind him.

Jonathan slapped a gold sovereign on the table. The old lady snatched it up like Jonathan might take it back. Jonathan went after Crow, who stood outside, leaning heavily against the building. His eyes were shut. "Are you all right?" Jonathan asked.

"Fine."

Which was an obvious lie. And what was he supposed to say to that? Crow wasn't his friend. It wasn't Jonathan's job to comfort him. So Jonathan just sort of stood there again. In time Crow straightened. He was breathing hard, though he hadn't done more than step outside. "If something is wrong, you need to tell me," Jonathan said.

"You almost killed me."

"I'm sorry. The healer thought she could help—"

"A two-copper witch with a touch of magic and half a brain," Crow hissed. "I expect this sort of idiocy from strangers. But you—" He pinched the bridge of his nose. "No," he said, calming down suddenly. "No, this was my mistake. If I were more in control of myself, I wouldn't need your help in the first place."

Jonathan raised his palms. "Look. I'm sorry I brought you here. It was clearly the wrong decision. Let's go sit down somewhere quiet and have a drink. We need to talk. If we're going to work together, you need to tell me what's wrong with you. Regis said you were sick; he didn't say how. You need to tell me the truth. You need to trust me."

"Trust you," Crow said.

The moonlight fell on half of Crow's face, highlighting the curve of his cheekbones, the slant of his nose. They looked at each other.

Crow began to shift. "No," Jonathan said, lurching forward. "Stop! You'll hurt yourself."

Crow collapsed to his knees. The shifting slowed and stopped. He gripped his head, and his face twisted in concentration. Then: triumph. His body burst into feathers, then reformed as a bird.

Jonathan watched him go. Within the space of three heartbeats, he was gone. Jonathan shut his eyes and leaned against the wall. So that was that. He and Crow were no longer working together.

Jonathan felt more tired than he ever had in his life. He walked to the Overlook lodging house alone in the dark. The hallway floor creaked when he entered, and the key made a lonely sound as he turned it in the lock.

Regis's books and notes still lay on the table, his boots by the door. Jonathan opened Regis's trunk and took out his favorite scarf—pale green, embroidered with silver thread. It still smelled like him.

Regis was still alive. He had to be. He was too valuable to kill. Besides, he was strong. He would escape, or he would be found. Jonathan collapsed onto the bed, curling into the indent. He felt overwhelmed, exhausted, and scared. He couldn't do this. He had barely been doing it with Crow. How could he possibly do it alone?

He dreamed of a woman calling him. The voice pulled at him. It wanted him to wake up. Eventually, he realized it was real. The room had been ransacked. The covers, ruffled. The luggage undone. Regis's things were strewn about the room. Cold terror shot through Jonathan. He'd always been a heavy sleeper, but to sleep through a robbery? And why was the garden door open? Where was Chartreuse?

Jonathan, Chartreuse said impatiently.

He lurched outside. Chartreuse sat beneath a tree, tail lashing. Up the tree, Crow sat squashed into the crook of a branch. He glared down at Chartreuse. "Your dragon is chasing me!"

I have treed him for you, beloved human. The creature broke into your room while you slept. He went through your things, then came out the garden door. And with that, she lay down and closed her eyes. Her tail continued lashing.

Jonathan stepped aside. "Get down from there."

"There's a dragon down there," Crow said, looking at Jonathan as if he were insane. Then he grimaced. "I'm not sure I can get down. The ground is several hundred feet away, Jonathan."

"You're eight feet up an ornamental shrub."

With some coaxing, Jonathan managed to get him down. Crow shut his eyes and put his feet where Jonathan told him, at last slipping on the last branch. He tumbled down. Jonathan caught him. Crow's shirt had come untucked, and he was barefoot, his hands dirty from damp bark. He looked up at Jonathan with hazy confusion. He reeked of the same smell that had infested the House of Red Silk. "Are you high?" Jonathan said slowly. There was a pipe on the ground. "Where did you get that?"

Crow turned red. "Get w-what?"

"The pipe, Crow."

Sulkily, Crow picked it up. "I went back to the House. I...." He listed to the side, and Jonathan caught him. "Useless," he muttered. "Nothing to find. A noble was passed out in the exhibition room with this pipe." Crow's self-conscious grace had abandoned him. In its place was a kind of relaxed disorientation that reeked of vulnerability. He leaned into Jonathan's arms. "I was wrong. She wasn't dosing us with hashish. It's opium." His eyes were red.

"And you smoked it?"

Crow closed his eyes. "I started going through Regis's things. I wanted to be close to him. I…. Jonathan, we need to find him."

"Of course. I know."

"No," Crow said. "Now, we need to find him now." And, without warning, he burst into tears.

Which was incredibly alarming. Alarming, the way Crow was clearly exhausted. The way Crow sniffled into his shoulder, eyes wet, raw emotion on his face—real emotion on his face.

"I think—I think I'm in love," Crow choked out.

Get rid of him now, before he steals your mate, Chartreuse said grimly.

"It's as awful as I always said," Crow moaned. "It's like a disease in me. I've tried so hard not to love him, but it's inevitable, like—like rain is destined to fall. A weight gathers in me, and I can hold it no longer. I drown for him, I want to breathe him like air, I want to be lost. If I had a heart—oh, if I had a heart, I'd give it to him, but I don't think I do, Jonathan. I don't think Myra made me with one."

"Um," Jonathan said.

"Well, go on. Hit me. Tell me what scum I am. It's true, all of it."

"You said you didn't believe in love," Jonathan said, desperate to end the conversation.

"It's stupid and dangerous." Crow laughed brokenly. "All it ever leads to is broken promises and hurt feelings. I want it to stop, don't you see? That's why I left. And coming back now—it kills me that he's happy with you. Isn't that awful? I should be happy for him." His hands bunched in Jonathan's shirt. "Hit me, please."

"Why?"

Crow shook him. "Because I love your lover, you idiot. Because I'd take him from you in a heartbeat."

"No," Jonathan said, dumbfounded. "Why do you want me to hit you?"

Crow collapsed back into a garden bench. "I don't know," he said miserably. "This would be easier if I hated you."

Jonathan sat next to him. "Is this because we couldn't find anything in the records room? It's all right. We'll find him somehow."

Crow shook his head and looked away. For a moment, it seemed like he would speak. He swallowed. "I'm not a real person."

"Crow," Jonathan said gently, "you're high."

"I'm not high," Crow said. "I mean, I am, but that's not the point. I'm a monster."

"I don't know what your mother did to you—"

"Literally," Crow said. "I am a monster. A thing. An *it*. Listen, damn you. Myra made me. A living bird, some of her blood, some of her magic. She's my mother, more or less. And now that she's sick, I'm sick too."

"What?"

The expression on Crow's face was the most abject humiliation Jonathan had ever seen. "Regis never told you about this?"

"No," Jonathan said slowly. "He said there was a spell on you that would kill you if Belcane died. She made you? That's why her death will kill you?"

Crow laughed bitterly. "That's more or less the gist of it. I learned to manipulate the magic early on, to control it so I could shift forms whenever I wanted. I think that's the only reason I'm still human now. But there's only bare traces left, and I can only do so much. When that old woman tried to break the spell—you nearly killed me." Crow slumped. "Pretty soon Myra will die, and the spell will fail."

"And then you'll die?" Jonathan said, horrified.

"Might as well. I'll stop being me, at least. The sentience I have comes from being human. Birds are incredibly intelligent, but it's not the same."

They were quiet for a time.

Chartreuse said, *I liked him better when he was high. Give him back the pipe.*

Jonathan pinched the bridge of his nose. He thought of explaining to her that she was being cruel and unhelpful, that it was wrong to hurt a man already in pain. Likely she would continue harassing Crow anyway. He stood up. "Come on. Let's go inside."

Crow laughed bitterly. "What does it matter, anyway? No one will care if I die."

"Ancestors, Crow. Don't say that."

"Don't say what? That I'm an abomination? That most people would burn me at the stake if they knew? That—" He stopped. Stared at Jonathan. Let his head tip back against the back of the bench. His eyes were still hazy.

"What?" Jonathan said.

"You're a very strange man," Crow said.

"I'm not sure what you mean."

"No, of course not. You're only being kind because you need me."

"Look," Jonathan said. "I don't get magic. Regis acts like it has rules, but mostly it seems like bullshit to me. I'm not going to sit here and argue about who made you and what that means. You say you're a man, and you act like a man, so I'm going to treat you like a man. If you turn into some sort of writhing pile of teeth and tentacles, I'll worry about your monsterhood then. Until that time, you're Crow, plain and simple. Fair?" He offered Crow his hand.

Tentatively, Crow took it. Jonathan pulled him up. This close, he smelled strongly of incense.

They made their way back inside. Jonathan left the garden door unlocked. He rested his hands on the knob. Without turning around, he said, "You can have the bed."

"What?"

"You slept on the floor last time, so you can have the bed this time. We'll trade off. I'm used to sleeping on the ground, anyway." He turned to take the coverlet from the bed.

Crow stood still, a half-shadow in the dark. He seemed too tired to cry anymore. He watched Jonathan as though expecting a trap. Finally, he sank onto the sheets. "You have a plan?"

"Sure. Just go to sleep, all right? I've got this."

Crow pulled the last remaining cover over himself. He closed his eyes. Started to turn away. Then he stopped, opening his eyes to slits. "Good night," he said.

"Do you remember being a bird?" Jonathan asked.

Crow took so long replying that, for a moment, Jonathan thought he'd passed out. "Yes," he finally said. "A little. Not much. To be honest, if the spell breaks, I probably won't die. Likely I'll just become an ordinary bird again."

"So you might survive, then."

"Survive? Well, yes, technically I'd still be alive, but my humanity would die. I have the mind of a man, Jonathan, and if the spell breaks, then Crow Belcane will cease to exist. Being a bird is no different from being a rock or a tree. It's nothing. I would rather die and be done with it." Crow took a shuddering breath. He sat upright. "I would. I mean it. I'd rather die a man than become a mindless animal."

"What are you saying?"

"If we don't reach Regis in time," Crow said, "I'm going to take poison."

He said it in a matter-of-fact way, like he'd been thinking about it for a while. It didn't seem real. Then Jonathan caught a flicker of fear in Crow's eyes, and the reality hit him. Crow meant it.

Jonathan got up and sat on the bed beside Crow. He didn't say anything for a long moment, putting the thoughts together in his head. Looking over their entire conversation and trying to figure out how to approach this. He'd never thought he would have to talk his mortal enemy down from suicide.

"Nothing to say?" Crow said. "Regis would panic if I told him."

"Regis was blessed with a lot of gifts," Jonathan said tactfully. "Levelheadedness was not one of them. Crow, don't kill yourself. Don't. I mean, strictly speaking, I can't prevent you, but... if you're going to, at least don't take poison. What if you take it too soon, and it turns out we could've saved you? Or what if you take it too late, and the spell breaks completely before you die?"

"What am I supposed to do? Cut my own throat?"

"No. Your wrists. It's more... it doesn't hurt. It's fast."

Crow's eyes slid over, knife-sharp.

A lengthy pause.

"This is off-hand knowledge?" Crow said.

Jonathan rubbed his neck. "I had a tough time, growing up." He grimaced. "Hell. Listen to me, whining. I was a jarl's firstborn child. I had a lot. But it meant—I don't know. It came with expectations I couldn't fulfill. So I researched ways to—I mean, I just wanted to know how."

"You tried to kill yourself?"

Jonathan rested against the headboard. "The night I first met you, I told you the story of how I got that scar on my mouth. Remember?"

"Your best friend bit you, you said."

Jonathan hunched over. He hadn't told this story in a long time. He hadn't even told Regis. "Part of that was bullshit. He wasn't only my friend. We were lovers."

Crow blinked at him. "That's not what you said before."

"Yeah, well, sometimes I lie about things I don't want to talk about." Just thinking about it brought back a surge of old feelings. "I was luckier than some boys my age. My father suspected that I preferred men, but he didn't turn me in or tell anyone. Cam was… less lucky."

Talking about it hurt. Jonathan steadied himself, then continued. "We were going to keep our affair a secret. How lucky, I thought to myself. I could marry a woman, have children, and love Cam in secret. People would whisper, sure, but rumors are just rumors."

"And then?"

"I didn't realize how—how dangerous it was. Someone caught us. I was an only child, and my father wanted me to remain his heir, so instead of having me arrested, he covered it up. He targeted Cam instead. My father, he…."

Crow was watching him intently. Jonathan grimaced. He could lie, or he could simplify the story again. But he'd already started telling the truth, so he might as well end it. "He sent my lover to an insane asylum. By the time I found Cameron, he was shell of his former self. I was the one who led him down that path. I put him in danger. Our love affair wasn't worth killing him. He liked women, not just men, and I thought that maybe if I left, he could recover and live a normal life without me. But the moment I was gone, he swallowed poison. His face… I don't think he actually wanted to do it. He died alone and afraid."

Crow toyed with the hem of the blanket.

"I know it sounds melodramatic," Jonathan said. "But I was young, and I had nowhere to turn. Suicide was the obvious option. I picked a random road and followed it out. I tried to kill myself every day, Crow, every bandit, every corrupt noble, every slaver, every monster hiding in the woods. You've called me stupid, before. Mad. You're right. I never expected to live this way."

"Does Regis know?"

He rested his head against the wall. "I've never told him in such explicit terms, no."

"And now? You're not suicidal any longer because… you're with Regis?"

"Grief never goes away. It has tides, like an ocean. Eventually, mine dried up. Sometimes I still think about it. It's like a black piece of my heart. There's no sudden will to live. There's no dramatic turning point. Being with Regis makes me happy, and that's enough for now."

It was a little odd, having such a calm conversation with Crow about suicide.

"And what's the point of this little story?" Crow said after a while.

"You don't deserve to die, Crow. You're worth saving. I wish I could have told Cameron that. I was lucky. I tried to kill myself, and I failed, because I had someone to stop me. Chartreuse saved my life over and over again, dragging me down from a cliff, defending me in battle. So if you want me to be that person for you, I will. I'll be the person that stops you. I'll help you off this cliff. I will take the knife from your hand. I will steal the poison from your mouth." Jonathan tilted Crow's chin. "Look at me."

Crow's eyes met his. They breathed the same air.

"Regis will fix you," Jonathan said quietly. "Understand me?"

"If we can reach him in time."

"We will."

Crow smiled wryly. "We will?"

"We have to. It's as simple as that, my friend." Crow nodded and looked away. He took something out of his pocket. It was a tiny pouch. Jonathan's heart leapt into his throat. "What is that?"

"It's iocane powder. I bought it today. I'm told it's painless."

"Give it to me."

Crow glanced up sharply. "Why?"

"Do you trust me?"

Crow was the kind of person who would deny it even if the answer were yes. Here, he said nothing.

"Give it to me," Jonathan said. "If you decide you want to die, then ask for it back, and I'll give it to you. This way you won't feel tempted to do something rash."

Crow handed it over.

Chapter SIX
Regis

REGIS AWOKE. The world was black, and he could not move. Were his eyes open or closed? He squinted into the dark. Nothing.

Panic shot through him. Had he gone blind? What was going on? There—a tiny crack of light not far from his face. He tried to roll over and encountered a solid wooden wall.

He was somewhere hot and confined. He tried to bang on the lid, but he barely had room to move. His hands were chained in front of him. He was on his side, and the walls were close enough that he had to lie curled. A trunk of some sort.

Regis shut his eyes and fought to breathe calmly. Someone had chained him up and shut him in a box. "Jonathan?" he called.

Idiot, he thought. There was no chance Jonathan was around. He hoped against hope, though, and he panicked again when no one responded. He kicked the lid. Nothing.

There was movement outside the box. It lurched and shifted, as if being carried by each end. Regis kicked again, and someone outside cursed and banged on the top. Muffled voices came from outside. A reprimanding tone. Something about not breaking the merchandise.

Merchandise?

He tried to use his magic, but he couldn't reach it. A weight lay around his neck—a collar? It must have opals, he thought. A mage collar. A box. Chains. Small space. He gasped. Oh gods. Did the box have proper ventilation? Would he suffocate? He prayed whatever idiot who kidnapped him wasn't that stupid.

The box stopped moving. Regis fought to breathe normally. Once the box was open, he could make a break for it. Advantage of surprise.

A woman had done this to him, he remembered, fighting through his hazy memories. Madam Karis, they had called her. They hadn't beaten him, only shut him in a cell. Was Crow a part of this somehow? Would Crow do that?

The box cracked open. The lid slid away.

Regis flinched, blinded by bright light. Two hands grabbed each of his arms and hauled him from the box like a corpse from a coffin. "Careful with him," said a man's voice.

The helpers guided him into an armchair, and Regis sank into it. He cracked his watering eyes open and scanned the room. Thick red carpet. Fancy tapestries. Expensive vases on sleek mahogany side tables. He sat in a very expensive dining room.

A man sat across the table. He kept his silver hair neatly trimmed, and his eyes were piercing gray. He laced his fingers together. "Regis," he said. "It's a great pleasure to meet you."

Crow wouldn't do this to him. Would he? No. It had to be some hideous coincidence. Regis took a breath. He wiped his eyes on his sleeve, straightened his clothes, and relaxed. The guards unlocked the chains from his wrists.

There was a fireplace ten paces to the right. Regis thought: *If I stab him with the fireplace poker, perhaps he'll be distracted long enough for me to jump out the window.*

Two men flanked his chair. Both were large. "You can go," said the man, waving them away. "I'd like to speak to my boy in private."

The door shut loudly behind them.

Regis darted for the poker.

A force slammed into him and threw him against the floor. Regis gritted his teeth. Another sorcerer. Dammit. Not content to simply hold him down, the man spun him onto his back and pinned his wrists like he was an insect.

The force dragged him like a puppet and pushed him back in the chair. Regis's jaw locked, and he glared at the man, who gave him an amused look. "A fighter," he said. "I like that. I was going to introduce myself as Master Aron, but you, Regis, may call me Septimus."

Septimus Aron. The Queen's Warlock. Court Sorcerer. Regis had never met him, but he was purportedly a very influential man.

Septimus leaned back in his chair. He toyed with a dinner knife.

Regis took a breath, then let it out. "A woman sold me to you. You have no use for a magical slave. What do you want with me?"

The windows were too far away to reach. If he could get out, someone might see him and help him. Septimus, though, was fast. If he could get a hold of that dinner knife, he might have a chance. Jonathan had taught him some tricks. All he needed was one lucky stab.

But then what? Where was he? Still within Tyrigaine? For all he knew, he'd been knocked out and shipped halfway across the kingdom.

Septimus watched him with keen interest. "You must be hungry." He rang a bell on the table, and a servant walked in. "Dinner, please."

The servant gave Regis a deeply sympathetic look before she scurried out. Septimus smiled and drummed his fingers on the table. "You must have many questions."

"If you wanted to tell me anything, you would do it already," Regis bit out. "I'm not going to pry answers out of you."

Septimus's smile vanished. "Boy, it's rude to talk that way to your elders. Have some respect."

Jonathan would kill Septimus for this.

Except Jonathan wasn't here, didn't know who Septimus was, and didn't know where Regis was. He recited medical notes in his head until he calmed down. He needed to focus on escape. Being rude to his captor would gain him nothing. "Why did you kidnap me?" he asked as calmly as he could.

Septimus broke into a smile. "Curiosity getting the better of you, huh? That's my boy. Well, I—" The servant walked in with dinner. "Ah, food! Talk will have to wait."

Finely sliced pork, deliciously charred and dripping with juices. Broiled potatoes. Sweet pink cordial in a glass. Regis's mouth watered as the servant cut his meat for him. He took a bite—politely—but didn't touch the alcohol. He needed his wits. "I assumed a noblewoman would buy me," he said through a mouthful.

"For your bloodline? To breed children? I can understand the assumption." The pitcher of water sat across the table, beading condensation. Regis's body ached from thirst. He glanced at the cordial next to him. It was alcohol or nothing for him, apparently.

Septimus drank deeply from a cup of water. "You know, I've done that myself before," he said, swirling the goblet. "Some women will pay through the nose for a magic bloodline. You're the perfect age, you know. Virile. Any child of yours would be guaranteed to have magic."

Regis recoiled. He dropped his fork. "You bought me to whore me out?"

Septimus burst into laughter. "Oh, heavens no! It was merely a piece of advice. You know, for your future. I'm not going to force you to do anything you don't want."

"Right," Regis said. "Okay. You're, uh, planning to let me go, then?"

"Oh no. I mean, not right away. But eventually, yes. Yes, of course. Slavery," Septimus said, "is barbaric. Frankly, I wouldn't have resorted to it unless I had no other option. And, of course, I spent an exorbitant fee. Just to meet you! You'll have to forgive the box. I had to get you here unseen, of course. It wouldn't do if anyone knew I was consorting with you."

Regis swallowed. His grip tightened on his knife. "Consorting. Right. Can I have some water?"

"Can you? Of course you can."

Regis stared at him.

"May you," Septimus said. "May you have some water. Say it."

Regis forced out, "May I have some water?"

The servant poured him a glass. He drained it. "There," Septimus said, sounding satisfied. "We'll teach you some manners yet. So, Regis. Tell me about yourself. You're doing well for yourself, eh? You've taken some of my clients."

"Clients?"

"Lady Redford bought your services. Her poor son fell off a horse and cracked his head open. You mended his skull and reduced the swelling in his brain."

"I," Regis said. "Yes. Sir. Yes, I did that."

"I'm impressed. You're very talented, aren't you?"

Regis hesitated. For once, he didn't feel like bragging. "I suppose. My, um, partner—you know, Jonathan—he's the real hero." He was desperate to change the conversation. "He saved Queen Isolde, you know."

"Oh yes. So I've heard."

"And Queen Isolde united the warring nobles. So. By extension, Jonathan sort of fixed everything." He was babbling now. He took a breath to calm down. "He's been picking up odd jobs for money. Mostly, um, looking for the Flesh Witch."

Septimus nodded patiently. "Yes, of course."

"He must be very worried right now," Regis said, "you know, since you—kidnapped me."

"Since slavers kidnapped you," Septimus corrected. "I only hired them."

Regis's jaw locked. He nodded jerkily. "Sure."

"I don't think we have to worry about Sir White. He seems like an honorable man. Even if he does somehow find you, he must have respect for the law. Slavery is legal now. I bought you, fair and square. I'm sure he'll see reason."

"Reason?" Regis said.

Fury twisted in his chest. He wanted to throw his plate in Septimus's face. How could someone just take him like this? What about Jonathan? What about Crow? And then a horrible anxiety gripped him. Crow. Oh gods. Crow. Crow was sick and dying. If he didn't get back soon, the spell would break.

Septimus drummed his fingers. "So tell me about yourself. What branch of the Teller family are you from?"

Regis shrugged. The Teller clan was quite extensive, but his mother had raised him alone, and she had never explained who he was related to or how. "My mother and I lived alone."

"Did you now?" He looked up, eyes suddenly cat-bright. "And what was your mother's name?"

"Sage."

Septimus set aside his silverware. He looked quite pleased with himself.

"Is that important?" Regis asked.

"It explains a lot. You look like her, and you're about the right age. You remind me of myself when I was young, which is only natural," he said, "given that you're almost certainly my son."

The crystal glass fell from Regis's hand.

It bounced on the carpet but did not shatter. Water soaked in. "Your son?" Regis said dumbly.

Septimus puffed up and said, "Well, unless Sage slept with some *other* outrageously gifted sorcerer."

Regis shoved his chair away from the table. "You... you kidnapped me because I'm your son?" He got to his feet. "You could have just asked. You could have approached me. You could have—you could have done anything else!"

Septimus set down his cup and in a very quiet voice, he said, "Regis, I am not going to remind you of your manners again."

Regis breathed hard through his nose. It felt as though no air was coming to his chest.

"Sit," Septimus said.

Regis sat.

A servant came by to clear Septimus's plate. "You're not special just because you're related to me," Septimus said. "I'm sure I have several sons. Sage and I were married before she left me, but she did leave me. Any man can be born with power. No, Regis. The reason I picked you up is entirely your fault."

"You have to let me go. I have a sick friend—"

Septimus waved his hand. "I have no interest in your friend." He drummed his fingers. "It's so rare that a sorcerer like you springs out of nowhere. Tell me. Who taught you?"

And he smiled coyly.

Chills shot through Regis. The aftertaste of food lingered in his mouth, but it tasted like ash, not pork. "I taught myself."

"Yourself? Really? Well, congratulations. That's quite a feat."

"I did. I can tell you the names of the books I read. *Body Magick*, by Septimus A—" Regis tripped over the name, bit his tongue. "By you. And others. I read them on my own."

Septimus smiled patiently. "Regis. Come now. Don't lie to your own father."

"I'm telling the truth!"

Septimus strolled to the bookcase and lifted a book. The title was handwritten: *Assorted Notes on Corbinian Anatomy.* Idly, Septimus flipped open the cover. The first page was a graphic illustration of a bird's skeletal structure. Corvus Albus, a crow with white and black. The notes were in Belcane's handwriting.

Septimus set the book down. "How long did you work for her?"

Crow was a good liar. Charming. Regis racked his brain desperately for some hint of how to get through this. Crow sort of—flirted his way around things. That wouldn't work here, obviously. Jonathan would try intimidation. No good. The only weapon Regis had was the truth.

"I was confined," he blurted out. "There, are you happy? She took me when I was nine. I had nothing to do, and I liked magic, so I stole her books. I read. I practiced. I was literate. I was lucky. I was in the right place at the right time. I'm fortunate she didn't kill me. I never wanted to help her. Never." He became desperate. "Look. You can't tell anyone I'm your son. It would look bad for you."

Septimus tossed the book aside. "Spare me the theatrics. I need your help. I've tried replicating her experiments, but I can't quite get them right."

Regis felt the blood drain from his face. "Replicating her experiments? She cut people up. That's unclean."

"Dead people," Septimus said. "Mostly. Haven't you?"

Regis flushed. A serial killer, once, that Jonathan had slain. And prisons were often willing to sell him the bodies of executed criminals. Medical magic required hands-on study. "Yes, but I paid for those."

There were only a handful of procedures that Myra Belcane had created. There was… there was longevity, the transfer of organs, a few shape-shifting pieces….

"I paid a great deal to have these journals stolen from Belcane's study," Septimus said. "My thief risked his life. They belong to me. I'll make you a deal. Explain these notes to me, and once we have a successful product, I'll allow you to leave."

"Allow me to leave? Just like that? What will happen to the journals?"

"My dear boy," Septimus said. "If I release these journals, you'll be arrested. Don't worry. I'll protect you. Provided, of course, you keep your mouth shut. I'll release Myra Belcane's discoveries as my own. No one ever needs to know. Understand?"

Septimus had blackmail material on him. Thank the gods. Maybe Septimus would actually let him go. "Fine. What do you want me to do?"

Septimus opened the journal to the first page. Regis read the first line. *Today I have created a servant.* Regis's breath seized in his chest, and his hands fisted as he fought not to react. No. No, not this one.

Septimus pointed. "This one here. Her greatest work. A monster unlike any other. Thinking. Feeling. Human. Tell me," Septimus said. "What do you know about Crow Belcane?"

Chapter SEVEN
Exposed

WHEN CROW and Jonathan returned to the House of Red Silk, a servant led them to Karis's chambers. The room was resplendent—an enormous bed draped in silk and fur, and to the side, two couches facing a decorated fireplace. Karis lay across one, examining her nails.

A well-dressed man sat on the other bench. "Ah, Lord Murtagh," Karis said. "Take a seat. I was just finishing up with another client."

"The slave you sold me is useless," said the man. "He's surly, defiant, and pig-headed. He refuses to help me no matter how I reason with him."

"Are you suggesting I cheated you? You have your slave, as you asked. If you don't like him, then return him to me."

"I can't give him back! I need him! Send someone to help me break him. Give me drugs. Give me advice. Anything. I can't use him like this. You owe me."

"No," Karis said. "I do not. You paid his value and nothing more. Break him yourself. Garlant, please escort Master Septimus from the property." Garlant took the man by his shoulders. With an angry look, Septimus stormed out. "Pay him no mind," Karis said with a wave of her hand. "You're here to buy Peter, yes?"

A small body stirred in Karis's bed. Peter uncoiled from beneath the covers. When he noticed them, he ducked his head.

"I think you'll find him very compliant," Karis said, voice slick as oil. "I trained him myself."

Next to him, Crow felt—rather than heard—Jonathan inhale. Jonathan gripped Crow's wrist tight. "I didn't know you were a sorceress," Jonathan said carefully.

Karis laughed and said, "Oh no! I'm not."

Peter sank onto the couch next to her. Her fingers slid into his shirt, and she pushed it aside. If he was old enough to grow body hair, someone had shaved it. Crow's stomach lurched. And—for a moment—he thought about drawing the knife from his boot and ramming it into her throat.

From the way Jonathan was gripping his wrist, he had to be thinking similar thoughts.

"Are you interested in my slaves or not?" Karis said. "My dear, I'm beginning to feel taken advantage of." Jonathan nodded. He took the bag from his waist and tossed it to Karis. She felt it. "What's this?"

"Half," Jonathan said. "Upfront. Convince me to buy a slave."

Another ruse. Regis might have been bought, but they still didn't know by whom. They only needed access to the House for a little while longer. Crow had to find out who bought Regis—here, today. Jonathan would stall her as long as possible. Worst-case scenario, they'd lure Karis out of the House, kidnap her, and interrogate her.

"Come, sit," Karis said.

Crow put his hand on the small of Jonathan's back, rubbing with his thumb. It might be mistaken for an affectionate gesture. Instead, a reminder: they were in a den of thieves and murderers, rapists, all of them. Step carefully.

Instead of relaxing, Jonathan tensed. Damn.

He scratched the back of Jonathan's neck, the fine hairline. Jonathan let out a breath of surprise, then relaxed. He smiled gratefully as Crow leaned into him like a lover.

There we go.

They sat on the couch together. Jonathan and Karis talked business. Crow tuned Karis out and focused on Jonathan. His fingers rubbed and found sore spots. If he paid any attention to what Karis was saying, he'd take the nearest brazier and swing it at her head. After a few minutes, he politely excused himself.

The House was nearly empty. He found the door that led to the courtyard and stepped out. He prowled around the perimeter of the building. Here in the back—he was certain the slave pens were nearby. A small barred window led inside. Crow stood on his toes. A small, empty room with a bed.

A bar came loose in his hands. Shocked, Crow landed on his ass. He stared in astonishment at the window, then at the bar in his hand. Someone had filed through it.

He tugged on the remaining bars. Solid. The slave that had filed away the first bar must have been sold before he could finish working on the others.

Crow shifted. Just a little. Slowly, agonizingly, his body shrunk. His bones crunched and his cartilage moved. Half bird and half man, he scrabbled through the gap, then fell on the bed. Immediately he focused on becoming human again.

He tried the door. Unlocked. It led to a long hallway with equally spaced small rooms. The slaves' quarters. At the end of the hallway, there were cages. Most were bare cells with only a bucket for waste. The good slaves, Crow thought, were likely rewarded with private rooms. There were only a few in the open cages, and all seemed injured. Beaten. Naked.

A tumble of curled red hair caught his eye.

His heart jolted inside his ribs.

It wasn't Regis. No, the hair was too long. It was the woman from before. Athea. Crow let out a shaky breath. He crept out to get a better look. Regis was nowhere in sight. Unless he was in one of the private rooms, of course, though Crow somehow doubted that.

Maybe Athea would know something. She seemed new. Likely she had been illegally acquired as well. And for some reason, Crow felt oddly drawn to her. Likely because she looked so much like Regis.

Crow slid his lock picks from his pocket. He knelt in front of Athea's door. He put his ear to the lock and slid the picks in. Eventually, the gears clicked. He took a vial of oil from his belt and wet the hinges, then swung open the door.

Athea stirred. Crow pressed a hand to her mouth. She jerked awake.

Crow held a finger to his lips. "I'm here to help you." He spoke as quietly as he could. "I'm looking for a red-haired sorcerer. A little shorter than me. About my age. Lots of freckles. Have you seen him?"

He took his hand away. She scanned the room, craning to look around Crow. One of the other slaves stirred, though the rest stayed asleep. "I saw him," she whispered. "What's it to you?"

"He's a dear friend. Please, I need to find him."

She bit her lip. Then said, "That sorcerer you're looking for is already gone. Karis had a buyer lined up ahead of time. Someone who asked for him specifically."

"Tell me who bought him."

Athea gripped his shirt and pulled him close. "I know everything. Get me out, and I'll show you where your friend is. I'll lead the way myself."

Crow hesitated. What if the guards caught them? How would he get her out? What if she was lying? "I can't right now," he whispered. "Tell me now, and I'll figure out a way to save you later."

"Get my collar off." Her voice was a hiss. "You can't just leave me here."

Crow hesitated.

"I'm not lying." Her face twisted with fear. "You're talking about Regis Teller, aren't you? See, I know him. There, is that good enough for you? His lover is Jonathan White. I know why he was taken."

Her chain rattled as she shifted to grab him. One cell over, her frantic whispering stirred another slave. A man jolted upright, staring at Crow, wide-eyed. He opened his mouth, then closed it.

Then, nearby, a second slave woke up and began to shriek. "There's someone in here! Get Lady Karis! A door is open, someone is trying to escape!"

Crow darted for the door. "I'll be back, I swear!"

Athea swore at him.

At the other end of the hall, two guards slammed through a door. Crow bolted. He ran into the room with the hole in the window. No lock on the door. Shit. He slammed it shut behind him and shoved the mattress against it.

They had seen his face. They knew it was him. If he could get out, maybe he could escape before they caught him—

What about Jonathan?

Shit. Shit. Shit. No, there was no time to think of that. He'd grab Jonathan if he could, and they'd run right out the front door. He fought to shift. Panicked as he was, he couldn't focus. The spell felt wrong inside him. He fought to fit through the window.

The door shoved open. Someone seized his legs and dragged him down, knocking him into the floor. A guard knelt over him and pummeled him in the head.

Darkness burst in his vision. It was all he could do to breathe through the pain. Reeling from confusion, he vaguely became aware of being yanked upright by two men. One of them slid a padlock through the rings on his cuffs, then locked it, binding his hands behind him. He fought uselessly. They had him.

"The bitch-slave," one said. Crow focused on him hazily.

It was the guard who had assaulted him. The one Jonathan fought off. Garlant smiled at him nastily. "Hi, beautiful."

THEY THREW him into the wine cellar in the kitchen, then locked the trapdoor. Crow curled in a corner. He thought of Jonathan.

He had been wrong. He couldn't do this alone.

The punch to the head had scrambled his thoughts. It felt as though he'd been dosed with opium again. The spell inside him roiled, out of his control. He fought the urge to vomit. His arms hurt where they'd yanked him, and he'd have bruises in the morning. Blood dripped from his nose. With his hands chained, he couldn't wipe it away.

For a time, he thought he'd break apart—lose himself completely and dissolve into feathers. He wasn't sure how much longer he could hold on. If he became a bird permanently, would he remember being human, or would he forget entirely? He wasn't sure which was worse. Either way, he'd stop being himself, and the idea was terrifying.

He didn't focus on being human; he focused on staying conscious for one more breath, one more heartbeat. At last, the spell inside him came back under control. Crow was so relieved he nearly wept.

The door opened. Relieved and yet terrified, Crow looked up, expecting to see Karis.

No, it was the same two guards. "Up," one said, but didn't give him time.

They seemed to enjoy dragging him about, because they did so with no regard to his health. At last, they reached a courtyard.

Five whipping posts lined the wall.

Karis reclined in a nearby gazebo. A servant fanned her, and Jonathan sat uncomfortably to the side. He jumped up when Crow was dragged in. The guards threw Crow on the ground. He breathed hard, a pit in his stomach.

Jonathan's boots approached. He stopped a foot from Crow's nose. "Is there a reason you've dragged my pampered pet to me in chains?" Jonathan said.

"We caught him trying to steal some of the merchandise."

Crow dared to look up. Jonathan's face was pale yet cold. They stared at each other. Crow could feel a swelling bruise on his face where the guard had hit him. There was a stretch of silence.

"Merchandise," Jonathan said.

"The young woman," Crow whispered. "Athea." One of the guards kicked him, and he cringed.

"Don't," Jonathan said sharply.

"You don't get to decide what happens to him anymore." Crow squeezed his eyes shut and tried desperately to block out the sound of Karis's voice. "He tried to steal my property," she said.

"Crow," Jonathan said. "Look at me."

Crow tensed. He didn't obey, at first. It was a mistake. A hand fisted in his hair and wrenched back. Crow's eyes watered. Jonathan's face was unreadable. Masked almost. There was tension there, and either anger or fear.

Every man in the courtyard wore a sword. Every man except for the two of them. It was the two of them against the rest. One wrong move, and they would be found out. Did Karis suspect the truth?

"What were you doing?" Jonathan asked carefully.

"Freeing a slave," Crow said.

Jonathan grimaced, then gave Crow an apologetic look. "Freeing a slave," he said loudly. "You conniving little bitch. How dare you try to steal from our host."

"I'm sorry, master." Crow thought hard and fast. He decided to play his only ace. "I was scared. Please forgive me. I'm so terrified of being replaced, master." He began to grovel. "I never meant to actually free her. I wanted to get caught. I thought—I thought perhaps if I got us thrown out, you wouldn't buy a new slave. I adore you, sir."

"So you were jealous?" Jonathan's voice was ice. "Jealousy is for men. You aren't a man, Crow. You're my pet. My toy."

"Yes, master," he said.

"Good. Kiss my boot and apologize."

Crow stared at Jonathan in disbelief.

"Go on," Jonathan said. "Show these men what a good slave you are."

Crow kissed the tip of Jonathan's boot. His lips parted around the curve. His eyes flickered up, but he did not move his head—held there, instead. With his wrists behind his back, he couldn't wipe his mouth.

Jonathan crouched to stroke his hair. "Good boy." He glanced at Karis. "Is that all? Can we go?"

"Is that all?" Karis slowly repeated.

"What do you want me to do? Kill him? It was one stupid escape attempt."

"I want you to punish him," Karis said. "Do it, or I'll do it myself. Beat him. Rape him. I don't care, just hurt him."

Jonathan froze.

"Fine," she snapped. To the guards, she said, "Strip him and tie him to the post."

Jonathan lurched to stop them. "Wait."

"A slave trying to steal a slave. You're responsible for him. If we get the City Watch involved, you'll be charged with attempted robbery."

The guards grabbed Crow's arms, wrenching him forward. Crow dug in his heels. He looked desperately at Jonathan. For a tense moment, Crow honestly thought Jonathan might break then and there. There were two armed guards, two slaves fanning Karis, and Karis herself. If Jonathan gave up the masquerade, what would happen? They were so close to being found out.

"I'll handle his punishment privately," Jonathan said. He pulled Crow away from the guards, and Crow staggered, unable to balance himself. Jonathan began to steer him away.

"Stop right there," Karis snapped. "If you want to punish him, then do it here. Now. In public. If you don't, I'll have you both arrested."

Arrested. Crow swallowed. Even if they explained their side of the story to the City Watch, there was no guarantee that the Watch would take their side. Karis was an influential woman; they had no proof that she was doing anything illegal; and technically, he had committed a crime by trying to steal from her.

"If I let you punish him, what will you do?" Jonathan asked slowly.

She settled back in her seat in the gazebo. "My men need some fun. They'll use him for an hour or two, then return him to you. No permanent scars, I promise. Fair?"

Ice filtered into Crow's veins. The two guards jeered. Beaten, raped, or arrested. Raped would be best. It would leave less damage than a beating, and arrest simply wasn't an option now. They had gone too far into this game; if they got the City Watch involved, Karis would use her influence to escape punishment, and Crow and Jonathan would stew in prison. No. The only option was clear.

Crow met Jonathan's eyes, praying he'd make the right choice. He could do nothing but wait.

"I can beat him in front of you," Jonathan said slowly. "Or I can let your guards have him. Or I can rape him myself. Is that it?"

"Unless you have a better idea."

Jonathan let go. "Tie him to the post."

None of the guards moved. In the end, Jonathan did it himself. He grabbed Crow's upper arm and pulled him, and Crow made a show of resisting. Only then Jonathan hesitated, glancing back at him, and Crow realized: Jonathan thought the resistance genuine.

Crow kept his head low and his eyes averted. "Free his wrists," Jonathan said.

One of the guards produced a key and unlocked the padlock. Crow rubbed his arms. "Tunic off," Jonathan said. "Face the post. Hands above your head—high."

Crow shrugged off his shirt. He rested his forehead against the wood and closed his eyes. He stretched his arms above his head.

Jonathan threaded rope through the rings in the cuffs, then passed the other end through a bolt high on the post. He cinched the rope tight, forcing Crow's body taut as he stood on the balls of his feet. Jonathan's body pressed close as he knotted the rope into place. His thigh shifted against Crow's ass.

Then his weight vanished, and fear bubbled up in Crow's throat. Footsteps could be heard moving back.

Then a crack.

Jonathan, testing a whip.

A whip. Jonathan was going to beat him. Crow didn't have to pretend anymore. Terror shot through him.

He'd never been this defenseless before. He rolled his shoulders and blew out his breath, trying to ignore the anticipation fluttering in his stomach. He expected Jonathan to speak—to taunt him, insult him, force him to count the lashes, make him ask for each blow.

"I'll give him fifteen," Jonathan said from somewhere behind. "Acceptable?"

"Acceptable."

The first blow landed, sending a searing stripe of pain down his back. Crow locked his jaw. For a moment, he forgot he was supposed to be playing the part of a weak and fragile slave. His arms tightened with the impact, pulling uselessly at the ropes before he regained control of himself. He stopped, breathing hard. The muscles in his back twitched.

The cuts would ruin the feather tattoos on his back. Especially if they scarred, he thought inanely.

"Count the lashes," Jonathan said.

Crow licked his lips, holding back his normally scathing tongue. "One," he said through gritted teeth.

There came a soft sound behind him, and he jerked, fearing the next strike. Instead, no pain came. Jonathan didn't snicker or comment on the flinch like Crow himself would have. Instead, footsteps approached, and Crow tensed, fighting the urge to turn around. He couldn't see behind himself even if he tried. The binding kept him stretched tight. He'd only look foolish, twisting like an animal caught in a trap.

A cloth was drawn over his eyes, leaving him in darkness with only a sliver of light on the bottom. It was only a blindfold, but he couldn't stop the tremor of fear that went through him. "I've got you," Jonathan murmured. "Pretend there's no one here but us."

To the audience, it would seem like a cruelty—depriving him of sight during the whipping. Crow knew it was a kindness. He waited, feeling eyes on him, as Jonathan walked back. The second blow hit.

"Two," he choked out. The third blow hit along the same spot as before, the fresh agony built upon the last. "Three." Jonathan would go easy on him. Surely. Was this easy? Gods, it hurt. Surely Karis didn't expect Jonathan to ruin his bedslave.

Along with the pain, he felt something else. It seared him with the heat of it, a flicker of shock and lust mixed in, coiling up his spine and electrifying his nerves.

Excitement.

Excitement?

Three more, and he counted each time. The metal dug into his wrists, and no matter how he twisted, they held. He had no hope of breaking the rope that kept him so tightly stretched. He fought. He didn't mean to fight, but he did. This was beyond his control, all of it. The lashes were inevitable. He could only hang there and take it, body arching and shoving.

Jonathan paused between each lash, sometimes for only a moment, sometimes for a full minute. Each second passed in an agony of waiting. No matter how he tried to prepare himself, each blow came as a shock, and he shrieked. Jonathan was good with a whip—very good—and though some strokes were hard, others were soft. The pain dulled. Heat grew.

Something was wrong with him. Something was wrong with his body. The blows felt shocking, exciting, and strange. Part of him recoiled; the other part cried out for more.

Before he could decide what to do, much less decide what it meant, the seventh blow landed, and Crow arched. "Seven," he whimpered.

Stomping footsteps in the dirt. A hand, wrenching back his head. "What was that?"

Something very much like arousal shot through him. The grip tightened. Jonathan shook him, and his eyes watered. "Please. No more."

The hand released, and Crow shook his head to clear it. His entire body ached. "I asked you what you said. Speak up. Did you lose count?"

He caught his breath. Jonathan moved away. The next strike was the most vicious yet. Crow gasped before he could stop himself, then went limp and hung from the ropes, panting. His back was on fire, and he couldn't do one fucking thing but hang there and take it. Gods, he'd never done anything like this before.

"Well?" Jonathan's voice was cool.

He wanted to spit at Jonathan's feet. He wanted to taunt Jonathan until he snapped—but he didn't. His sense of self-preservation was too strong. So instead he said, "Eight." Loudly, this time.

A hand running through his hair, soothing the ache. "Good boy," a voice murmured in his ear, too low for the crowd to hear. And that thought made the heat in his gut spark into a blaze, and he shuddered, pressing back, moaning. "Just a few more." Jonathan let go.

This was not a game. This was the only real thing between them. He had thrown Jonathan off a building, and now here he was, tied to a post. At Jonathan's mercy.

Crow rested his face against the post. The next blows came rhythmically. They were no longer a surprise. How many was it? He was supposed to be counting. No matter. He choked out a laugh, then groaned and rolled his shoulders to ease away the pain.

"You know," Jonathan said, "it's not my intention to cause you permanent damage, but the less you pay attention, the harder I'm going to have to hit."

The next strike landed before Crow was ready for it, He jerked and screamed before he managed to bite down on the cry, gritting his teeth and groaning through them.

The agony had him feeling more aware, more real, than he had in ages. In a freakish way, he enjoyed it. What was wrong with him? His pants were tight, and there was no way to remove his belt, much less the restrictive cloth.

He wished fervently that he'd discovered this little fact about himself in a safer environment. Say, while loosely tied to a comfy bed, not chained and half-naked, stretched out tightly like a willing victim for his rival.

It was a struggle not to press his hips against the wood. He wanted to grind against something, anything. He wanted to fight the ropes until his wrists bled. His hard cock made an obvious ridge in his pants—he could feel it—though hopefully the wooden post blocked it from view. He prayed that when he was released, he could grab his tunic quickly and put it on.

His mind went fuzzy. He didn't want to be here, tied to this post. He wanted to rest on a bed of soft furs and blankets, alone. The manacles were fine. They could stay. He trusted Jonathan. He wanted to moan as loudly as he liked and rut against Jonathan's thigh—

No, his hand. He wanted Jonathan's hand on his cock. Wide. Thick. Callused. His thumb smearing liquid from the tip of his head. He wanted something inside him, fucking him open—hard and desperate—

Jonathan hit, again and again. "Fifteen," Crow gasped. "Fifteen. Jonathan, please, let me down, let me down, let me down—"

He was incoherent, begging. He did not hear Jonathan come up behind him. The ties released suddenly, and Crow fell. Jonathan caught him. Crow pressed his face into Jonathan's shoulder, wrapped an arm around his back, and just breathed. The rope was neatly severed. Oh. Jonathan had cut it.

Jonathan smelled faintly of leather, and his skin was warm from exerting himself. He jerked a little when Crow's groin accidentally pressed against his hip. "Hell, Crow," Jonathan breathed. Quietly, so only the two of them could hear.

Oh, Crow remembered. He was hard.

And now Jonathan knew.

The blindfold was tugged away, and Crow flinched, blinking into the bright light. Jonathan supported him, keeping Crow's body angled away from Karis and away from the guards.

His pain was obvious enough, and from the sympathetic looks of the guards, Crow knew his reaction to the whipping had been mistaken for agony.

It had been agony. What was wrong with him?

Karis's face had gone white, as if she had been slapped. She seemed to be searching Jonathan's face for something—something—though what it was, Crow couldn't fathom. "Satisfied?" Jonathan asked. "I'll make sure he doesn't do it again."

Her lips thinned. She nodded, then swept up her skirts and left.

Jonathan led. As soon as they were alone, he slipped under Crow's arm, taking part of his weight. "Are you all right?" he whispered.

The words seemed to come from far away. Jonathan picked up the pace, and Crow stumbled, unable to keep up. The way back to their room was a slow, agonizing journey. Jonathan eased Crow onto the bed, then shut the door and locked it. Immediately he was by Crow's side again. "Crow. Crow, look at me."

His eyelids were too heavy to open.

There was the sound of water being poured. Then a weight shifted the bed. Jonathan dragged him into a seated position, then held a goblet to his lips. "Drink."

Crow drank.

Jonathan set the goblet aside. The rim made a loud wobbling noise as if he'd set it down wrong, tilted. "I tried to keep the blows light."

"Not your fault." There, he managed that.

"How badly did I hurt you?"

Crow summoned all his energy and shook his head.

"I thought that going slowly at first, giving you more lashes but more lightly—I thought it would give your body time to dull the pain."

He'd done an excellent job. Crow felt incredibly dull. Imparting this fact to Jonathan, however, felt like it would take more effort than it was worth. Crow simply sat. Jonathan would care for him.

Something niggled in the back of his mind. Something was wrong. He'd missed something.

Jonathan helped him into a facedown position on the bed. Then footsteps moved toward the door, and Jonathan could be heard exiting, then speaking. "Could you bring me a salve? Something to stop his cuts from getting inflamed."

A sullen voice. One of the servants. "He should have expected correction. You shouldn't spoil him."

"Get me a fucking salve," Jonathan said.

The door closed. There came the sound of rustling cloth, then a slosh of water, and then a weight pressed beside him. A cool cloth eased across his back. Crow took a sharp breath. "Cold?" Jonathan asked, and Crow nodded. The touch stung, but only in a few places. Skin had not broken with every lash. When Jonathan finished, he laid a hand on the back of Crow's neck, stroking the soft spot behind Crow's ear with his thumb. "Does it hurt?"

"Aches." Pleasantly, almost, like the sensation that came from bruises and scraped knees as a child. It left him with a sense of accomplishment. He had survived a flogging, and there was no more flogging in his future.

Time had no meaning anymore. He existed to lay on the bed. He shifted his head so that Jonathan's fingers were in his hair, making a small noise when—after a moment—they began to move.

Eventually, Jonathan muttered something about lazy servants, then left. He returned shortly. "She left the salve beside the door," he said sourly. "Without knocking." There came the sound of a bottle popping open. "Hold still."

A shock of cold fingers. Liquid smeared across the cuts. Crow arched. He was safe. The pain was inevitable. He accepted it.

The stinging woke him a little. "Why did you whip me?"

It was all he could manage. He was weak and perverse for reacting the way he had. Jonathan was dangerous. He forced himself to believe that: Jonathan was dangerous.

And yet this room felt like the safest place he could be.

"It was whip you or let them have you," Jonathan said.

"You could have fucked me."

Jonathan didn't answer.

"Too loyal?" Crow said.

"Good gods, Crow. Do you really think Regis would care? He's possessive, not insane. He'd be angry we were forced into that situation, not angry we had sex."

Crow made a noncommittal noise. "I don't know how that fidelity nonsense works."

Jonathan still hadn't answered his question. After a while, Jonathan said, "A whipping seemed more merciful than rape."

"It would have been just sex."

"Would you have preferred that?"

Crow turned his head aside. Karis would not have been satisfied with slow preparation and a boring fuck. The sex would have been framed as punishment. Being humiliated, fucked without oil, degraded in front of people who thought he deserved it, all under fear of discovery…. Fear slivered through him. The idea made him shudder. "No," he said. "The whipping was better. Thank you."

Jonathan's thumbs made circles on Crow's back.

"About yesterday," Crow said slowly.

"Hm?"

"When I ran off. I'm sorry. It was an idiotic tantrum."

"Do we have to talk about that?"

"I was out of line. I'm being honest."

"Honest. You. Crow Belcane."

Crow laughed. He felt like crying. "I can't fix this, can I?"

He recoiled, pulling away from Jonathan's hands. He sat on the opposite side of the bed and wrapped an arm around his knees. His back blistered with pain. He sort of liked Jonathan. And how sad was that? He'd never asked Jonathan for anything, never done him any favors. Crow had made his own mess, and yet here Jonathan was, helping him out of it.

Jonathan's eyes were like ice, like glaciers. "Come back over here. I need to fix your back."

"Fix me?" Crow said. "Why? What use am I now?"

"Crow. You're headstrong. You're unstoppable. Yeah, you're hurt right now, and I have to protect you, but you're not a liability. We're not enemies, are we?"

The words hung heavy in the air between them. Crow considered the man before him, the hard set of his shoulders and the pinch of honesty around his eyes, and found himself responding with a grudging lack of hate. "We're not," he said, after a breath. He had meant it as a question. It didn't come out that way.

"I don't like you. I won't deny that. Regis still cares about you. Not in the same way he loves me—"

"He loves me like a brother," Crow finished for him.

"I really don't think so," Jonathan said.

Another long silence.

Crow bit the inside of his cheek until it bled. He couldn't stop the surge of hope inside him. "He still—really?"

Jonathan grimaced. "He tries not to talk about you. I can tell when he's thinking about it, though. He gets this sad, hopeless look, like an abandoned puppy."

"You're jealous," Crow said, disbelieving. "Are you kidding? You, the love of his life, are jealous of me."

"You had him first."

"You idiot. I said that so you'd hit me. I was trying to make you look bad. Who cares? *You* have him *now*."

Jonathan took the cloth from the bowl and wiped his hands. He set it aside. "We should go."

"Jonathan. I…."

"What do you want me to say?" Jonathan said. "That I hate you? That I don't know how to feel about you? That I want you stay away from him? I can't tell when you're being genuine and when you're manipulating me. You killed people for your mother. You stole things. You kidnapped Regis for her. What if she sent you to kill me instead of Regis? What if you took the oathspell?"

"I would kill a stranger to save my own life," he said. "I'm not ashamed of that."

There it was. The bare truth between them. How could they ever trust each other?

"You really were kind that night in the tavern," Jonathan said. "The first time we met. It felt real. Crow. Why were you nice to me?"

Because I didn't hate you then, Crow thought to say, but he kept his mouth shut. He didn't hate Jonathan now. This conversation was becoming incredibly confusing. "I do what I need to," he said. "My life is worth more than a stranger's, and so is his. If I'd let you kill Myra, I would be dead. It was you or me."

"It was you," Jonathan said, "or the queen. Your life or everyone else's. The fate of the kingdom. And you picked yourself."

"My life is worth more than a thousand strangers'."

The truth pervaded the very air.

They were no longer strangers.

Crow caught his wrist. "For what it's worth—things are different now."

They were gazing at each other.

"You're right," Jonathan said, and Crow let go. "They are."

Crow stopped there. He meant to say something. Something important.

"What?" Jonathan said.

Something was wrong. He could feel it. And then it hit him. Crow leapt off the bed as if it were made of fire. "We have to go. Now."

"What?"

"Karis found us out."

"How do you know?"

"Because," Crow said. "After the fifteenth lash, I called you Jonathan."

The door swung open.

Karis stood framed in the doorway. A guard to her left, her boy Peter to her right. Crow tensed, and beside him, Jonathan gripped his arm.

Karis wore her usual sunny smile. "Master Murtagh. I apologize for this unfortunate incident that's come between us. It's so difficult to discipline a favorite, isn't it?" She bowed her head. "If you would allow it, perhaps I could heal your slave?"

Jonathan's grip neared bruising intensity.

"Come, dear." She motioned for Crow. "Let's get you fixed up. I'd hate to scar your lovely back."

Slowly—so slowly—Jonathan let go and got up off the bed. Crow took a step closer, then another. The guard at her right ushered him into the hall. He stood inside their little group. Peter stood outside the door, and he watched Crow suspiciously.

Karis's shoes clicked as she strode down the hall. As she passed him, Crow caught sight of her expression. She looked murderous. The guard followed, pulling Crow along, and Crow looked back desperately, searching for Jonathan. Jonathan snatched up Crow's shirt and followed.

He could barely walk. His back burned. The guard was nearly dragging him. At last, they came to the exhibition room at the front of the building. A slave had been beaten to death on the floor.

A woman. Long ginger hair bound back by a strip of cloth. A slim build. Athea. He fell to his knees, feeling sick. She had been stripped naked and whipped. Blood trickled from welts on her back.

"Forgive the mess," Karis said. "See, this is what I do to disobedient slaves, Master Murtagh. You're so very careless with yours. Almost like he's not a slave at all."

Crow scanned the room. Three guards, Karis, and Peter. Jonathan was a talented swordsman, but could he take out three men while unarmed? Unlikely. If Crow could disarm one of them and give the sword to Jonathan, maybe they'd get out of this alive.

Athea stirred. She cracked an eye open at him. Not dead, he realized, washed by a wave of relief.

One of the guards—Garlant—seized him by the arm and dragged him up. "Don't touch the merchandise."

Jonathan yanked Crow away from the offending guard. He held Crow close. "My slave is badly injured, Karis," Jonathan said quietly. "You said you'd have someone heal him."

"Oh yes. Of course. In a moment."

"You know, it really doesn't matter. I think I'll just get my own healer. Crow and I will be leaving now."

Karis didn't fall for it. "No," she said flatly, and she met his eyes.

A long silence.

"Look at this." Karis nudged Athea with one booted foot. "See how badly she's hurt? I regret such damage, but it's the way of things. I discipline my pets, hoping they learn."

The doors to the foyer were shut, but not barred. Crow calculated the distance between them and the street. If they could reach the outside, Karis would not dare attack them. But the distance was far, and the guards would surely seize them before they reached the doors.

"Girl." Karis kicked Athea in the ribs. "Girl, look at me."

Athea's lips cracked open. "Girl," she hissed. "I… am… a woman."

"Miss Athea. When I acquired you, you seemed like such a nice young lady. Do you think I like hurting you? No. I hate punishing my pets. Alas, punishment is necessary for discipline. I hurt you because I love you, little one. Imagine all the nice things you could have if only you learned to behave. Real clothes. Books. A private room." Her voice was liquid smooth.

Athea stared at her, white-faced.

"I will give you one last chance," Karis said quietly. "Tell me why the black-haired slave came to your cell. Tell me what he said to you."

"Fuck you," Athea said.

"Foul words have no place in reasonable debate. The simpleminded resort to spitting insults when they are beaten."

Athea's face brightened with sheer fury. She spat at Karis, who daintily wiped spittle from her cheek with a handkerchief. "If you insist on acting like a child, I will treat you like one. Garlant, Avard, take her back to the cells, bind her to the bars of her cage, and finish her."

She dropped the soiled handkerchief on Athea's face. "A wise woman finds opportunities even in the most unfortunate circumstances. Use Miss Athea as an example. Make sure all the other slaves are awake and watching. When you are done, reward the slave who alerted the guards. Do you hear me, Athea? Your nasty attitude has reduced your value. You are unsellable. A scrap to be thrown to my men."

Athea's face lost all color. The guards dragged her to her feet. "No." She wrenched against their hold. "You can't do this! It isn't fair! You can't just—you can't just take away my life like this!"

"Perhaps," Karis said, "if someone else told me why he spoke to you, then I would not need to kill you."

The guards didn't take Athea away. What were they doing? Was this a show? Karis looked at Crow, and chills shot down his spine. "Perhaps I wouldn't have to kill her," she said quietly, "if someone else would confess."

She knew why they were there. This was a game. Crow's heart pounded.

If he said nothing, then Athea would be murdered. If he confessed, she would throw them out and destroy her records. If he attacked her, then she'd call the City Watch and have them arrested. She wanted them to do it. It would gain her sympathy and credibility. Even if they explained what was going on, they had no evidence against her. They could not possibly win. This was provocation. The beating, the nudity, the display. She was using Athea as a pawn.

Crow took a leather strip from his wrist. He tied back his hair. It would only get in the way during the fight. "Jonathan," he said.

"Yeah, Crow?" Jonathan said.

"If you can handle the guards, I have a plan."

"If you're certain," Jonathan said.

Crow darted toward Karis.

The two guards moved to stop him. Crow ducked beneath a swung sword, then snatched his first attacker's ankle, and the large man fell hard. Crow seized a nearby brazier and knocked it over, scattering coals and smoke.

Jonathan picked up the poker from the fire, still glowing. He moved between Crow and the guards.

They fought. Sharp steel on hot iron. Sparks. Jonathan dove and ducked past strikes. He played them against each other, dodging attacks rather than parrying them, and their swords often hit each other. One swipe nearly caught the second guard across the face. Each backed off after that. They didn't seem to know whether to attack Jonathan together or separately.

Jonathan speared one in the side, and the man shrieked, burned. Crow watched him in amazement.

Karis backed into a corner. She pulled Peter in front of her. The boy's face was pale, but he stood his ground. A golden shield flickered in front of his palms, and sparks lashed out at Crow. Crow flinched. "Hiding behind the boy you abused," he said. "You think he can defend you?"

Karis laughed mockingly at him. "You think you can beat my pet?"

Peter flinched. There was hesitation on his face, but Karis didn't see it. "Peter," Crow said. "Are you really going to die for her? This controlling bitch? Run. Go on. We're going to kill her if we can."

The boy's mouth wobbled. He glanced between Crow and Karis. Crow snatched him by his thick necklace. "Run," he roared in the boy's face, and shoved him toward the door.

Peter ran.

"Peter!" Karis shrieked. She backed against the wall. "Garlant! Avard! Help!"

Crow rolled his eyes. He pinned her to the wall. She fought like a cat, clawing at him. He felt her down. There, a lump in her pocket. He pulled out the keys, then looked around wildly. There. Athea lay on the floor.

He ran to her. He prayed Jonathan would see what he was doing, and he prayed Jonathan would defend him.

Jonathan stepped between him and the guards. They attacked, and Jonathan parried, his fire-poker ringing as it met the swords. Crow fumbled with the keys. Too large. Too small. There, a medium one—no, it wouldn't fit. "The old-looking one," Athea rasped. "Two down. Medium size. Hurry."

He shoved it in, unlocked the collar, and tore it from her neck. The collar bounced on the floor. It landed hard on the opal, and the gem cracked.

Athea laughed.

She didn't seem to have the energy to drag herself upright. Silver sparks crackled around her, and her body rose up, as if by magic. Her head rolled back. Blood dripped from her back. "Get behind me," she said. Crow grabbed Jonathan's arm and dragged him back, and they huddled against the wall.

Athea raised her arm, then threw out her palm.

Silver lightning lashed out, throwing the first guard into the second. Both traveled backward, hitting Karis. Athea threw out her hand again, this time at the door. It ripped off its hinges, then swung. The edge hit the first guard. It went through him cleanly. He stared down at it in shock, then collapsed.

"That's for beating me," Athea spat. The fallen brazier rose into the air. Individual coals hurled at them. The drapes set fire. Karis bolted, vanishing into another room. The second guard stayed behind, pinned.

Smoke choked the air. Athea stumbled after Karis, leaving bloody footprints on the floor. She tore open the next door and flung it. There was no delicacy to her magic, just brutal force.

Jonathan looked at him, and their eyes met. His eyes were blue again, no longer brown. His disguise was undone. Crow scanned the floor to see what had happened to the little crystal. Had it bounced out of Jonathan's pocket? There. A pile of broken glass on the floor. It had escaped during the fight and shattered in the confusion.

So they were themselves again. Not master and slave any longer.

"The slaves," Jonathan coughed.

"We can't do anything."

"The keys." Jonathan snatched them up.

Crow leaned against the wall, overcome. The welts on his back had cracked open. Wetness dripped down his shoulder blade. The shock of the fight had worn off, and the pain hit him again full-force. They stared at one another. "I don't think I can," Crow said honestly.

Jonathan shoved him toward the exit. "Go. I'll be right back."

"I—"

"Wait in the alley."

"I need you," Crow insisted.

"Trust me. Give me five minutes. Five minutes, then run."

Crow nodded. He snatched up a sword from one of the fallen guards, then ambled out the exit. The foyer was slowly filling with smoke. He slipped out, then into the alley entrance.

A crowd had gathered around the front. Crow rested heavily against the wall. A trail of blood had come from his shoulder to his wrist, and it wet the grip of the sword. He let it slide from his hand.

The back of the House began to burn. Too quickly to have been set by the fire in the front. Athea must be sowing destruction inside. A crash brought down a nearby wall, lit by silver—she was tearing at the walls. The crowd gasped. Residents fled from nearby buildings. People milled and moved back, but Crow didn't, glued to the spot. He could feel the heat of the growing fire.

After a minute or two, her active destruction seemed to stop. Either she had been killed, or she had escaped, or she had stopped to do something else.

A few slaves ran from the door. Members of the City Watch had arrived, and they seized the runaways. One punched a guard in the gut, and two more bolted. Crow fought to catch his breath. Where was Jonathan?

It had been longer than five minutes. Maybe he was hurt.

Going back in would be outrageously stupid. Logically: Crow was injured, the fire was dangerous, and Jonathan was able-bodied. Only a courageous fool would risk his life for no reason.

Crow swore at the gods, then Jonathan, then Karis. He dragged himself to the hole in the wall, then climbed through.

Smoke. Much heavier smoke than before. Slaves ran from the door, a whole group of them. Crow stopped one. "Jonathan," he shouted. "Brown hair, nice clothes, set of keys?"

The slave pointed back where he'd come.

Crow trotted. It was as fast as he could manage. Then—a dirty mop of hair. Jonathan and Athea stood among the slave cells. Her magic supported a falling beam. Jonathan fought with a locked cell. It was the last closed door.

Crow added his grip to the key. Jonathan glanced up, startled, and Crow met his eyes. Together, they forced the lock open. The slave hurried out. "Karis?" Crow panted. Jonathan shook his head and coughed.

Athea heaved the beam aside. She stood naked, mottled with bruises and streaked with soot. There in the collapsing building, she was not a victim. She was a goddess. Standing tall amongst her own destruction, her hair wild in a tangle down her back. "Come on," Jonathan coughed. "'Thea. Miss. Come—with us."

She shook her head. With her magic, she shoved them out the door. She padded after them, blood at her feet. She shoved them farther, this time up the rubble and out the hole in the wall. They stumbled down.

Crow turned back to look.

Karis emerged from a nearby door. She held a tumble of little black books in her hands, documents of her business. Thick ropes of jewelry around her neck. A heavy pouch of coins at her waist. She saw Athea, and she dropped the books. She raised her hands to defend herself.

With raw magic, Athea picked up the brazier. She ripped it apart in the air. Metal rods and spikes whirled above them. Athea held out her hand, then clenched it.

The largest spike shot downward. It pierced Karis through the chest. The spike stuck in the wall. Karis gripped it, shocked. Crow turned his head, not willing to give her the dignity of witnessing her death. He watched Athea instead.

Athea sank to the floor. The rods clattered around her. The last Crow saw of her was her bloody back, streaked with soot.

He climbed down the rubble. In the confusion, the two of them slipped away. Crow leaned heavily on Jonathan and tried to ignore the blistering pain in his back. Jonathan supported him with an arm around the hips. "Were you injured?" Crow asked.

Jonathan clapped a hand across a small cut on his neck. "During the fight, Garlant nearly got me across the throat. But no. Not as badly as you."

"Then let me go." Crow forced himself away. He steadied himself on the alley wall. A wave of dizziness overcame him, and he slid, unwillingly, to his knees. "You need to go back," he said through gritted teeth. "Get Athea. Convince her to come with us. Knock her out if you have to. Carry her."

"Crow. Just because she looks like Regis, you can't—"

"You don't understand." Crow fought to breathe through the pain. "She knows where he is. She told me."

Jonathan knelt by his side and was quiet for a moment. He pushed Crow's hair aside. "Did you promise to help her if she told you?" he asked eventually.

"She wasn't lying just to get free. She said your name. She said *his* name."

"She saw us in the foyer when we first came in. Some people know who I am. She must have recognized me through the disguise. Did you describe Regis to her and tell her that we were looking for him?"

"She's our only lead!"

"Then we'll find her once the confusion is over. She destroyed a building. Everyone will be talking about this."

Crow moaned. "She'll be arrested. Jonathan. Please."

"They won't sentence her to death," Jonathan said quietly. "There'll be controversy. She'll speak up about the horrors she endured. Self-defense. Karis will be investigated. Witnesses interviewed. It will take months."

"And so?"

"We'll visit her in prison. She'll tell us then. Or the investigation will reveal something. We'll be okay. This is good, anyway. We need the City Watch looking into this."

"I—"

"Crow," Jonathan said in a much lower voice. "I love Regis as much as you do. But I'm not leaving a half-naked man to bleed to death alone in a back alley."

Crow shut his eyes. He breathed.

"Are you hurt?" Jonathan asked.

"Yes," Crow said.

"I mean more than before."

"No. The whipping was enough, thank you."

"Then you can't force me to leave you."

They sat there for a time. Then Jonathan heaved him up, supporting him. Crow gripped him and focused on moving his feet, one after the other. His earlier bursts of energy had drained him. The salve on his back had attracted dust and dirt, and it itched.

They stepped onto the street. Empty buildings, quiet sidewalks. Everyone had gone to gawp at the fire. A few people passed them, giving them a wide berth, but no one stopped them. "There's someone following us," Jonathan whispered. "I keep catching glances around the corner. I don't think it's the Watch."

"Athea?"

"No. Whoever it is has short hair." Jonathan glanced behind. "We shouldn't go home with someone tailing us."

A small garden was nearby, a bench on its outskirts. Jonathan gently set Crow down. "Come out now," he called behind them. "I know you're there."

A boy edged out of the alley. He wore the fine silk of a pampered slave, but he wasn't wearing a collar. Peter. His hair was mussed, and his face was flushed like he'd been running.

He stopped in front of Crow. Crow struggled upright. "Your mistress is dead," he said. "Her record books are certainly destroyed, you know. You could run."

Peter bit his lip. "I know." His voice was fine, like a flute. Surprised, Crow realized it was the first time he'd ever heard the boy speak. "I just wanted to say thank you."

"Oh," Crow said. "Er."

He shifted from foot to foot. "My ma sold me when I was five. Said I was lucky. Picked up by a lady like Ka—Kar—like *her*, given a better life. Paid special attention to." His voice wavered. "I wanted to run, but I didn't know where to go. I don't know what to do. Karis gave me everything I ever wanted. I was going to be her special boy, she said. Make her so much money. Sell me to someone good."

Jonathan began to look sympathetic.

Peter's eyes were wet. He scrubbed an arm across them. The bangles on his wrists jingled. "Doesn't matter. I'm not asking you for anything. Your back's hurt, that's all. I can, um. I can fix that." He averted his eyes, still red. "It's just cuts."

Crow sighed and turned around. Cold hands touched his shoulders. Gold magic sealed the cuts. Peter stepped away. "Wait," Jonathan said suddenly.

Crow groaned.

"If we send him off on his own, he'll end up on the streets," Jonathan insisted.

"He's a sorcerer. He's among the most privileged people in Tyria. He'll be fine."

"Where's he supposed to go? Someone will take over Karis's business now that she's dead. He'll be claimed as an asset. We should take him with us. If we don't, he'll just end up a slave again."

"Damn you."

"Only until we find a better solution. Maybe Regis could use an apprentice."

"Regis is a bitter, angry hermit who tolerates you for sex. Come on," Crow said. "If he's meant to survive, he will. I survived my childhood just fine, and my mother didn't even feed me."

Jonathan gave him a hard look. "If you hadn't come back to help me in the fire, I might be dead. And if we don't find Regis soon and get his help, you might be dead. Good people help each other, Crow."

Crow opened his mouth. Closed it. Glanced between them. Peter's guarded look had disappeared, and in its place was a kind of desperate hope. Crow's heart squeezed involuntarily. "Dammit," he said.

"See? I knew you weren't evil." Jonathan offered him a hand and pulled him up. "Well. I didn't, but Regis insisted."

"Well, maybe not evil-evil," Crow said. "I mean, I've been known to kick the occasional puppy. But it's not like I'm going to grow a mustache to twirl."

"You'd look hideous."

"Yes, exactly. I'm glad you understand."

"We should get outside the city," Jonathan said, waving Peter along. "My friend needs to rest."

Crow dragged his feet as they walked. His eyelids felt heavy. "Maybe you're right about the whole 'helping people' thing. I mean, it's a group-survival instinct. If you help other people, they'll help you. It's just logic. It's not like you're actually better than other people. You're just obeying your instincts."

"Sure. Yeah. Absolutely."

"You're not even listening to me."

"Does your back still hurt? You're limping."

His back twinged a little. He moaned loudly. "Oh, it's awful." He leaned heavily on Jonathan for extra effect. Jonathan rolled his eyes.

Peter spoke up. "That lady with the long hair. Is she okay?"

They passed The House of Red Silk. The building was mostly sandstone. All the wooden parts—the roof and two side buildings—were blackened. The walls continued to crumble, bit by bit. Civilians gawked, but the City Watch kept them back. The fire brigade had arrived, and they passed water buckets down a line. A few slaves huddled together under the protection of a red-clad guard.

Athea was nowhere in sight. Had she been arrested? Had she escaped?

"I'm sure she's fine," Crow said.

Chapter EIGHT
Cheat

CROW'S LEANING, at first, seemed like a joke. Jonathan went along with it mostly because it amused him. In time, though, Crow's weight became heavier and less balanced, and Jonathan found himself providing more and more support. At last, they passed through the front gates of the city, and they made their way down the street to the Overlook lodging house.

He arranged for a separate room for Peter. The boy could probably use one after everything he'd been through. Crow closed his eyes halfway through the conversation, and he made a sleepy noise into Jonathan's neck. Prickles shot up Jonathan's spine.

He gave Peter a key to the separate room, then gently guided Crow into their own room. He helped Crow onto the bed, then sighed and stretched. He unlaced his jacket, stuck to him with sweat. "Damn," he said, fumbling with the buttons. Crow dragged himself upright. He began to help.

Jonathan held perfectly still, barely daring to breathe. "Become accustomed to slavery?" he asked lightly.

"Mhm." Crow's eyes were at half-mast. "Glad it's over." He finished unbuttoning, then let his hand drop.

"I arranged for a hot bath," Jonathan said. "They said the water would take a half hour to warm before they carry it here."

"Do you mind if I borrow some decent clothes?"

"Go ahead."

Crow shut his eyes but remained standing. "Thank you for...." He listed to the side. "For all of this."

Jonathan caught him. "It's okay. I got you."

Crow's eyes flickered open. Black, like obsidian. "I owe you."

"There's nothing I want from you."

There were, in fact, several things. For a second, just a second, Jonathan missed the freedom of being single. Taking whoever he pleased to his bed. For a moment, back at the slavers—for several moments—it had seemed like—

Like what? Like Crow had enjoyed being whipped?

"I'm sure we can come up with something," Crow said. "I'd hate to seem ungrateful."

Jonathan swallowed.

It wasn't his fault he wanted Crow. It wasn't like he could turn off his own emotions. But wanting wasn't the same thing as doing. He'd stop himself. He'd hold back. Fidelity was a choice, and he'd abide by it until Regis returned. Simple as that.

"We might not find Regis in time," Crow said. "I'm not sure how much longer I have left." He collapsed into the armchair. "Belcane is a rat."

Crow's hair lay in beautiful disarray, his body languid and loose. He seemed physically exhausted. Jonathan sat beside him and pushed a mug of water at him. "Here, drink."

"Are you deaf? I'm telling you something important."

Jonathan laid his hands on Crow's shoulders. They both tensed at the same time; he could feel corded muscle beneath his fingers, nothing like the delicate bones of Regis's body and yet… familiar. Here was Crow, who he knew not at all and yet who he had lain with before Regis. He murmured, "You should go to bed. You're hurt. You're tired."

The tension in Crow's back ratcheted up another notch. He shoved himself upright and spun around, then shoved Jonathan into the wall. Surprised, Jonathan offered no resistance. "I am not exhausted," Crow said.

"Let me take care of you."

"I don't need anyone to care of me. I do fine on my own."

"You need Regis."

"I don't *want* to need Regis." He took a breath then, and let it out. He slumped, let go, stood back. "No. That was cruel of me. You've been… helpful." His voice had an odd quality to it. He turned aside, running a hand through his hair. He looked troubled.

"Belcane is a rat," Jonathan said quietly.

This was growing dangerous. "She is," Crow said. "She's in her tower, in a small iron cage."

Jonathan slid down the wall. He sat heavily on the ground. "A cage," he said in disbelief. "So—when you said she was a rat, you meant—you meant she's been a rat. Ever since Regis turned her into one. That's why she's been missing? You're completely mad."

Crow let out a breath of laughter. "It was an impulse. I knew it would take time for her to become human again, so I put her in a cage lined with opals the moment I could. And once she was in there, I thought: well, shit, I can't let her out now. Gods." He sat down next to Jonathan. "I'm fucked if she ever gets out. But, I mean, I'm kind of fucked anyway. Rats don't live very long. Certainly not as long as human men, at least."

Jonathan wrapped an arm around Crow's shoulders. He squeezed. "That's why she's ill?"

Crow nodded. "I thought I had time. Another two years, at least. I never imagined…." He curled his arms around his knees and laid his head down. "I should have gone to Regis ages ago. I was stupid. Prideful. I miss him."

"I miss him too."

Crow sat up and drew his arm across his eyes. He cleared his throat. "When I die, I recommend killing her through the bars," he said matter-of-factly. "I doubt she'll take food from you, so poison is out, but you could always toss the cage in a lake or something."

Jonathan swallowed. He said, "You're not going to die."

"Damn you."

"You need to have hope."

"Fuck your hope," Crow said. "Promise me, Jonathan. Please."

"I swear."

Crow pressed into the crook of Jonathan's arm. Sometime during their conversation, the last of twilight had faded, and the world was dark. The lamplight flickered, throwing shadows on Crow's skin. He eased back now and to the side. He seemed to be studying Jonathan. "We should go to bed," Jonathan said.

"Your clothes are filthy."

Jonathan shrugged.

"Let me," Crow said, and he reached forward, unpinning the clasp of Jonathan's cloak. It did not fall, glued to his skin with damp.

Crow's fingers were unerring. His hand slid beneath the heavy cloth, easing it aside, and the cloak dropped. Crow took it and arranged it over a chair. Jonathan stood, unmoving, waiting.

With precise movements, Crow pulled out the laces of Jonathan's tunic. With the touch of his hand came heat soaking through thick cloth. Jonathan peeled the shirt off himself, then held it loosely. It dropped and landed on the floor beside the bed, forgotten.

His boots were coated with dust. He sat on the chair, lying back against his cloak, and raised his foot, then looked at Crow. Slowly, Crow's gaze traveled from Jonathan's boot, up his legs to his bare chest, his face. "Am I your servant?"

"No," Jonathan said. "You're my slave."

Crow's mouth curved. Without a word, he knelt. Small buckles clinked as Crow undid them. He pulled, then tossed the boot aside. Jonathan raised the other, and it received identical treatment. Crow stayed on his knees. His hands rested on Jonathan's calves. "Is my master pleased?"

"Your master is still dirty."

"Your slave knows how that feels," Crow said, plucking at his tunic.

"Stand," Jonathan said.

Gracefully, Crow rose to his feet. His hands rested on Crow's hips, gathering cloth. He was in Crow's personal space now. He had been before, but not quite touching, not like he was now—small brushes of their nearest parts, damp skin on soot, skin on skin.

Crow moved backward, his breath shallow and fast. Jonathan moved with him. Crow's back hit the wall. "We should go to bed," Crow said hoarsely.

Jonathan nodded. His heart beat like a drum. He wanted to kiss Crow, but he was too rational for that. He pushed himself away.

Crow kissed him.

It was like the first sip of water after a long drought. Relief and desperate wanting hit Jonathan, and he groaned.

Crow's fingers dug into Jonathan's back, dusty with ash. Jonathan yanked at Crow's tunic, tearing it over his head and tossing it aside. As soon as the cloth was gone, Crow kissed him hard, dragging him back close. "Hit me," Crow hissed.

Jonathan slapped him. Crow's face went slack and flushed at once, a white mark on his cheek. He kissed Jonathan again, and his mouth tasted like iron.

Jonathan grasped Crow's throat, squeezing. Crow made a strangled noise into his mouth, hips bucking, and Jonathan shoved him against the wall so hard that the nearby table rattled. He kept one hand tight on Crow's neck, keeping him pinned and upright, and hit him again. Harder this time. A thrill went through him when he saw the look on Crow's face, shock mixed with hunger.

He slid his thigh between Crow's legs and pressed, and gods, Crow was as hard as he was. He leaned back and just watched—Crow helpless, caught, gripping the hand at his throat. His fingers dug in, stinging.

Jonathan pressed harder, and Crow whined—whined, with all the breath he had left, and Jonathan covered his mouth with his own. Crow kissed back like Jonathan was air itself. "Wanna fuck you," Jonathan whispered. "Wanna tie your wrists behind your back and make you scream—"

A knocking came on the door. Jonathan let go, and Crow sank against the wall, gasping. Jonathan's mouth found the juncture of Crow's neck, and Crow moaned loudly. The heat of his erection pressed against Jonathan's hip. Jonathan was dizzy with lust. He'd done that. He'd pinned Crow down, the twisty bastard, and gotten the better of him.

Stopping was like heaving himself back up a cliff. He flattened his palms on either side of Crow, then pressed his forehead against Crow's shoulder. Crow's arms were still around him. They both held there, breathing hard. Stepping away was impossible, so Jonathan did the next best thing. He shut his eyes and tried very hard not to move.

He felt Crow swallow. They were that close. "Regis," Crow whispered hoarsely.

"I know."

"If you keep touching me, I'm going to kiss you again."

"Please don't," Jonathan said weakly.

Crow seemed to be breathing shallowly to minimize skin contact. He slid down the wall until he was sitting against it. "We're so fucked."

Someone banged on the door more insistently. Jonathan shoved himself away, ears pounding with blood. He wanted to kiss Crow again. He wanted to throw Crow down on the bed and take him like an animal.

He wanted to cover Crow in finger-sized bruises and make him beg. Instead, he stormed to the door, unbolted it, and yanked it open.

A young woman with long, curly hair stood there. Jonathan gripped the door and said, "What the fuck do you want?"

She stared at him, openmouthed.

Behind him, Crow said, "Athea?"

Jonathan took a step back. It was Athea. She had acquired a dress somehow—blue, and far too large for her—cinched by a makeshift rope belt. She'd tried to wipe off the soot, and her face was covered with a thin smear of gray.

Yanking and fumbling. A belt buckling. Crow shoved past Jonathan and threw his arms around her neck. "Oh, thank goodness."

Athea pushed him back at arm's length. Her face was scarlet. "Er," she said, eyes darting between them.

Jonathan collapsed onto the bed and put his head into his hands.

"You have no idea what a relief this is," Crow said. "Come, sit. Come on. This is Jonathan. I'm Crow—oh, you already know our names, don't you?"

Athea shut the door behind her. "Did I interrupt something?"

Crow's shirt was half-tucked into his breeches. His belt had missed a loop, and his hair was undone, loose against his neck, perfect for gripping. He rubbed his throat and glanced back at Jonathan. He had a lovebite on his neck.

Jonathan took several deep breaths. "No," he said. "Give me a moment." He got to his feet and headed toward the garden door. Outside. Fresh air.

Crow caught his arm. "Are you all right?"

Jonathan tore his arm away. *"Give me a moment."*

He slammed the door behind him.

He crouched in the grass and fought to breathe. Cool night air stirred around him.

The first thing he did was shut everything out. The kiss. The stray boy he'd picked up, one room over. Athea. And, ancestors, everything that had happened. He focused, instead, on the grass. His father had taught him this. A warrior did not allow emotion to dictate his actions. He wanted to hit something, or—

Or shove Crow against the wall and kiss him again, harder.

Once the urge subsided, he added things back in. He thought first of Regis. The way Regis looked when he woke, sleep-mussed and agreeable, usually at noon. It was easy, those mornings, to hold Regis down and stroke his hair. Sleepy mumblings. Soft, contented noises. Eventually, he'd squirm awake and complain loudly until Jonathan let him go.

And then Jonathan thought of what he had just done, and a pit opened in his stomach.

Regis doesn't have to know.

Did he?

He did. Jonathan sat against the wall. Sure, he didn't believe in honor, but—he believed in love, didn't he? If he couldn't be honest with Regis, then who could he be honest with? And, frankly, the thought of forcing Crow to keep quiet was ludicrous. Crow would just blackmail him or something.

It was a stupid mistake. He'd apologize and do his best to make up for it. Simple as that.

A small creak. The door opening. Crow slipped out, then shut the door behind him. He crouched. "You okay?"

Jonathan forced himself to nod.

Crow rose and stepped away. He stayed a careful two feet back.

"Sorry," Jonathan forced out.

Crow said nothing.

"Is Athea all right?" Jonathan asked.

"She's fine. You need to come inside."

"We just—" Jonathan cut off there, not willing to say it. *I put my tongue in your mouth*, he thought.

Crow rubbed his neck where the mark was, then snatched away his hand once he seemed to realize what he was doing. "Yeah. I know. We don't have to talk about it. Actually, you know what? Let's not. Let's promise not to. But right now, I need you to push all of that away. All of it, all right?"

Jonathan fisted a hand in the grass and counted silently to himself. "Okay," he said through gritted teeth. "No talking."

"Look at me," Crow said. "You and I are the same, all right? We're strong people. And the difference between us and everyone else is that when we get knocked down, we get back up. When we're upset and angry, we fucking shove those emotions down and keep walking. We do what needs to be done. And right now, it doesn't matter who you are or what you did. It doesn't matter whether you kick puppies or fuck prostitutes or burn down houses. Regis needs you. And right now, we need to go inside and talk to Athea."

Crow's voice lowered. "I'm here to help you. I'm willing to do whatever it takes."

Jonathan took a breath. Crow was right.

"I've done everything I can on my own," Crow said. "Peter is inside healing her up. She's resting on our... on your bed. She says she knows who bought Regis."

Crow had circles under his eyes. He seemed to be keeping himself upright with sheer willpower. He offered Jonathan a hand, and Jonathan took it, and together they heaved him up. "Better?" Crow said.

Jonathan nodded. "What happened," he said, then hesitated. "That can't happen again."

Crow's mouth twitched. It was almost a smirk. "I could blackmail you."

"I thought the exact same thing."

Crow rubbed his head. "Regis won't be happy." He shook his head. "We'll decide what to do about it later."

Jonathan's pulse beat in his throat. "The kiss was an accident. We're both under a lot of stress. It's natural that we... we...."

Crow gave him a look. "You can't even say it."

"That I pinned you to the wall, slapped you, choked you, and told you I was going to fuck you until you screamed," Jonathan said, just to prove he would.

Crow's face darkened red.

A beat of silence.

"Don't say that to Regis," Crow said seriously. He motioned Jonathan through the door.

Peter leaned over Athea on the bed. His orange magic healed her cuts. "Ouch!" Athea said. "Ow. Ow, I said. Cut it out!"

"B-but, miss. Master Crow asked me to... to...."

"Look, you've gotten half of it already. So stuff Master Crow." The door shut loudly. "Oh!" She startled upright. Her dress—which was unfastened—lay across her lap. She had freckles on her chest, and—Jonathan tried desperately not to notice—she was unusually well-endowed. He hadn't noticed while she was burning down the House of Red Silk.

Tyrians. He felt his face heat up. He cleared his throat and turned around.

"Could you do up your top?" Crow said. "Jonathan's Northern. They have weird taboos."

Jonathan peeked behind himself. Athea fastened her top back up. "I heard you were a woman-hater, but this is ridiculous," Athea muttered. "They're just breasts."

"I don't hate women! I just prefer having sex with men."

"Well, I prefer having sex with blondes, but you don't see me shrieking every time I see a redhead's tits."

"You don't get it," Crow said. "He's never had sex with a woman. Ever. He's homosexual. I looked it up in a book of sexual fetishes. He can't get aroused by the opposite sex, but otherwise he's pretty normal. Weird, huh?"

"So seeing breasts makes him panic?"

"Guess so."

Against his common sense, Jonathan tried to explain. "In the North, we have taboos about, um—seeing the opposite gender naked—"

"Really?" Athea frowned at him. "Oh. So everyone from the North is homosexual? How do you have children, then?"

Jonathan tried, several times, to speak. Nothing would come out. He gave up. He sat down and put his head in his hands.

Crow leaned against the dresser. "Tell me how you found us."

"Everyone knows Sir Jonathan White is staying at this inn. You've got a dragon out back," Athea said. "You want the person who took that sorcerer, right? Well, I said I'd help you, so here I am." The cadence of her voice was precisely like Regis's. The rapid pace, the way she bit off her words. It was unnerving to listen to.

Crow tapped his fingers on the dresser. He had a bruise forming on his wrist. Was it from being chained? Or the whipping? Or when Jonathan had—

He couldn't think about that now. If he thought about it, he'd drag Crow outside and fuck him then and there. Normal people did not have these kinds of urges. Normal people did not try to fuck their lover's best friend. Normal people did not want to fuck shape-shifters.

"His name is Septimus Aron," Athea said. "A powerful sorcerer. He offered that slaver a substantial amount of money to have your friend kidnapped, but once she found out who the target was, she demanded more. He didn't have enough, so he sold me to her. Fifty gold sovereigns and one sorceress in exchange for Regis Teller, bound and gagged."

"Sold you," Crow said. "By what right?"

"I was his apprentice. Sorcerers are allowed to do that, you know. Sell their failed apprentices. Failed! Ha. Just because I don't like his overcomplicated book-reading nonsense." She bit her lip. "Also, he's, um, sort of my father."

Crow started to laugh.

"It's not funny," she snapped.

"Sorry," Crow said. "I know exactly how you feel. My mother was awful. I bet you and I could swap stories." He folded his arms. "How old are you?"

"Oh." Her face slowly colored. "Sorry. Er, I'm eighteen. He sold me right before my birthday. The rat bastard."

"And your mother was okay with this?"

"I don't have a mother. She left after I was born."

"Huh," Crow said. He tipped his head back against the wall. He seemed to be thinking something over. After a long moment, he said, "Your magic is silver, right? How common is that?"

"I don't know."

"Do you have any male cousins?"

"How should I know? I mean, I have an aunt and an uncle, but Septimus is kind of a snob, so I'm not allowed to talk to them." She sniffled. "I'm sorry I'm here," she burst out.

Jonathan winced. He never knew what to do with people when they cried.

Crow immediately sat down and wrapped his arm around her shoulder. "Here, now. You'll figure this out."

"I know." Her lips trembled. "I suppose I've got to cry a bit first, that's all. Oh, I can't believe he sold me! I want to get out of Tyrigaine. Someone might have seen me k-kill Karis." Her eyes darted to Jonathan.

"You. You have a relationship with the City Watch. Why didn't you go to them when your friend was kidnapped?"

"I did," Jonathan said.

Crow spoke up. "I'm pretty sure they knew that Karis was breaking the law. The queen's hold on Tyria is still weak, and cities like this are often ruled by the wealthy."

"The law is weak and ineffectual," Jonathan said. "Corruption takes years to root out. I wasn't going to sit around waiting for someone else to save the man I love. She brutalized you, Athea. People like that need to be stopped. It doesn't matter what the Watch thinks. You did good."

Crow's eyes flickered up, black. He held Jonathan's gaze.

"What?" Jonathan said.

"You're not as honorable as you pretend."

Jonathan shrugged. "People make assumptions about me. Sometimes I take advantage of that."

"Must be the blond hair and blue eyes. Mister Goody-Two-Shoes. I never expected you were such a criminal." He rubbed the back of his neck. "If we go to the Watch now...."

"What are you saying? We tell them that Karis was corrupt?"

They had disguised themselves. Broken into her records room. Stolen a slave. And Athea had burned down the House of Red Silk and murdered the wealthiest woman in Tyrigaine.

"No," Crow said.

"No," Jonathan agreed.

"Miss Athea, can you show us where Regis is?"

Chapter NINE
Reunion

THUNDER RUMBLED in the distance. The air was hot. Humid. Thick. Athea led the way through the North Quarter of Tyrigaine, between towering manors and wrought-iron gates. "Here," she whispered, motioning them through an alley.

Septimus's manor was small but extravagant. Double doors, intricately carved. Rotting shingles. It spoke of a man who had quite a bit of money and not a lot of sense. Athea stood in a patch of daisies and craned her head to look up. "That's my room," she whispered, pointing.

Crow pulled her back out of sight, into the alley. "The one with the light? Top floor?"

"Yeah."

"That must be where Regis is, then." He began searching for handholds. Windows. Out-of-place bricks. Anything he could use to get himself up there.

"Hold on," Jonathan whispered. "We can't do this now."

"Why not?"

"Because Septimus Aron is in there. If he's keeping Regis locked up somehow, we need to get rid of him first."

"But Regis is *right there*. I've always protected him. I need to... need to...."

"We can't save him if we both get arrested. Regis is my partner for a reason. You love him, don't you? You trust him? Have faith. He's a grown man. He's not your helpless toy anymore. He'll be okay a little while longer."

Crow grimaced. He nodded grudgingly.

Then—movement in the window. Someone peered out. Jonathan dragged Crow further out of sight. Crow fought. "I only want to look!"

A cloth fluttered in the window. Green, like Regis's favorite cloak, like his scarves. "Someone saw us," Crow breathed. "Someone's trying to *show* he saw us."

Athea shuddered, rubbing her arms. "I'm going back to the inn."

"Why?" Jonathan said.

"About to start raining," she said. "I hate rain. Besides. You got a dragon there. I figure even if my father comes looking for me, well, Miss Chartreuse can eat him, can't she?"

"She'll definitely try," Jonathan said.

Athea looked relieved. She pulled her hood over her face. The first raindrop pattered down, sliding off the oiled cloth. She hurried off. Crow's heart was in his throat, and for a moment, all he could do was stand there, pressed into the crook of Jonathan's arm.

"Can you turn into a bird and fly to his window?" Jonathan asked.

"It hurts when I shift. I might get stuck again."

"Maybe you could climb."

"What's the point? If he could fit through that window, he would've escaped already."

"Yeah," Jonathan said. "And you... you're probably exhausted, anyhow."

The rain shushed the cobblestones.

"Give me your cloak," Crow said.

"What? Why?"

"It's oiled. It'll keep off the rain." Crow toed off his shoes. He checked the small satchel at his waist. Lock picks, a knife. Gloves. He pulled them on.

"The neighbors might see," Jonathan said. "This is a bad idea."

"Yeah. Well, I'm sick of good ideas. Shout if you see anything." Crow put his foot in a windowsill, gripped a gargoyle, and slung himself up. He felt for another handhold.

A voice called out softly from below. "Tell him...."

Crow glanced back down. Jonathan looked lost and alone on the ground. "What?"

Jonathan averted his eyes. "Tell him I love him."

Crow crouched on the gargoyle. Jonathan's lips had been slightly chapped, and he'd kissed hungrily, like a man starving for sex. Because it was obvious—and because Crow was not above being petty—he said, "Should I also kiss him for you?"

"Crow."

"I could bring you one back," he offered.

"Tell him he's going to be okay," Jonathan said. "That we're going to get him out of this no matter what."

"I don't think he needs to be told that," Crow said, and he went back to climbing.

The rough stone crumbled between his fingers. He picked his footholds carefully and only moved when he was certain. By the time Crow realized how exhausted his body was, he was already halfway up, and well, he could hardly turn back.

His foot slipped, and his grip tightened on a windowsill. Inside, on the third floor, a flickering light passed by. A servant, perhaps. Crow's toes scrambled—he couldn't find a foothold!

He gritted his teeth, closed his eyes, and shifted shape the smallest bit. His body grew light as his bones hollowed and his frame became more slender. His hair feathered. His foot found a niche to rest in.

One of his fingernails came loose.

He couldn't pick it off right away. He steadied himself as best he could, then examined it. It had turned black like the talons on a bird's foot. A chill shivered through him. He pulled the nail off with his teeth and spat it out. It was just a fingernail, he told himself. No big deal. He was still in control of his body.

The wind blew hard through the alley, like a tunnel. He unfastened the clasp of Jonathan's cloak and let it fall, exposing himself to the rain. Water plastered his hair to his face. His fingers reached Regis's windowsill, and Crow found a solid niche to rest his fingers in.

He peeked over the sill.

The room was small but luxurious. The bed was unmade. A vase smashed. Notes all over the desk. Five books open, one propped up. One of them looked like Myra's handwriting. Regis sat in a chair at the desk, tapping one finger rapidly. A plate of food sat in front of him, uneaten.

"Regis," Crow called quietly.

Regis glanced up. His face went slack with shock. He bolted upright, blew out the candle, and came to the window.

His hair was mussed and tangled. His neck had red marks from the heavy collar he wore, and he looked thin. "Are you all right?" Crow whispered.

"Fine. Who cares? What about you?" He touched Crow's cheekbones through the bars.

Crow fought to speak. Nothing came out. Overwhelmed, all he could do was hold on.

"You have no idea how good it is to see you," Regis whispered. "What did you do to yourself? Your face looks different. Your eyes are black. Please tell me the spell isn't about to break."

"I tweaked it a little to get up here. That's all."

Regis's face lost color. "Please don't do that."

Crow bit the side of his tongue. *I wanted to see if you were all right.*

Regis tried to peer out around Crow. "Is Jonathan down there? I saw three people."

"Yeah. A friend led us here, but she left. You should meet her," Crow said. "She's a lot like you." He reflected for a moment. "Well. Actually, you'd probably kill each other."

Regis's tired face broke out into a smile. "I want to hug you so badly."

"It's okay."

"It's not okay," Regis whispered. "All I can think about is you and Jonathan. Are you getting along? No. Of course not. Are you tolerating each other, at least?"

Crow laughed. "Actually—"

I kissed him.

Regis would be furious. Especially if he found out now, and he was forced to deal with it alone, trapped in a room with nothing to think about but his partner's betrayal. By the time Jonathan had the opportunity to apologize, Regis would be too angry to reason with. It would be so easy to destroy their relationship. Right now.

He kissed me. That's all he had to say.

"Are you okay?" Regis said. "You seem flustered."

"Jonathan... he...."

Here it was. The moment he would destroy everything.

"He, um, wanted me to give you a message," Crow said. A weird feeling came over him. His throat tightened. "He said: Regis, I have tried not to love you. But we are destined to be together like rain is destined to fall—not because it wants to, but because it's inevitable, the weight of it gathering until it can no longer be held. I drown for you, and so long have I been without sense I crave to breathe you in and lose myself entirely. I love you, and you will be safe soon."

Regis's face softened. "Did he really say that?"

"His precise words."

"Some were lent by a book of poetry, I'd wager. Jonathan's never been an artist."

Crow wordlessly shook his head, looking away. "He is an artist."

Regis reached through the bars. "Are you all right?" Crow closed his eyes and rested his forehead against the bars. Regis sifted his fingers through Crow's wet hair, settling on the back of his head. "Hey, come on. It'll be okay."

"You don't even know what I'm upset about."

"Well, I'd ask you, but this isn't exactly the time for a heart-to-heart. Besides, you're Crow Belcane. You survived your mother. You can survive this."

I love you, Crow thought. It would be so easy to say. He opened his mouth, but nothing would come out. *You fucking coward*, he thought to himself. He pushed those emotions deep inside and locked them away. "I can survive this," he said.

"Tell Jonathan I love him," Regis said.

Crow swallowed a lump in his throat. "I can survive this," he said again in a murmur. He gripped a bar tight with one hand. His fingers were beginning to cramp. With one stiff hand, he undid the straps of his lock-picking kit. It nearly fell; he snatched it from the air. He pushed it through the bars. "Here."

Regis set it on the desk. "Another lover's token? A strange one at that, my friend."

"Just try them, all right? I know you're not good with lock picks, but who knows, maybe you'll get lucky. Does Septimus ever leave?"

"All the time."

"Jonathan and I will watch and wait until he's gone. We'll break in and get you out. Just hold on awhile longer, sweet. We'll have you rescued in no time."

He began to climb down. His fingers gave out a few feet from the ground. He landed hard.

Jonathan caught him. Pulled the fallen cloak around Crow's shoulders, pinning the clasp in place. Not far from the alley, there were voices. "Let's go," Jonathan said in a low voice. "Hurry."

Boots splashing in the rain. Crow was nearly too tired to run, and he ran anyway. Several streets away, they slowed and slipped beneath the shelter of an overhanging roof. "The Watch?" Crow said.

"Someone must've seen you and thought you were housebreaking." Their thighs pressed together. Crow was startled by the heat of it, the closeness. The rain made him shake. He focused on the spell inside him. Focused on being human.

For a single, terrifying moment, nothing happened. He couldn't feel the spell at all. Then a cold shudder passed through him, and he felt his bones harden again. Thank the gods. It seemed like it was getting easier to shift.

"I think the Watch passed us one street over," Crow said. "We should double back and head home."

"In a moment. How's Regis? Is he all right?"

"He says he's fine."

Jonathan gave him a sharp look. "Really?"

"Yeah. Wait, what's wrong?"

Jonathan was silent for a moment. Then he said, "When Regis gets a splinter, he complains for an hour straight. One time he sprained his ankle walking and made me carry him around for a whole day. After he healed himself."

"So?"

"If he's not complaining... he might actually be hurt."

Crow put together the pieces out loud. "He looked thin and tired, but he had a full meal on the desk. Septimus is feeding him, but he hasn't been eating."

Jonathan groaned. "He never looks out for himself. He needs me."

"There was a bruise on his neck. Someone yanked his collar, or he's been pulling at it. There were a lot of notes on the desk—don't know why. One of them looked like Myra's handwriting... don't know why or what it was. I gave him my lock picks, and there's a knife and file inside. He'll be okay."

"Did you tell him—?"

"He loves you too," Crow said.

Jonathan nodded stiffly, averting his eyes. They walked back to the lodging house in the rain.

Chapter TEN
Laudanum

IT WAS dawn. Jonathan barely had the energy to close the curtains before he collapsed into bed. There was a bath, but it had long since gone cold. Crow stripped off his clothes and stepped behind the partition. Water splashed.

Jonathan dozed. He awoke to the sound of Crow dressing himself. Jonathan rolled over to his half of the bed, but Crow didn't lie down. "Stop messing around and come to bed," Jonathan grumbled.

Crow shook his head. He combed his hair, then began to braid it. "I can't sleep like this."

"Where are you going?"

"What business is it of yours?"

Jonathan rolled onto his side. "Crow," he said petulantly.

"I haven't had sex in… a while. I'm going to find someone to fuck me." He pulled a few strands from his braid, then artfully swept them aside and pinned them in place.

"Stay here."

And Crow seemed to stop breathing.

They looked at each other from across the room. The bed was undone. Jonathan recoiled. "I didn't mean—" Except he had meant that. Sort of. If he weren't committed to Regis, Jonathan would gladly tire Crow out.

What was wrong with him? "Never mind," he said. "Go."

Crow left. Jonathan beat his pillow into submission, then closed his eyes.

A WEIGHT dipped the bed. Jonathan groaned in protest as he was dragged from sleep. Crow sat on the side nearest to the wall. He didn't lie down. "Hey," he said.

Jonathan rubbed his face. "I thought you were going to sleep somewhere else."

"I changed my mind."

He smelled like sex. Semen, sweat, and the undeniable stench of a man. A man who wasn't Jonathan, wasn't Regis—was some fucking bastard in a bar. Jonathan shoved aside those feelings. "You might get more rest if you slept in another bed," he said roughly.

Crow tipped his head back against the wall. "I feel like we should be honest with each other."

"Honest?"

"I wish we could have sex."

Jonathan swallowed. His fingers dug into the sheets.

"I keep thinking about the first time I met you. We should've fucked more. You know, while we had the chance." Crow slid down the wall until he lay flat on the bed. "My mind won't stop working. It can't shut off. I can't believe we were master and slave yesterday. I keep trying to remember why I hate you, but I can't. Maybe they were stupid reasons."

"You're delirious."

"I can't sleep."

"So you decided to harass me?"

Crow laughed weakly. "Do you want me to leave?"

Jonathan shut his eyes. He counted silently to himself. "No. I can handle myself."

"I can handle myself," Crow echoed. "Well, that's certainly one way to look at it. I'll keep myself in check, you keep yourself in check. We'll work together at it. 'It' being not having sex, that is."

"Go to sleep, Crow."

"Do you know how tiring this is? I spend every moment—every tiny second—not having sex with you. It's an exhausting task. I've wasted every ounce of energy. It's like an orgy of repression. I thought it was regular sexual frustration, at first. So I found a man, a blond man, and offered to suck him off. It went pretty well up until the point I started moaning your name—"

"Crow," Jonathan said weakly. "Please stop talking."

"I slept with another after that. A woman. Don't remember her name."

"You've only been gone two hours. And still you want more?"

Crow's eyes were lidded. "Neither of them were you."

"You're insatiable."

Crow laughed. His head lolled. "I'm not used to denying myself what I want." He curled up. "Like a fat, gluttonous noble." He pushed himself up. "I should go."

Jonathan caught his wrist.

Corded tension. Bone and muscle. Cool skin. Crow looked back, black eyes unfathomable. Jonathan kept hold, though he wasn't sure why, or why he'd grabbed. It had been instinct—

—just as it had the night they'd met.

A flood of heat and desire, against all reason. Once they were rested, they'd rescue Regis. He had to stop this, now. They were both delirious. If he waited another night, maybe more, he'd have Regis back, and then he'd remember why he thought monogamy was a good idea. But his grip only tightened, and it took all his willpower not to drag Crow back into bed. He couldn't let go.

Crow took a hoarse breath. He pried away Jonathan's fingers. "We could kiss again. We've done it once already. It wouldn't matter."

"You're still riled?"

"No, I'm spent. I came twice already. It would be safe. No temptation for me. See? I wouldn't even get hard, and then you—" He stopped there. He wet his lips.

"I can control myself. I think."

"Yeah," Crow said. "I mean, as long as I don't sink to my knees and beg to suck your cock."

Jonathan's heart beat wildly. "Right. If you don't do that."

"As long as I don't beg, and as long as you don't unlace your pants and shove it in—"

Jonathan nodded. "Exactly. Both of us would have to lose our minds at the same time. We both have far too much self-control for that. We're strong people. Strong people."

Daringly, Crow took a step forward.

He bent. The ghost of breath on his mouth. A touch of lips. It was the epitome of self-control. Wasn't that just like Crow, Jonathan thought, half-insane with need, and he gripped Crow by the shirt and by the root of his hair, then slung him down on the bed. He kissed Crow, kissed him like they were both drowning, breathed him like air. The feel of his body—lean and hard and a little bony—was nothing short of ecstasy.

Jonathan meant to stop. He tried to convince himself. But a moment longer wouldn't hurt, would it? It wasn't like one second would make a difference. One second became two, then five, then ten, then....

Jonathan pinned Crow's wrists. He pressed a thigh between his legs, that needy place. "Jonathan," Crow gasped, and he squirmed, shoving upward. Jonathan kissed him again. Crow's groan was muffled, and it reverberated in Jonathan's mouth. Full-throated and desperate.

Crow bit Jonathan's lip. Sharp teeth, a shock of pain. Jonathan snarled, gripping Crow by the hair and forcing him down. He licked a taste of blood off his lips.

Crow's eyes glazed over. He whimpered. "Oh fuck." He pushed up in Jonathan's grip. "Oh fuck! Jonathan. Jon, we need to stop." He squirmed out from under Jonathan, landing on the floor. He bolted upright, backing away. His hair was tangled, and all Jonathan could think about was fisting his hand in it, throwing Crow against the bed, and fucking him.

Jonathan wiped his mouth. His lips stung. He got up and took a step toward Crow.

Crow bolted for the door, slamming it shut behind him.

Jonathan sank into the bed. His head hurt from sleeplessness. He couldn't calm down. And Regis....

Just thinking his name hurt. This was a mistake. But it would always be a mistake, wouldn't it? And there was less harm doing it now, while Regis was away, while it was more understandable.

And then he realized he was looking for an excuse—any excuse—to have sex with Crow. For some reason that struck him as strange. But then the door opened, and Crow shut it and locked it. Jonathan jumped a little.

Crow had a small glass bottle of clear liquid in his hand. His grip on it was tight, white-knuckled. Jonathan's gaze darted from it to Crow's face. Oil. He had gone to get oil. It would be so easy to fuck Crow right now. So easy. All he had to do was give in.

Crow tossed Jonathan the bottle.

The front said *Laudanum* in Tyrian script. Jonathan stared at it dumbly. "Laudanum? Isn't this a healer's medicine?"

"The innkeeper had some. I told her it was an emergency."

"It's opium and alcohol. This isn't oil. It's a drug. How is this going to help us…?"

An impossibly long stretch of silence.

Jonathan's hand tightened on the bottle. A wave of hysteria hit him.

"We should both have a capful," Crow said. "It'll help us sleep." He inched forward, then—keeping his body as far from him as possible—extended his hand. Jonathan gave him the bottle back. Without warning, Crow unscrewed the cap, measured out a dose, and drank it.

He wiped his mouth and handed it back. "You must be joking," Jonathan said, shaken.

"Well, I already took mine." He sounded relieved by it. "Unless you're planning to fuck my unconscious body, then we're not having sex tonight. I don't consent to that, by the way. So." He motioned to the bottle. "Up to you."

Jonathan shoved himself off the bed and stormed out the garden door. "Chartreuse!" he shouted.

She slunk out of the bushes. *What's wrong, little one?*

"Don't go hunting anytime soon. Guard the inn. If anyone breaks into the room while Crow and I are asleep, shriek until they leave. Break down the wall if you have to."

Are you all right?

"No."

He went back to the room. Locked all the doors tight, double-checked the handles. Stripped off his boots. Crow listed to one side. Jonathan caught him and gently lowered him onto the blankets. "You're welcome," Crow mumbled.

"Thank you," Jonathan whispered.

But Crow's eyes were already closed. Jonathan drank the laudanum, then curled up beside him. They fell asleep arm in arm, white skin on tan, black hair on brown.

CROW FLOATED awake, curled next to a warm body.

Their limbs were entangled. A hard knee was wedged uncomfortable against his side, and short hair tickled his face. Crow let out a long, shuddering breath. He hadn't shared a bed with anyone since he'd abandoned Regis. He'd forgotten how much he liked mornings like these, waking in the arms of another man.

Crow leaned back to study his bed partner. Jonathan looked defenseless when he slept, much like everyone else did. Somehow that came as a surprise. The idea of Jonathan being defenseless at all seemed unnatural.

It was the afternoon, and orange light dimmed the room. They had slept all day. Jonathan's eyes cracked open. "Good morning."

He didn't push away. This was fine, Crow told himself. Two people curled together for creature comfort. It didn't mean anything. Tomorrow, they would save Regis, and both of them would come to their senses. "Evening," Crow replied. "We slept all day."

Jonathan inhaled. "You smell like a man. Normally you smell like… lavender and treachery."

"Lavender and treachery," Crow said, amused.

"Hush. Still sleepy." Jonathan shifted and looked up. A strange expression came across his face. Shock and discomfort and unwilling affection.

"Is there something wrong with my face?" Crow said lightly.

Jonathan reached out. He touched Crow's cheekbones. It took an act of sheer willpower for Crow to remain still. Jonathan brushed aside a lock of black hair, and Crow fought the urge to lean into the touch. If he leaned, it would mean admitting what was happening inside him—a strange new feeling blossoming, filling up his chest and squeezing his lungs. It was dangerous, as he had always said.

He looked at Jonathan and thought: *This is the man who destroyed my life.*

It was hopeless. He seized Jonathan by the wrist and pulled him closer. They were pressed against the headboard. Crow was aware of the heat coming from Jonathan's body, the brush of his clothing, the shallowness of his breath—the shallowness of his own breath. "Jonathan," he whispered.

"I need to tell you something. And when I do, I need you to remain calm."

"No. Please. Don't say anything. Let's just… lie here a moment."

"It's not that. It's your eyes," Jonathan said. "They've gone black. Completely."

Crow bolted upright. He went for the mirror. His eyes were black, pitch black, no whites, no pupils. The floor dropped out from under him, and he collapsed against the wall. "Oh fuck." He looked again. "Oh fuck!"

Jonathan got out of bed. "This has never happened before?"

"No." He fought to reach the spell inside him, but he couldn't grip it. The spell felt different today. He fought to shift back into his proper shape, to turn human completely. His skin rippled. A wave of sickness hit him, and his hair feathered. His skin lost a shade. He didn't look like himself. His face was wrong. Everything was wrong. This wasn't his body.

Jonathan lurched forward. "Stop! You're making it worse."

His left foot itched weirdly. He glanced down. Black scales went from his toes to his ankle, crawling up. His toenails darkened and curved like talons. He collapsed on the floor. He heard himself hyperventilating and—in a distant sort of way—realized that if he didn't get himself under control fast, he was going to pass out. He'd fucked up trying to mess with the spell again. He focused, instead, on holding it in place. Not turning human. Just trying desperately to stop himself from getting worse.

His fingernails felt loose.

Jonathan knelt beside him and smoothed his hair from his face. "Shh. Just breathe, okay? Calm down."

"Give me the poison," he whispered.

"What?"

"Give me the iocane. I won't take it right now, I swear, I just want it back. Please, Jonathan. I'm begging you. I can't—I can't—"

"You can. Just focus."

"I am focusing!" Crow lost it. He shoved Jonathan back, flew to his feet. Grabbed Jonathan and shoved him against the wall. "I've been focusing my entire fucking life! I lived through an insane mother, soldiers coming to the tower and trying to kill us both, a dangerous world, wretched secrets I couldn't tell anyone. Every single day, Jonathan, every day was about staying in control, every day was about trying as hard as I could. Being pushed to my limit. I survived because I forced myself to survive. Because I refused to die. And now... and now...."

He let go and stumbled back. Dimly, he realized his face was wet. "This isn't my body anymore," he said pathetically. "I don't look like me."

Jonathan held him. "You're you no matter what you look like."

Crow sank to his knees. "If the spell breaks, I'll stop being me. I can't let that happen. What am I? Just some fucked-up spell gone wrong? I can't just come undone. I'm begging you. Let me choose how I die."

Jonathan winced. He seemed to be thinking about something. Finally, he said, "I already threw out the poison."

"You *what?*"

"I emptied it in a ditch."

Crow's mouth hung open. He was speechless. Then he put his face in his hands and choked out a laugh. "You dirty, rotten, lying, cheating bastard."

"You were threatening to poison yourself. Yeah, I lied. I lied because I wanted to get the poison out of your hands before you did something stupid. And you know what? I don't regret it. Look." He knelt in front of Crow. "I know how you feel, I promise. But you're acting rash. We still have time, don't we?"

"Time? Time to do what?"

Gently, Jonathan helped Crow into the armchair. "I'll go get Athea."

Crow laughed bitterly. "You think she's an experienced caster who specializes in shape-shifting? How convenient that would be."

"We'll find someone else. We'll… we'll…."

Crow closed his eyes. They had been so close.

"We'll go get Regis," Jonathan said suddenly.

"We need to wait until Septimus leaves."

"How long can you hold out?"

"I don't know," Crow said.

He hadn't realized that until he said it. He didn't know when he was going to die. His entire body shook. He'd saved the Flesh Witch to save himself, and now he was going to die anyway.

He couldn't fucking breathe. He was going to die, and he had no way to fix this himself.

The fear hurt too much to bear. He gripped his wrist, sinking his nails in, fighting to focus on the pain. It didn't work this time. So he pressed harder. As long as he had the hurt to focus on, he could ignore the terror.

Gently, Jonathan began to pry away his fingers. Crow refused to let go. Jonathan had to force away each finger one by one. His nails had cut the skin. Ugly little marks. It was his one bad habit, a weakness he tried to keep secret. There were small silver scars on the inside of his wrist from where he'd done it before.

Jonathan noticed them. His lips parted, and he started to speak, then seemed to think better of it. He fetched a rag and wet it with alcohol from his flask, then pressed the cloth to the cuts. "It's okay. We're going to save him in time."

Pathetic tears tracked down his cheeks. Crow loathed his own weakness. If he were a stronger man, he wouldn't need help. He was lucky Jonathan was being kind. Lucky he had this breakdown in front of someone relatively safe. "And—what if—we d-don't?"

Jonathan smoothed hair out of Crow's eyes. "We'll go now. We'll get in, get the collar off, and Regis will fix you."

Crow tried to laugh. It came out as a choking noise. "That's insane. What if we fail? You might lose your chance at rescuing Regis."

"No matter what happens to Regis, he'll be fine. Septimus wouldn't dare hurt him. It's worth the risk."

"And if we're arrested?"

"Then I suppose I'll be a criminal," Jonathan said. "It's happened before. It's not a big deal. Crow. Regis would kill me if I let you die. Let me have this one, all right? Let me save my own skin."

Crow nodded unsteadily. "All right." Blearily, he noticed that his hair had fixed itself again, though his eyes were still black. "This is humiliating," he moaned. "Why am I crying on your shoulder?"

"Temporary weakness," Jonathan said with a straight face. "The spell must be interfering with your emotions somehow."

"If you tell anyone, I'll ruin you."

"See? You're already back to normal. Come on. Athea might know a back way into Septimus's manor."

Chapter ELEVEN
Release

PANIC WOULD only make their job more difficult. Jonathan told himself that repeatedly. If he wanted to keep Crow calm, he needed to be calm himself.

Crow removed two knives from his boots. He cut into the lining of his belt to reveal two small vials. Each held a different liquid—one purple, one green. Colored, doubtless, to tell the vials apart. He coated the knives. When he caught Jonathan staring, he smiled wryly. "This one's a paralytic," he said, twirling the first knife. "The other is a knock-out drug."

"How do you keep track of which knife is which?"

Crow put the knives back in their proper places. "The left one is always the knock-out drug. The right is always the paralytic." Jonathan fitted himself with leather armor. Thin panels that fit close to his chest. Crow tossed him a tunic. "Here. We need to remain inconspicuous."

Jonathan shrugged it on over the armor. "If someone catches us, what do we do?"

"You grab them. An arm across the throat and a hand across the mouth. I cut them, they go to sleep for a while."

"And Septimus. What about Septimus?"

"Same thing."

Jonathan's mouth thinned. Neither of them said the obvious: that Septimus was a powerful sorcerer, and unless they found Regis first, they were fucked. "Sure," Jonathan said.

THE UPPER District was filled with lights.

People. A smoke-filled haze. Gaudy nobles spilled out of the yard of a nearby estate. Someone was having a party, and servants filtered through the crowd, offering drinks to any who pleased. Jonathan and Crow stopped near the outskirts. "People," Jonathan breathed. "Fuck."

A servant breezed past, barely glancing at them and their plain clothes. "No, this is good," Crow murmured. "Keep your head down and look like you know what you're doing."

"What? Why?"

"You'd be surprised what people will ignore," Crow said. He led the way through the crowd. Jonathan tried not to look suspicious. Which was—he suspected—very suspicious-looking. How did Crow do it?

He kept his mouth shut and his eyes looking straight ahead. He hadn't been at a party like this since he'd run away from home. And for a second—a split-second—Crow's black hair looked like the hair of Jonathan's childhood sweetheart, the friend he'd fallen for and abandoned. Jonathan was forcefully reminded of his teenage escapades, running around behind his father's back. Wanting someone he shouldn't.

Crow and Cameron weren't the same person, of course. But there were some striking similarities between them.

Crow took his hand and pulled him along.

UP IN his room, Regis had been working with the lock picks all night. He scratched this way and that until finally they caught, then pushed in. It was more or less chance that he'd get the correct amount of pressure in the correct places.

It was unlikely, but so what? The file had broken when he'd tried it. He wanted to be out. His whole body screamed for it. Meeting Crow through the window had been torture, though of course he couldn't have told Crow that.

He tried the lock picks on his collar, but they did nothing. He didn't know what he was doing. He flung them on the floor, bit down onto his wrist, and let out a muffled scream. He thunked his head on the desk and lay there until he calmed down.

Then he picked up the lock picks and tried again. More patiently.

Belcane had never bothered teaching Crow to read. Crow was thirteen, and he'd asked Regis to teach him. A bargain was struck: Regis would teach him letters and the sounds they made, and Crow would teach him practical things.

Crow had an unusual mind. He had no patience for studying, but he could solve almost any problem he was confronted with. He liked to think and fiddle. He'd taught himself to pick locks and pick pockets. He'd passed a few skills to Regis. He'd tried, at least. Regis had never been good at flirting, or stealing, or....

Or any of it.

His eyes stung. He missed the touch of Crow's hands. He remembered how Crow had guided the picks into the lock, showing him the motions and telling him what to listen for. He remembered the press of Crow against his back. The fluttery, panicky shock of a new infatuation with an older boy. A boy who, for the longest time, had not noticed.

But then years had passed, and eventually, Crow had noticed. Crow started giving him lingering looks. Toying with him. Trading him kisses for favors—

Now wasn't the time to think of that.

The picks fell into place. The lock clicked, and the collar shifted. A chill shot through him. He set down the picks and carefully—oh so carefully—took off the collar.

His magic smelled like catmint. The scent was so normal to him that he usually didn't notice it. His magic roared inside him; he was at full strength. He ached to use it, like a limb too long restrained. He could use it. Now.

Septimus will be asleep.

He could creep into his father's room and take revenge. He'd have to wake him, though. There was no point in murdering a man in his sleep.

No. He couldn't kill his father over something this stupid. Besides, what if Septimus was stronger than him? He had to get out quickly. He needed to find Jonathan, and he needed to fix Crow.

JONATHAN KEPT a close eye out for City Watchmen. Despite how plainly he and Crow were dressed, none of the gaudy nobles paid them any attention. He followed Crow around a corner to the back of Septimus's house. Rustling and moaning came from the bushes. Through the branches, a woman's gaudy skirts were visible. No, actually… two sets of skirts, one purple and one pink. One of the women peeked out, then ducked, giggling.

Athea had said there was a key under the top left flagstone. He found it and unlocked the back door. They were in.

Septimus's manor smelled of wood polish and old paper. Jonathan turned in a circle, searching for anyone nearby. "Fourth floor, on the south side of the house," he whispered. "I see stairs. Let's go."

Footsteps descended a nearby set of stairs. Jonathan looked around wildly, then—quietly as he could—opened a large closet. He and Crow pressed close in the tiny space.

The footsteps passed by. Jonathan held his breath. Next to him, he could feel Crow's heartbeat. He peeked out. He caught a glimpse of fancy green robes as whoever-it-was left through the back door. Jonathan relaxed. "I think Septimus just left," he whispered. "Someone dressed in expensive clothing."

They held their breaths and strained to listen. They stayed there for several more minutes.

"This is going to be even easier than I thought," Crow said.

THE WINDOW was the best option, Regis decided. He gripped the bars and said, "Heat."

Almost immediately, the metal became blistering-hot. Regis snatched his hands away. Damn. He tried it again with his hands a few inches back, but before the metal melted, he had to pull back. Maybe he could blast the whole thing from a distance.

That would wake up everyone in the manor, though. First he needed a way to get down. He glanced at the sheets and blankets. Too thin, and not enough of them. His gaze landed on a brush sitting on the dresser.

An idea struck him. He ran his fingers through his hair and said, "Grow." His scalp tingled. His hair rapidly grew past his shoulders. He began to braid it.

It reached the floor, then doubled, then tripled. Giddy, Regis took the knife out of the lock-picking kit. He cut his hair. On a whim, he left it long, a foot past his shoulders. He tied it into a low ponytail.

He glanced at the window.

If he went through the house, he might encounter Septimus, who might force him back into captivity. If he left the house immediately—loudly—he would be in public, making him much safer. Septimus wouldn't dare attack him in the middle of a crowded street.

He summoned his anger. He thought of his father refusing to let him go. He thought of Crow dying, his organs losing function, his skin growing feathers. He thought of Jonathan, angry and alone.

He threw all his rage into his power. A rush of lightning shot through him, exploding from his palm. The window crumbled. Half the wall went with it. Regis ducked under the desk. Once the rocks settled, he crawled out, wiping the dust from his face.

Outside, there were people calling out in alarm. The air was thick and warm. Regis tossed out the length of hair, then peered over the edge. The rope didn't quite reach the ground, but it would be enough. People gathered below his window. He eased himself over the side, holding on tight.

The hair bit into his palms. All of his weight was supported by his arms, and his arms were weak. If he'd thought to wrap his hands in cloth, he could have slid down. Now he had to either hold on or fall to his death, though, so he held, and he began to move. He was twenty feet from the ground, now. Fifteen. Ten.

Flush with victory, he let himself relax. He'd rescued himself. Jonathan was going to be thrilled.

PAINTINGS RATTLED on the walls. Jonathan leaned against the banister to steady himself. "Did you hear that?" he said, glancing around. "It sounded like an explosion."

"Maybe it was Septimus."

"Can't be. He left ten minutes ago." Regis's room was on the north side, top floor. Jonathan headed up the grand staircase. "His door will be locked. We need to find the key. Septimus's bedroom, maybe?"

"I can pick the lock."

"You gave your lock picks—"

"Regis can slide them under the door. It'll take me a few minutes, though." Crow said it quietly, as though he meant it. As though he was asking for Jonathan's help.

Jonathan ran scenarios over in his head. The explosion had been loud. The Watch was probably on their way. People might enter the manor. With some improvisation, maybe they could pull this off. But they couldn't run, not now, not with Regis so close. Leaving the house was unthinkable. "This way," he said. He went to the north side of the house.

He pounded on the first door he came across. "Regis?" he hollered.

No response. He moved to the next door and repeated the shouting. No servants appeared or stopped them.

At last, they came to a door at the end of the hall. Last one. "This must be it," Jonathan said. He knocked. They held still, silent, holding their breath. Was Regis all right? Maybe he was unconscious. Maybe his captor had moved him.

No response.

Downstairs, there came banging, then pounding footsteps. Crow leaned over the banister, then jerked back. "It's them."

Jonathan backed down the hallway. He rammed the door with his shoulder. The oak shuddered but held, and pain lanced through his arm. Fuck. He needed to get through. He hit again, then looked back.

Guards pounded up the stairs. Others fanned out to check the rest of the manor. Four came down the hallway with swords drawn, faces grim.

Jonathan backed against the door. These were honorable people. They worked to defend the city. They probably had families to feed. Some of them might have children. He'd killed bandits before, sure, and killed in self-defense, but he couldn't cut down innocent men.

Wordlessly, he held up his hands. One gripped his wrist, slammed him against the wall, and punched him in the head. Dark spots burst in his vision, and the floor pitched beneath him. Only their grip kept him upright. They unbuckled his sword-belt and began to drag him out of the manor.

REGIS LANDED on the pavement. He stood at the entrance of an alley. The Watch had come, predictably. Only two men stood outside, and they seemed focused on the house's entrance. They were a ways away from him.

A few hungry spectators glanced between him and the Watch, but no one waved their hands and shouted, "Look! There he is!" All he had to do was walk away. It even looked like Septimus was gone.

And then the Watch dragged two men out of the house.

Regis's breath caught. He could see only their backs. Each was dressed in dark clothing, and both were armed. Had someone tried to rob Septimus?

Long black hair. Slender body.

Crow.

The other man had brown hair, a touch too long, and he stumbled as though dazed. There was blood on his temple. He lifted his head. Blue eyes and a straight nose. The scar across his mouth was gone, but those eyes....

It was Jonathan.

JONATHAN'S EARS RANG. At last, he got his feet under him. "Isn't that Lord Murtagh?" someone said from a distance.

Another voice echoed in the crowd. "And his pet."

The men let him go. He regained his balance, and he and Crow leaned on each other. He lifted his head. The Watch surrounded them in a circle. Karis pushed through.

For a moment, Jonathan thought he'd hit his head again.

Her chest was wrapped in white bandages, and her face had peeling pink skin, recently burned and healed. Her perfect mouth twisted into a smile, and the scar tissue tightened. "I told you he'd come here," she said to the Watch captain.

He had not watched her die. Classic mistake—he should have killed her himself. He should have climbed back in and cut her throat. A blow through the stomach wouldn't have killed her immediately. It had been a major fire. Of course there would be city-employed healers on the scene. Of course.

"I'll tell you everything," Jonathan said to the captain. "She kidnapped my partner. She can't be trusted."

The guard captain said, "Jonathan White, your days of vigilante justice are over. You are under arrest for housebreaking, interfering with an official Watch investigation, theft of human property, arson, and the attempted murder of Madam Karis Du Bois."

The truth crystallized. The Watch was in on this. They worked for her. It explained everything. Of course they had never looked for Regis. They knew.

She was untouchable. Burn her building, and she'd build a new one. Drive a spike through her chest, and she'd be rescued and rushed to a healer. Have her imprisoned, and she would be out the next day. Septimus would lie for her. Peter would be caught. Athea would be arrested. They hadn't stopped Karis, only set her back. It was like dealing with a viper; there was only one solution.

"Okay," Jonathan said. "I'll come quietly." He held out his hands.

The guard captain moved to put him in manacles, stepping away from Karis.

Jonathan shoulder-tackled him. He drew a dagger from the guard-captain's waist, seized Karis by the arm, and—in full view of the Watch and several dozen witnesses—drove the full length through her throat.

Chapter TWELVE
Fall

REGIS WATCHED, stunned. The woman Jonathan had impaled collapsed, dead. At once, several people in the crowd began to scream, and others fought to get away from Jonathan. Others stood stock-still, gaping. Jonathan disappeared among the moving bodies. Regis fought to say close. "Get out of my way," he roared.

His voice was lost in the crowd, which was to be expected, given that Regis was not terribly good at roaring.

Regis held his hand in the air. Energy ripped through his body as he discharged an enormous lightning bolt. A warning shot. Everyone within five feet of him immediately backed away, save for one woman who fainted.

Jonathan and Crow stood in the middle of a circle. The Watchmen backed away from them, and away from Regis. One of them went white, then turned and fled. The rest stayed behind, clutching their weapons.

The Watch captain hollered orders, though Regis could not make out the words above the noise. The remaining Watchmen retreated with the nobles.

Jonathan turned. A glorious smile broke across his face. He whooped, then dropped the dagger and threw his arms around Regis. For a moment, Regis's body wouldn't seem to work. The touch of his lover's arms was like sinking into a hot bath after days of filth. It made him weak with relief, helpless with love. He hugged Jonathan back. It was all he could do. "I missed you," Jonathan whispered.

Regis took a shuddering breath. He pushed him back at arm's length. "You moron," he said. "Who the hell did you just kill?"

Jonathan's grin widened. "I'm glad you're okay. I mean, you're being a prick, so you must be okay."

"Just peachy! I mean, it was only a kidnapping. Why, they barely tortured me at all."

Jonathan's expression dropped. He scanned Regis's body. "Tortured? They tortured you?"

"Not really," Regis said, caught off-guard. "I was exaggerating. I mean—I thought—weren't we teasing each other just now?"

"I was worried," Jonathan said. "If someone tortured you, I'll kill them." Crow nodded as if that were the most reasonable thing in the world. It was probably the first time they had ever agreed on anything. Regis gave up.

The Watch hadn't left, only stopped a ways down the street. The partygoers were gone, save a few who remained to lollygag. The captain spoke rapidly to an underling, who nodded and left. They were looking at him, Regis realized with a jolt. They'd only backed off because he was a sorcerer. They hadn't fled or given up, only changed tactics.

"We probably need to get moving," Crow said.

Crow seemed unusually thin. His skin, too white. His eyes were black. "What happened to you?" Regis said.

"I'm okay. It's fine. The spell is breaking, but I'm still in control."

"He's not fine," Jonathan said. "He's dying. We need to get somewhere safe and fix him. Top priority."

Crow dug his heels in. "We *need* to get somewhere safe because *someone* murdered the most influential woman in Tyrigaine. Honestly, Jonathan, stop babying me. I can handle myself for five more minutes. What happened this morning was a fluke."

"We need to go," Jonathan said, putting a hand in the middle of Crow's back. Watching them touch gave Regis an odd feeling. Something he couldn't place. A week ago, they would have been at each other's throats. Now they were fighting side-by-side. What had happened?

Most of the Watch had fled. The rest stood at the ready. Were they waiting for reinforcements?

Something clattered by Regis's foot. A crossbow bolt. He glanced up.

Three crossbowmen crouched on the rooftops. One of them wore dark clothing, and as she notched a bolt in her crossbow, the head glinted oddly. It was tipped with something. "Go," Crow hissed, shoving at him, and they darted for the nearest alley. Two bolts clattered behind Regis.

The third bolt punched into his arm.

The force made him stagger. Pain hit a moment later, deep-seated and aching. Numbness spread through him. Was the bolt tipped with an opal? Was this how the Watch handled sorcerers?

Two hands gripped him, one on each side. Together, Jonathan and Crow dragged him down the alley. "The eastern gate," Crow panted. "It's only a half-mile away. Can you make it, Regis?"

Jonathan's voice was low. "It doesn't matter. I caught sight of a few men circling from that direction. If we go that way, they'll box us in."

"The city walls," Regis said through gritted teeth. "Let's go that way. They won't expect it."

One street over, a tall stone staircase led up. They could climb up to... what? The battlements? And then what? They'd make a stand? They'd jump? The forest was close to the wall on this side. If they could get down somehow, they could escape into the trees.

Jonathan and Crow pulled him down the street, then ran for the stairs. He caught sight of the crossbowmen following them across the rooftops. They needed to hurry if they wanted to stay out of range. "We need to get the arrow out," he panted as they climbed.

"Leave it in," Jonathan said. "It's the only thing plugging the hole. If we take it out, you'll bleed to death before we can reach safety."

"No magic. Tipped with opal. If we leave it in, I'm useless."

The stairs went on forever. His lungs burned for air. He was only weighing them down. He was too soft for this sort of activity. He spent his days writing and working magic, not running. At last, he staggered over the last step.

The wind blew hot and humid here. The sandstone wall stood fifty feet tall. There were no trees to climb down, no ladders, no handholds. Not far behind them, the crossbowmen made their way across the rooftops and took aim.

Regis sank down below the battlements. He gripped the shaft. Jonathan knelt. "Let me," he murmured.

Crow held the arm still. Being held by both of them at once gave Regis a fluttery sort of feeling. They had him. He wasn't alone. They would be okay. He had to believe that.

Jonathan teased the shaft out. Regis bit down on his tongue to keep from screaming. He pressed a hand to the wound. White-hot pain dizzied him. He couldn't focus long enough to heal himself. "Steady," Jonathan said. "You can do this. You know how piercing wounds work. Blood vessels and skin, right?"

"The bolt-tip punches through muscle," Regis groaned. "The barb—causes further tearing as—it's pulled out. So I need to heal muscle, and…."

He couldn't fix it manually. He couldn't concentrate well enough. Instead, he sped up his body's natural healing process, and the wound scabbed over, then scarred.

Heaving wingbeats came from outside the city. Regis looked up, then almost laughed. Chartreuse glided toward them from the direction of the lodging house.

A person rode on her back. A young woman with wild hair. Chartreuse skidded to a halt atop the wall, tearing long grooves in the stone with her claws. A chunk of the battlements fell into the grass.

The young woman slid off her back. She pushed her hair from her face with a dramatic toss. She looked delighted. "Oh, good, you found him." Then she cleared her throat. "Oh damn. I was going to say something heroic. How's this?" She struck a pose. "Need any help? I was just in the neighborhood."

Crossbow bolts rattled against the battlements, and down below, five men with swords began to climb the stairs. "This isn't the time for heroism," Jonathan snapped. He shoved Regis toward Chartreuse. "Chartreuse, how many people can you carry?"

Down to the ground and back? Two at a time.

"Take Regis and Crow first."

Huh, Regis thought, glancing at him. It was the rational decision, of course. The spell on Crow could break at any moment. The two of them needed to get away the fastest. He was surprised, though, that Jonathan had thought of it.

What about you and Athea? Chartreuse said.

"Come back for us," Jonathan said.

There wasn't enough time. Whoever Chartreuse left behind would be arrested. Jonathan would be thrown in the deepest and darkest jail cell Tyrigaine had to offer. They'd execute him. The young woman might be fine, but Jonathan was a murderer.

Crow swallowed. He and Jonathan looked at each other. Crow didn't say anything, but he clasped Jonathan's hand. Jonathan squeezed, then let go. He shoved Crow toward Chartreuse.

I won't abandon my favorite hatchling. I'm not doing that.

"You have to," Jonathan said. "It's the only decision that makes sense."

No. I mean factually. Factually, I am not doing that.

And—ignoring Crow entirely—she snatched up Regis and Jonathan. Talons wrapped around Regis, furnace-hot and snake-smooth. Jonathan snarled and kicked. He shouted curses at her in his native tongue. Chartreuse didn't let go. She leapt off the battlements.

She didn't have enough room to take off properly. They plummeted toward the ground. Chartreuse beat her wings hard, and they slowed.

Above the roaring wind, Regis could hear Jonathan still cursing. She released them five feet from the ground, then hit the grass, rolling on her side. Jonathan shoved himself upright. "Go get them!" he roared.

She pushed Jonathan with her tail, shoving him toward the forest. *You and your mate are more important than that nest-wrecking cripple.*

"If you don't save him right fucking now—"

She crouched, then launched herself into the air. It was too late. The Watchmen had reached the top of the wall, and they had Crow and the young woman backed into a corner. Crow leaned over, looking out over the forest. The young woman climbed onto the battlements. Just as Chartreuse passed, she jumped.

Crow jumped after her.

Chartreuse caught the woman, then dove for Crow. Her claws missed him by an inch. Immediately, Crow began to shift. His body shrunk.

Of course. Crow had never intended for Chartreuse to catch him. Crow never trusted anyone to save him. He intended to save himself.

The dark-clothed crossbowmen aimed at him from the wall. The bolt struck Crow in the chest. He tumbled through the air.

And then the shape-shifting spell broke.

Regis felt it break, like a window shattering. Something gave way. With a crack, the last vestiges of Myra Belcane's magic exploded from his body. Red light rippled outward. A small black bird hit the ground, the opal-tipped crossbow bolt sticking from its chest.

Regis fell to his knees.

There was a roaring in his ears. He couldn't balance. He collapsed onto his hands, gripping the earth just to stay on all fours. Crow was dead. His best friend was dead. His adoptive brother was dead. Crow had come to him for help—just this once—and Regis had failed him.

A wall of grief and rage hit him. He'd kill Septimus. He'd murder every slaver bastard in the city. He'd hunt down Belcane and rip her limb from limb. Everyone involved in this would pay. He'd become the worst villain in Tyria if he had to.

He cradled the bird in his hands. Weakly, it twitched. Still alive. Still bleeding. Was it too late?

Chartreuse landed. She dropped the young woman next to him.

"Regis." Someone shook him hard. Jonathan. It was Jonathan. "Regis, we have to go. The Watch is coming. They circled around through the gate."

"I can fix this," Regis whispered. "I can fix this. I need time."

The young woman stood up, looked at the Watch, looked at the dragon, then looked back at Regis. "I think I can get you a few minutes." She raised her hands. She made a ripping motion with her arms, and a wave of power lashed from her fingers. She pulled down a nearby tree.

She wasn't particularly good at magic. There was no precision or control, only strength and brutality. The magical discharge was enormous; there were silver sparks everywhere. Her lack of skill, though, didn't seem to matter. She had enough raw power to hold off ten guards. She ripped down another tree, then another, making a wall between them and the Watch.

Chartreuse launched herself on top the pile, screaming. A man fought to climb the limbs, and she slapped him away with her tail.

Jonathan knelt by the bird. "Don't worry. If anyone reaches us, I'll protect you. Focus on Crow."

Regis laid the bird on the ground and held his palms over it. He began his breathing exercises, inhaling for a count of five, then exhaling. It calmed him. Sparks flickered from his fingertips. He wove his magic into the body, teasing in each spark one by one. Piece by piece, the bird became human. Feathers into skin. Wings into arms. He worked the flesh first, then grew the bones to fit. He pulled out the arrow shaft, then healed the wound. The bird didn't bleed. Its heart had stopped beating.

His magic touched something inside it.

Something… not physically there. When he closed his eyes, he could sense a ball of glowing light inside Crow. A presence of sorts. He reached out to it and snatched his hands away, stung. Touching the presence hurt. "What?" Jonathan asked. "What's wrong?"

"I don't know," Regis said. "There's this energy inside him. I… I think I touched his soul or something."

"His soul?"

Regis shut his eyes. "Some cultures believe each person has an immortal spirit which inhabits—"

"Regis. I know what a soul is. I don't need a history lesson."

"It's coming out," Regis said. "He's coming apart completely."

He steeled himself, then put his hands back on Crow. The soul inside Crow withdrew. "Oh, Crow," he whispered.

"What is it?"

"Nothing. It's just—" He shook his head. "He, he won't let me touch him. I'm not sure I can fix him like this." He reached out to it again. It didn't like being touched. It didn't like being vulnerable.

He sculpted Crow's body. His sharp hipbones and his white legs, his flat and bony feet. The elbows that had often prodded him in the night. No other sorcerer could have done it, but Regis had spent his childhood in a room full of books with nothing to do. He'd spent days learning the precise shape of Crow's body.

When he was done, he looked down at his work. He'd made a corpse. "It's empty," he said.

"You can do this," Jonathan said. "Just breathe. You can fix him."

"I can fix him," Regis muttered. He shut his eyes tight again. "You only use that voice when you're upset."

"I'm upset enough for both of us." Every word was quiet, strong, and soothing. "We can do this together. You'll work your magic, and I'll keep you calm. We'll stick to things we're good at. Okay?"

Regis nodded, throat tight. "Okay."

He placed his hands on Crow's chest. The consciousness was still there inside, but it was disconnected, as if all contact between it and the body were severed. It broke apart, bit by bit. He didn't try to grab it this time. He gave it space and tried to think calm, friendly thoughts.

He touched it, and this time, it didn't withdraw. He worked it back into the body. Tied the two together again, fixed the consciousness deep into those bones. At last, Crow's soul was reunited with his human form. Regis pressed his hand over Crow's heart and sent a jolt of lightning through it.

Crow's eyes flickered open. Hazily, they focused. He squinted.

Regis half laughed, half sobbed. He threw his arms around Crow's neck and squeezed. "You're all right."

Crow squeezed back weakly. "What happened? Did I fall?"

Then, hazily, his eyes focused on Jonathan. Jonathan didn't hug him, but he squeezed Crow's shoulder and helped him up. "You were dead, my friend. Regis brought you back."

Crow leaned heavily on Jonathan. "You—you *brought me back?*"

Regis scrubbed his teary eyes with his dirty hand. "Yes, well," he said airily. "Most powerful sorcerer in Tyria, all hail me. You were only dead for five minutes. Can we go?"

Guards were climbing over the downed trees. The young woman held them off with branches. "Oh, Crow's back?" she said. "Good. I hate this magic nonsense."

They fled into the woods.

Chapter THIRTEEN
Confession

REGIS WAS exhausted. But they needed to get away from the city as fast as possible.

Jonathan liked to call himself a professional hero, and like any professional, he had plans for situations like these. They both did. They had been together two years, and they had learned to work together.

A trail would lead the authorities right to them—footprints, broken branches, bruised leaves. Jonathan led the way and found the quickest path, making sure they didn't cause too much of a disturbance. Regis erased their footprints and mended any broken branches.

"Chartreuse," Jonathan said. "We need you to lay a fake trail for us."

Chartreuse nodded, then padded off in another direction. She clawed the ground with her paws, swept her trail behind her to disturb the prints, and trampled right over bushes.

The redheaded sorceress from before looked concerned. "How will she find her way back to us? I don't want to leave her behind. She's the only funny one."

"She's a dragon. She'll sniff us out later." Jonathan motioned for them to follow him. "We need to stop by the lodging house briefly. There's something we need to pick up."

Regis lingered in the woods with Athea and Crow while Jonathan slipped through the back door. He returned with the three journals Regis had stolen from Belcane... and a boy. The boy was young, fourteen maybe, and he smelled like a sorcerer. He fidgeted and picked at his clothes like he didn't like wearing them. "Regis, this is Peter," Jonathan said. "Peter, this is Regis."

Regis scowled. "Dammit, Jon. We've had this discussion before. You can't just pick up strays."

"Do you need an apprentice?" Jonathan said, like he wasn't asking Regis to waste years of time banging knowledge into some kid's head.

"No," Regis explained.

Peter ducked his head and stared at the ground between Regis's feet. "Don't mind him," Jonathan said, clapping the boy on the shoulder. "We'll find something to do with you."

The sorceress struck a pose like a commanding general. "I know a place we can stay."

"A place?" Jonathan said. "Where?"

"I'll show you. Follow me."

SOON, THE afternoon cooled off. Regis was too exhausted to move quickly. So, it seemed, was everyone else. He stumbled over tree roots and tripped in the underbrush. He didn't bother covering their trail anymore. No one had come after them yet. Even on the unlikely chance that someone sent soldiers after them on a suicide mission, Chartreuse was probably leading them on a merry chase through the woods.

The young woman kept turning to look at him. She seemed familiar, though he couldn't place her. The shape of her nose... her thin lips... her dull blue eyes.... She gave him a warm sort of feeling. She seemed powerful, and her magic carried the tang of ozone and lightning. "I'm sorry," Regis said. "Who are you, exactly? I'm Regis Teller."

She offered him her hand, and he clasped it. Delicate and bony, like his own. "Athea Aron. My father wouldn't shut up about you."

Aron. Prickles shot through his hand at her touch. She was related to him? She watched his face carefully. "Your father?" Regis said lightly. He knew better than to get his hopes up.

"Oh, you know." She waved her hand. "The man who had you stolen from your partner and dragged off to meet him. Sorry about that, by the way. He's a git, isn't he?"

Regis had to steady himself on a tree. "Septimus. Septimus is your...? Septimus is my father. You—you're related to—I have a *sister?*" And, without really knowing what he was doing, he hugged her.

She clutched at his back, burying her face in his shoulder. The hug was awkward and overwhelming. "I knew it!" she said. "He kept talking about how you might be one of his children, and well, I didn't want to get my hopes up, but—I have a brother! Oh, Regis, I'm so glad it's you."

Regis pounded her on the back. It seemed like the sort of thing a brother would do. "Who's your mother? What happened? Why were we raised apart?"

"Who cares? I'm so glad my entire family isn't made up of jerks. Well," she said, immediately reconsidering. "I mean, you are a dangerous criminal, apparently, but other than that, you seem fine."

"I bet you had a nice, safe childhood," Regis said. "A rich father, a quiet home, plenty of time to study…."

"Well, yes. It was awful."

Regis shoved her back. "Awful? That sounds fantastic!"

"It was boring," she said, looking at him as if he were insane. "I bet your boyfriend teaches you sword tricks and how to wrestle. I'm not even allowed to have a boyfriend. Oh, Father was awful. You know, when I was little, he told me I could be whatever I liked when I grew up. So I told him I wanted to be a knight. 'A knight?' he said. 'Like a magic knight?' No, I told him. Like a person who hits things with a sword."

"I know some prostitutes that would give their right tit to have magic," Regis said.

"Yes, well, I'm not one of them. Just because you're born with a gift doesn't mean you're obligated to use it. I mean, imagine if a witch made you the greatest cocksucker in the world. Would you go around sucking cock all the time?"

"Yeah," Regis said. "I mean, probably."

She elbowed him. "You're filth."

AN HOUR passed. Chartreuse slunk out of the underbrush, shockingly quiet for such a large predator. She nuzzled Athea, and Athea clambered onto her back. To his shock, the dragon did not immediately buck her off; instead Chartreuse just kept walking with Athea perched atop her like a jockey.

Regis fell back to meander beside Crow, who walked at the back. He kept staring at the insides of his wrists. He jumped when Regis touched him. "Something wrong with your body?"

"No, it's good. It's—it's fantastic. My scars are gone. Will you check my back? You know, for the tattoos?"

Regis checked. "They're gone."

Crow glanced at his wrists one last time, then dropped his hands. "Huh. Clean slate."

"Guess so."

"Listen," Crow said. "We need to talk."

"Talk?"

Crow lowered his voice. "It's about Jonathan. Something happened while you were gone."

Regis grimaced. He wasn't looking forward to this conversation, whatever it was. Probably they'd gotten into another stupid fight. They barely pretended to get along when he was around. He couldn't imagine how cruel they were to each other when he was missing. "What did you do? Punch him?"

Crow seemed to be moving options around in his head. Plotting things out, probably. After a while, he said, "We kissed a couple times."

Regis stared at him dumbly. For a moment, he assumed Crow was joking. But Crow looked back at him steadily, white-faced, hands clenched.

Jonathan had been unfaithful? Jonathan?

Jonathan was the one who demanded fidelity in the first place. Monogamy never made a lot of sense to Regis—what was the point?—but he did love Jonathan, and well, people made sacrifices when they were in love. He hadn't cared at the time. They hadn't even talked about it much.

Regis's mind raced. Why now, and why Crow? They hated each other.

Maybe that was why Crow had done it. Crow hated their relationship and would do anything to end it. Crow fucked people over all the time. This was another stupid attempt at manipulation, wasn't it? Regis's hands clenched, and he kept trudging through the grass. He kind of wanted to hit Crow.

"Please, say something," Crow whispered.

"Let me get this straight." His voice was deadly quiet. "A week ago, you hated Jonathan. But the moment I disappear—the moment you're alone with him—you're so overcome with lust you can't stop yourself from sticking your tongue in his mouth. Bullshit." He shoved Crow. "Why did you do this? Is my life a game to you?"

It was obvious why Crow had done this. Crow had always been a liar and a cheat. The next step would be for Crow to blame Jonathan and twist this into a fight. Regis crossed his arms and waited, glaring.

Crow reached out, then seemed to think better of it. He averted his eyes. "I'm sorry. I understand why you're angry. But I want you to hear my version first. Regis, I love—I adore you as a friend, and you deserve to be happy."

Here it came. The lies and manipulation.

"It was me," Crow said. "All of it."

Regis's arms loosened. "Wait, what?"

"We barely escaped Karis alive. Her records were destroyed, and we thought we had no hope of finding you. I was exhausted. He was exhausted too. I took advantage of that. Don't blame him."

"All right," Regis said, taken aback. "And the second time?"

"I came into his room in the middle of the night, reeking of sex. I told him I wanted him. We decided to—to kiss, just once, just because we'd already done it. It seemed harmless." Crow's tone took on an oddly light edge. "Look, just don't blame him. It wasn't his fault. I should've backed off earlier. I kissed him first both times."

"And then you stopped?"

There was a long pause. Finally, Crow said, "Jonathan suggested we drug ourselves so we could sleep. We did that."

Something was off. Crow was never this straightforward. But why would Crow lie about this?

"I wanted you to hear my version first," Crow said. "He'll probably tell you his eventually. I'm certain he'll try to take the blame or something equally stupid. He's that sort of idiot. Just let it go, all right? Don't tell him I said anything."

"Okay. But—"

"You know me," Crow said. "Usually I'm the sort of person who lies to make himself look good. I'd hardly tell a lie to make myself look bad, now would I?"

Apparently Crow didn't want to destroy his relationship with Jonathan after all. But if Crow wasn't trying to destroy his relationship, why had he kissed Jonathan in the first place?

Had they—

Had they kissed because they genuinely liked each other?

The possibility was too ridiculous to consider. It was, however, the only option left. Regis pinched the bridge of his nose. "You're giving me a headache."

"I'm sorry."

There was a stretch of silence. For once, Crow looked honestly apologetic. Regis cleared his throat. He was going to have to be sincere, he realized sadly. He hated doing that. He glanced around to see if anyone was nearby enough to hear, then spoke softly. "Crow. You were dying. You were terrified and alone. It's okay. I forgive you."

Crow looked relieved. He wrapped an arm around Regis's shoulders. He squeezed. "Thank you."

"If you're lying to me again, I'm going to kill you."

Athea called out ahead. "Look! I think I can see my hideout." She pointed. There, between the trunks, a ramshackle cottage was visible. She thrust her hand into the knot of a tree and pulled out a key. She unlocked the door and kicked it open. "I've been planning to run away for ages. Isn't it lovely?"

It was filth. Regis made a face, but he stepped in.

The entrance was a bare kitchen with a table and a stove. Jonathan, in his typical fashion, immediately began checking the place for enemies. He circled around the furniture, then set off through the hallway. He came back a moment later. "Two bedrooms and a privy," he said. He dressed down the cabinets. "Some moldy apples... two weeks' worth of dried tack and jerky—" He nearly tripped over a barrel. He dusted off the top, revealing burnt-in letters. "A barrel of ale?"

"Victory ale," Athea said. "For when I finally got the courage to run away."

Jonathan considered this a moment, then—in that uncomplicated way of his—announced, "I like you."

Crow was largely silent. His lips were white. He had been staring at Jonathan during the entire walk. He noticed Regis watching him and quickly looked away.

Huh, Regis thought. That was weird.

When Crow stumbled over a loose nail, Jonathan's arm shot out, and he held Crow up. Crow leaned into the support like a man seeking shelter, and Jonathan let go as though burned. They stepped away from each other, each looking away. Jonathan had a guilty look on his face, which was weird, given that all he'd done was touch Crow.

"I need a drink," Crow muttered.

Regis settled back against the counter to watch them. "You? You never drink."

"That's not true," Jonathan said. "He drank the night I met him. We were tipsy."

Crow's fingers played on the counter. "Oh, that. Actually, I faked that."

"Faked getting drunk? Why?" Jonathan said.

"It puts people at ease."

Regis heard the implication clearly: *It's easier to get people into bed.* He watched Crow carefully. "Maybe we should have a drink later. I bet you two have been through a lot together."

Jonathan winced like Regis had hit a sore spot. He and Crow said nothing, and they certainly didn't look at each other. And as they maneuvered around the cramped kitchen, they did not touch at all.

For some reason, the idea of them together took root in Regis's mind. Jonathan and Crow lying together in the bedsheets, still clothed from a long day. Kissing. In a hurried way, clumsy and exploratory, both of them too exhausted to think straight. Hands bunched together. The tension between them must have been unbearable, and it would have shown. Bodies ratcheted tight, both of them fighting to stop but too desperate to succeed.

Oddly enough, the idea didn't make him jealous. It gave him a warm feeling, instead.

Huh.

THE NEED to tell Regis about the kiss was a burning coal in Jonathan's chest. He bit his tongue each time it almost came out. He couldn't bear the thought of what Regis would think of him.

Then again, the rules were different here. His family had always placed such emphasis on monogamy, but in Tyria....

Marriage was rare. Tyrians were very clan-like. The women picked lovers to father children with, then raised those children with the help of their family. The queen herself was whispered to have several children, all hidden away until they came of age. Women only married to gain status, and men only married to gain parental rights.

He'd asked Regis not to sleep around. He'd wanted Regis for himself. And Regis had always abided by that rule. Several women had made passes at Regis before. Beautiful women who wanted magical children. Regis had turned them down. If it weren't for Jonathan, Regis might be fucking his way through half of Tyria's nobility.

And yet here Jonathan was. Panting after Crow. Breaking his own stupid fucking rule.

Jonathan shut his eyes. He should have expected this. Crow had gotten him into bed the first night they'd met. Of course they were compatible. Of course Crow was handsome, and charming, and funny, and....

...sometimes, when Crow let his guard down—when he was exhausted—he seemed nice. Vulnerable, even.

Crow, Athea, and Peter filtered outside. They lounged in the shade, chatting with Chartreuse. He was alone in the kitchen with Regis. Now. He had to say it now.

"Give me your hip flask," Regis said.

He did.

Regis knelt to fill it with ale. "Athea says there's a stream nearby here. I think I'm going to take a dip."

"You hate water."

"Yeah, but I like watching you naked. Come with me." He offered Jonathan the flask.

Outside, Crow leaned against a tree. His hair cut a sleek line across his shoulder, stuck with a twig. He smiled as Athea played with Chartreuse's tail. Athea said something loudly and yanked her hair as though frustrated by it. Crow rolled his eyes and began to braid it out of her face. He glanced up and happened to meet Jonathan's eyes. His smile faltered.

Jonathan looked away to find Regis watching him. "What?" Jonathan said.

"We need to talk," Regis said.

JONATHAN DUG around in the cottage and found a hook and line, then followed Regis to the stream. He flipped rocks until he found some bait.

A nearby tree made a good anchor point, so he tied off the line there, then tossed the hook in the water.

Farther upstream, Regis stripped off his clothes, then began blatantly watching Jonathan. Jonathan smiled against his will. He wanted to feel depressed—he deserved to feel depressed—but it was such a relief to be with Regis again.

He'd missed this. Selfishly, he wanted to ignore all the bad things that had happened over the past few days. Forget all that and go back to roughing it with his best friend. Maybe it would be more merciful not to tell Regis. He'd been held captive for a week. He needed a rest, not more drama.

He eased the shirt off, then began on his pants. Regis whistled. Jonathan laughed. He dragged Regis into the water while he shrieked and struggled.

Regis was a sorcerer. He could throw Jonathan in a moment. Instead, Regis squirmed and let him pin him against a nearby boulder. He kissed Regis. Sweetly and softly, cradling his body. "Are you really all right?" he whispered. "I don't mean just physically. I mean… mentally. Being imprisoned like that—it isn't good for you. Did he isolate you?"

"I'm fine, you giant lug."

He smoothed a curl out of Regis's face. "Is this a good time for you to yell at me?"

"It's always a good time for yelling."

Jonathan looked around for a moment. Satisfied no one was nearby, he said, "I want to apologize for the way I acted before you were kidnapped. The way I acted towards Crow, I mean. I was being an ass to him. It isn't fair to you, and it isn't fair to him."

Regis blinked at him. "Really?"

"Yeah," Jonathan said. "If you want to hang around him, then hang around him. That's your business. I trust you. But—but there's something I should tell you." He couldn't even get the words out. His throat wouldn't work.

He swallowed.

"I kissed Crow," he said.

Regis's expression did not immediately change. The evening light reflected off the water and onto his face, warming his skin tone. He was all golden skin and fire-lit hair. Slowly, an odd emotion came across his face. Curiosity? It was the sort of look he got when he latched on to an interesting new theory. The sort of look a cat got when it saw a ball of string—an intense interest that bordered on predatory. "Go on," he finally said.

Jonathan settled his feet in the silt and braced himself. "You did hear me, right?"

"I want details. Facts. Specifics. Give me data."

Data? Jonathan was at a total loss. "It, uh, happened twice. Well. Technically, it was three times, but the first time—the first time wasn't our fault. And there was some…." Some choking and some slapping and some really inappropriate suggestions, none of which Jonathan dared to mention. He was still figuring that part out himself. Hitting Crow gave him a sense of satisfaction so powerful it scared him. He loved the look on Crow's face, the desire. "There was some grinding," he said weakly.

Regis scooted up onto the boulder. He sat on it. "Crow told me."

"He *what?*"

"That's why I brought you out here. I want you to tell me the entire story, start to finish. Crow is lying about something, and I can't figure out what."

JONATHAN TOLD the entire story. He didn't rush. He wanted to be precise, straightforward, and honest. This wasn't the time for misunderstandings or lies. Finally, he reached the part where Crow came to his room.

Regis picked moss off the boulder. "Did you have sex with him?"

"No."

"Huh. What's he lying about, then?" Regis leaned forward, swinging his foot against the rock. "Crow says he initiated the kisses."

"He did." Jonathan winced. "But he's also the one that stopped first. He even pulled this really mean trick. He left—he came back with a bottle—I thought we were going to fuck. Turns out he decided to drug himself unconscious so we couldn't have sex."

Regis slapped a hand against the boulder. "That son of a bitch," he said, sounding pleased with himself. "He did lie. He told me you drugged him."

Jonathan stumbled. He took the soap he'd borrowed from Athea (she'd come very prepared for her eventual escape) and scrubbed it into his hair. "He took the blame?"

Regis slid down into the water again. He ducked his head under, then took the soap. "He insisted everything was his fault. He asked me not to tell you."

"And here you are, telling me everything."

"Look. I like Crow, but he's Crow. I'm sure he has good intentions—deeply buried good intentions—but he has a long history of lying to get his way." Regis's face softened. "Only I suppose he wasn't trying to get his way this time. He was lying to…."

"To protect me?" It hit Jonathan. "To protect you. He wants you to be happy."

Regis began scrubbing suds into his hair. "I left you two alone for a week. I guess I should be glad I wasn't gone longer. You'd be married with children."

"I can't believe you're not angry at me."

Regis dunked his head to rinse it. "I'm not sure if you remember this or not, Jonathan, but the first time I slept with you, I was planning to kill you."

Jonathan hunched over. "That was different."

Regis wrapped his arm around Jonathan's back. He rested his head on Jonathan's shoulder. "We lead unusual lives, beloved. It was a kiss. We'll get through it, all right?" His arms slid around Jonathan, slick. It was such a relief to be held. To hold someone without feeling guilty about it.

Jonathan cracked a smile. "This is unusually nice of you."

"If you tell anyone, I'll deny it."

"They'd never believe me, anyway. Black-hearted Regis."

"Well, obviously. Everyone knows I just keep you around for sex." He finished washing off, then climbed back on his boulder, where he was safe from the water. Jonathan stood between his legs and wrapped his arms around his waist.

Regis gripped his hair tight. Jonathan inhaled, going weak. The grip kept him from moving. It thrilled him, knowing Regis was one of the few people in the world who could hold him down. If Jonathan's father knew he'd developed a kink for magic, he'd be even more disgusted.

Regis twisted his hand. "If you'd like, I can pretend to be mad. Throw something at you, call you names. We could get into a fistfight and everything."

"I could grovel a little." His voice was hoarse with lust, and he was half-hard.

Regis smirked. "I do like groveling."

Jonathan mouthed a kiss on Regis's hipbone, then trailed a line to his cock. He sucked the head into his mouth. Regis moaned and relaxed, his body loosening against the moss. He pulled Jonathan's hair like the reins of a horse and pressed him farther down.

The taste of him was intoxicating. Jonathan toyed with his own cock, long pulls from the base to the tip that made him shudder with pleasure. He sucked Regis off lazily. Neither of them was in a hurry. He loved the fantasy of servicing Regis.

He loved everything about this. The little noises Regis made when he was close to coming. The halfhearted thrusts as Regis tried not to choke him. He worked them both up to climax slowly.

Salt teased his tongue, and Regis bunched up, arching. "Ah!" Jonathan backed off, holding Regis's cock still in his mouth. Regis lay there, panting, on the edge of orgasm. He moaned. Slowly—without moving up or down—he began to suck. Regis jerked, gasping.

He wanted to enjoy this. He tortured himself the same way, waiting until he was close, then forcing his hand away. It was torture, trying to concentrate on oral sex while so close to his own orgasm. He reveled in it. The water swirled around him, cooling off his overheated body.

He wanted to come when Regis came. He wanted to share that special moment. So he timed it. He waited until he was close, then sucked hard and down. He couldn't erase the fear and desperation of the past few days, but he could give Regis this, and he would.

When Regis threw his head back and tensed his body, preparing for orgasm, Jonathan allowed it. He teased it out, slowing down but not stopping. When Regis's essence filled his mouth, he let himself climax. Shuddered it out. He spat into the river, then rested against the slimy rock, closing his eyes. Relief and joy filled him.

Regis flicked a hair away from his nose. "I kind of like you with brown hair," he mused.

"I hate it," Jonathan admitted.

Regis's mouth quirked up. He tugged Jonathan's hair, and Jonathan's scalp tingled painfully. The grip on his hair loosened. No— his hair was growing longer, that was it. He checked his reflection. Long blond roots with brown tips. Close enough.

Regis picked up a knife from the riverbank. "Come here. I'll fix it for you."

THE ALE wasn't much. They drank it, then sat on the bank for a while. Jonathan dragged a salmon out of the river, and they made their way back to the house, tipsy. Lazily, he rubbed small circles on Regis's shoulder, and Regis leaned against him.

Their companions were outside, playing cards. One of them had started a small fire in a ring of stones. Jonathan checked it over automatically. The wood was dry and smokeless. Good. No helpful plume of smoke to lead the authorities to them.

Chartreuse flicked her tail at him rudely. She huddled up to Athea, curling around her like a protective mother dragon. It seemed they had already become close friends. *Good evening, thin-scaled hatchling of mine.*

She was a dragon. She didn't understand the subtleties of human relationships, and she'd never understand why he wanted to rescue a rival. Jonathan tried to remind himself of that. He wasn't going to argue with her again.

Still, the insult rankled him. Thin-scaled hatchlings never survived in the wild. When people insulted him, they usually called him stupid, cruel, or self-righteous. They never called him weak.

Jonathan scaled the fish and set it above the fire. Regis went to gather herbs, then came back with wild onions and carrots. They stewed nicely with the fish.

Athea rolled the barrel of ale out of the cottage, then flopped down on the grass. "You and Chartreuse are making me uncomfortable," she announced. "You should get drunk and make up."

Chartreuse raised her head. *Is that the burning drink?*

"Alcohol," Jonathan bit out. "It's called alcohol."

"Yes, and you can have some," Athea said. "Just let us get ours first. Peter, you first."

Peter colored. "Karis never let me have alcohol before. She said it was for patrons only."

Athea fussed over him, and eventually Peter drank.

THE BARREL of ale didn't help. Mostly because Jonathan didn't bother drinking it. There might be soldiers or guards after them, and he needed to be alert in the morning. Regis had a cup or two but stayed sober. He leaned against Jonathan, loose and relaxed.

Athea lay in the grass, face bright red, her skirts floating up around her. "You've never been drunk before, have you?" Regis said wryly.

"Father says alcohol kills your brain." She rolled over. She prodded Jonathan. "Hey, White. Lady Chartreuse and I have been talking."

Chartreuse slurped the last of the ale out of the broken barrel. *Don't tell him.*

"Don't tell me what?"

"Chartreuse and I are going on an adventure," Athea announced grandly.

Athea. Sweetheart. It was a secret.

"We're leaving in the morning. We're taking Crow and Peter. Well. We're taking Peter. He's going to be my apprentice. I'm going to try to commandeer Crow." She giggled. "Commandeer. Crow. You know. Because—because he's a slave."

Crow didn't say anything. He'd been oddly silent the entire night, sitting across the fire and looking over his shoulder occasionally. He wasn't drinking, either.

Jonathan touched Chartreuse's tail. "You're leaving?"

Ever since he'd left home, she had been the only constant thing in his life. Chartreuse kicked away the barrel. She trundled over and snuffled in his hair. *You're not a hatchling anymore.*

"Damn right he's not," Regis said from the ground next to Athea.

"Shut up, Regis," Jonathan said.

Chartreuse sat on her haunches like a dog. *Dragon hatchlings are headstrong but stupid. We confine them. When they are large enough, they fight us and must win to leave the nesting cave. It occurred to me today, Jonathan, that you are not a dragon, and therefore you cannot fight me.* She sounded like a drunk woman pondering her life.

"Yeah," Jonathan said. "Guess not."

I am sorry, little one. I did not notice how much you had grown, and I never considered leaving you. You don't need me anymore. Her eyes flickered back to look at Crow. She bent her head. In a whisper no one else could hear, she said, *If you are building a harem, I would recommend that you clear it with your other mate first. Females can be territorial if they feel threatened.*

Jonathan put his head in his hands. "Regis isn't a female."

I know that, Chartreuse sniffed. *You know what I meant. He is the female in your relationship, isn't he?*

"No. There is no female in this relationship. We're. Both. Men. Okay? Both of us."

"Oh gods," Regis groaned. "What did she say? Are we going to have to explain this again? Chartreuse, no, I am not female, and human males can't impregnate other males. We aren't going to have an egg. Ever."

All mating is done for the production of offspring, Chartreuse insisted. *If humans are biologically wired to sometimes desire their own sex, there must be a reproductive reason. Perhaps you should keep trying.*

"Oh, believe me, we are," Regis said.

Jonathan kicked him.

Chartreuse settled down next to Athea again. She rubbed her cheek on the drunk girl. *I have grown very fond of this female. She needs looking after. I am going to follow her.*

Athea spoke up. "She didn't ask me. She informed me. It was not a mutual decision. She's stalking me, apparently, whether I like it or not."

"Yeah," Jonathan said. "That's pretty much what happened to me too."

He curled up next to Regis and Athea, lying against Chartreuse's scaly hide. Her furnace-like heat seeped into him and lulled him to a drowsy state. He was a criminal now, but it wasn't the first time. He was a criminal in his homeland too. And right now he was free and had a full stomach. He had a partner who trusted him and stood at his back. He could handle the future, whatever it was. He laced his arm through Regis's, and he fell asleep.

JONATHAN WOKE to someone shaking him. He had always been a deep sleeper. He groaned and cracked his eyes open. He didn't have the energy to tell Regis to stop, so he pushed the hand away instead.

It wasn't Regis.

The dying light of the fire cast shadows on Crow's skin. He sat beside Jonathan. "Regis stepped away," he said quietly. "I want to talk to you."

Jonathan was awake in an instant. The touch of him—the smell—had all of Jonathan's senses on alert. He glanced around. Athea and Peter were gone. Chartreuse was asleep, and he still rested against her hide. He was alone with Crow.

"How did it go?" Crow said. "Did you tell him?"

"I did. It went a lot better than expected."

Crow nodded. He toyed with the hem of his shirt. His gaze flickered over. "Is he angry at you?"

"Don't think so." Jonathan rubbed his eyes.

"Is he angry at me?"

"You're overcomplicating this. If he was angry, he'd let you know. Trust me. Relax, okay?"

Crow ran a hand through his hair. Grudgingly, he nodded. He leaned against Jonathan, shoulder to shoulder. Jonathan's heart beat faster. Daringly, Jonathan slipped an arm around his shoulders. He squeezed.

Crow didn't pull away. It struck Jonathan, then, how odd this was. He felt like he was getting closer to Crow. Was this how Crow and Regis's friendship was? Cautious support mixed with restrained desire? Crow seemed different now. Still guarded, still unsure, still tightly controlled… but a tiny bit less tense.

He remembered vividly how Crow had slept beside him the previous night. Vulnerable. Open. Crow had taken the drug without hesitation; he'd left himself helpless in Jonathan's bed, and trusted Jonathan to do the right thing.

Two years ago, Crow wouldn't have trusted him. Two years ago, Crow never would have trusted anyone.

"I really don't think you should touch me," Crow said quietly.

"It's a hug. You're a friend. It's not like I'm sucking your dick."

"Strange things set people off. Did you talk to him in detail? You were gone an hour."

Jonathan shrugged. "Not really. There was a lot to discuss." He let go. "What am I supposed to tell him? That the moment I started lusting after you, I stopped hating you?"

"That's not what happened."

"Isn't it?"

"No," Crow said. "You were jealous and possessive because you distrusted me. You stopped distrusting me, so the possessiveness stopped."

"And the lust," Jonathan said. "What about that?"

"I suppose those feelings were always there. Hatred stifled them." Crow shifted. "Just be honest with him. I'll stay out of it this time. Take care of him for me."

Jonathan twisted around to look at him. "What do you mean, take care of him? You're actually leaving? I thought Athea was kidding."

Crow groaned. "I'm not sure how much I can be around you two. I thought watching you two was torture before. Now—now it's unbearable. Every little kiss. Every fond look. It's like being suffocated. I'm leaving before I lose my mind. I can't tell which of you I hate more, or which of you I—" He stopped suddenly.

The dying embers glowed faintly. Crow's expressions were hard to read, and never had it been harder than now. He turned his head away, and his hair shifted over his shoulder. He hunched his back.

Crow was a young, attractive man. Not even thirty yet. It would be easy for him to find other friends. Another lover. But somehow—despite all common sense—the idea of him leaving was intolerable. Even though it made no sense for him to stay, Jonathan had sort of expected him to anyway. What was he supposed to do? Hang around and be a third wheel?

Seeing Crow in such pain suddenly lit something up in Jonathan's brain. "You know," he said, "I always sort of thought you were a sadist."

Crow turned to stare at him in shock.

Jonathan winced. "Sorry. What I mean is, you're not the person I thought you were. I guess I just sort of expected you to be a sadist. You know... black clothing, charming, debonair smile. And you did tie me up to threaten me."

Crow laughed. "Debonair? Look. Threatening to skin someone isn't sexual."

Jonathan hesitated. He was about to say something stupid. Very, very carefully, he said, "Is being whipped sexual for you?" And Crow went absolutely still, his entire body a rigid line.

Jonathan swallowed. "Sorry."

Crow sucked in his breath. He loosened a little. "It's fine."

"You don't have to say anything if you don't want to. We don't have to talk about it. I'm just curious. Regis never mentioned anything like that about you."

Crow seemed to struggle with his reply. "You won't press?"

"No. No, we can drop it."

"My relationship"—the word sounded odd in Crow's mouth—"with Regis was not sadistic. Or masochistic. At all. If that's what you're asking."

"Okay."

Crow relaxed against their dragonhide backrest. "The whipping. That's never happened to me before. I didn't know."

"What? Really?"

"I do not regularly let men tie me up and beat me," Crow said flatly.

"Oh," Jonathan said. "Right."

A painful pause.

"I suppose you think I'm perverse," Crow said.

Jonathan laughed. "Crow, where I come from, sleeping with other men is perverse."

"Still." Crow blew out his breath. He let his head fall back. "Everyone has flaws. I suppose masochism isn't a bad one. It's not like I have to let people hurt me."

Jonathan was taken aback. "Crow. You shouldn't—it's not a flaw. Why not just embrace it and enjoy yourself? It's not hurting anyone."

Crow let out a breath of laughter. "What person could I possibly trust enough to be that helpless with? They could torture me for their own amusement. They could kill me. I suppose it wouldn't be so bad if I were in a relationship with someone." His voice was wistful. He closed his eyes. "You're good with that whip. You were patient. You tried to stop it from hurting too badly."

"This is a strange conversation to have with an enemy." With anyone, actually.

"With an enemy?" Crow repeated.

They looked at each other.

Before Jonathan could figure out what to say to that, Regis came out of the woods, whistling. The whistling trailed off as he noticed them sitting close together, but Jonathan didn't move. This was fine, he told himself. They were just sitting next to each other.

Jonathan caught his wrist and pulled Regis down into his lap. Regis laughed, tumbling down easily. His leg lay against Crow's, and the three of them were tangled together. The three of them had always been tangled together, enemies and lovers.

Regis had been drinking earlier, but only a little. Jonathan liked him best like this: somnolent-eyed, loose, relaxed. These were the moments that Regis might allow himself to be petted, stroked, and cuddled. Regis's prickly demeanor slid away, leaving a rare agreeability in its wake.

"I wanna get drunk," Regis said, stroking Jonathan's face.

Crow chuckled. "I don't think you need to be drunker, sweet."

"I think I do. I think *you two* need to be drunker." Regis rolled on his back. He was on both of their laps, and his ass was between them. "Tell me about your grand adventure. I want to hear all the slave bits. Jonathan glossed over them."

"We spent the entire time pretending we were fucking," Jonathan said. "I really don't think I want to hear about it."

"Crow half-naked and in chains? I definitely do."

Jonathan bit the inside of his cheek. He didn't miss the ripple of stifled surprise from Crow, either, the shift.

Regis smiled lasciviously. He reached up and caught Jonathan's face in his hands, then kissed him. Slow and hot and in control. Regis tasted like wheat-grass ale and stew, unsurprisingly. It was different from their usual kisses. His tongue begged for entrance, and Jonathan parted his lips, letting it deepen. Regis made a small sound into his mouth. Beside him, he heard Crow inhale.

A blaze of heat tore through him at the knowledge Crow was watching. Of course Crow was watching. Regis was sitting on them. The shift of his body on top, the small noises their mouths made—it had to be driving Crow insane.

Regis only had a few drinks, Jonathan registered dimly. Was Regis deliberately fucking with him? At last, they parted for breath.

Crow gracefully extricated himself. He cleared his throat. "You two must be tired. Do you want the room?"

Jonathan gave Crow a puzzled look. They weren't in a room. They were outside, around a fire.

"There are two bedrooms in the cottage," Crow said. His voice had a hoarse undertone. "Athea and Peter took one. There's one left. Obviously you two—" He stepped back. "I should go."

"Why?" Regis said, sliding a hand up Jonathan's shirt. "I like having you here."

Crow just shook his head. He went into the cottage and shut the door.

They idled by the fire awhile longer. At last, Jonathan spoke. "We should talk."

Regis traced circles on Jonathan's stomach. "Talk about what?"

"Crow."

Images played in Jonathan's head. Regis bent over the bed, Crow pushing inside him. Bodies twining together. Crow's face, twisted with ecstasy, Regis urging him to go harder, faster, more. He felt his body warm, and something hungry stirred inside him.

Regis waved his hand dismissively. "We already talked about that. You were alone. You were both upset. You needed each other. Emotional reactions are common in situations like that. I forgive you. Can we *please* stop talking about it."

Jonathan stroked Regis's stomach and didn't say anything.

"All right, fine," Regis said. "Sometimes I do feel a little threatened. People flirt with you, you know. People nicer than me. I mean, you're—" He gestured up and down Jonathan's body. "You know, tall and exotic and dangerous, and I'm… skinny and mean and awkward. Sometimes I worry you're going to stray. I don't even understand why you like me. But I love you, Jonathan, and I trust you. I love being *with* you. And Crow—Crow is…." He shifted. "There's always this tension between the two of you."

"Tension, huh."

Regis sat up. "You know that play we went to last year?"

"The comedy you dragged me to? Yeah."

"Remember how the entire time, that man and woman wanted the same thing, but they were both too afraid to say it? You know—so they spent several weeks dancing around the subject and getting into hilarious misunderstandings?"

"Yeah," Jonathan said.

"I want to have sex with Crow," Regis said.

He watched Jonathan's face very carefully when he said it. Jonathan swallowed. "Oh." Their legs pressed together, cloth on cloth, heat bleeding through. His reaction could change a lot of things very quickly, and he had no idea what direction to go in.

"Are you mad?"

He stole the flask from Regis's hip. "No."

He took a very deep drink to avoid seeing Regis's expression. Then, dying of curiosity, he set down the flask to look. Regis's face had gone scarlet. Jonathan started to laugh, and the flush darkened. Regis elbowed him in the ribs. "Stop laughing. That was difficult." He leaned against Jonathan again. "It's a pity you two didn't hold off until I was here. You know, you'd probably stop obsessing over him if you just had sex with him. Trust me. Sex solves everything."

"Yeah," Jonathan said reasonably. "Pity that's not going to happen."

The alcohol settled into his stomach, lighting a warm fire through his veins. Regis's eyes glittered like a greedy merchant looking at a pile of gold. He seemed to be considering something.

"You're a filthy pervert," Jonathan said.

"I didn't say anything!"

Jonathan leaned in. The alcohol made him giddy. If he had any sense, he told himself, he'd stop here, take Regis to bed, and let this remain unsaid. Instead—very bluntly—he said, "So what are you thinking about? One of us has sex with him, the other watches? Or both at the same time?"

"*Jonathan.*"

"We don't have to," Jonathan said. "I'm not going to pressure you. I'm just saying. We could."

"We need to talk about this first," Regis said. "In detail. Rational adults. Reasonable discussion."

"Absolutely."

Regis twitched a little. "Or… or we could go have sex with Crow. Right now."

It would be so easy to go inside and grab Crow. He was dying for it, to be honest. He stopped Regis as Regis shifted to stand up. "Hold on. Does this mean we're not exclusive anymore?"

"Do you want to be exclusive?" Regis asked warily.

Jonathan grimaced. "The idea of you sleeping with strangers makes me want to hit something." The idea of Regis having sex with Crow, specifically, made Jonathan so hard it hurt.

"Okay," Regis said. "So let's talk."

CROW SCOPED out the bedroom. One cover on the bed, two pillows. He could steal the cover and leave Jonathan and Regis the bed, but then where would he sleep? The ground outside would be softer than the floorboards, he supposed.

The three of us could share the bed.

There was no point in torturing himself with thoughts like that. Jonathan and Regis wanted each other so badly they couldn't keep their hands off each other, even lying next to him. He'd bed them both if he could, but he wasn't willing to risk it.

A bottle of old whiskey lay under the bed. He picked it up and felt the weight. It was dusty. The ale was gone, but this was enough to get all three of them blindingly drunk, just like Regis wanted. Crow was good at flirting with people. So why didn't he go out and flirt with them?

Except he didn't sleep around like he used to. Casual fucks had lost their appeal. And this didn't seem casual. He cared about Regis too much. And Jonathan… they had history.

He tried to remember how he did it.

The night played itself out in his mind. They would each have a few glasses. He'd test the waters by running his fingers up Jonathan's thigh. He'd sit too close, let his hand linger, make his intentions apparent. If Regis got angry, he'd back off.

But maybe Regis wouldn't get angry. Maybe he would smirk, lean back, and watch. It would become a game—the three of them flirting and drinking together. Teasing would become innuendo… and then he'd slyly suggest they go to bed together. And then, and then—

Crow swallowed. They would be outside talking. He fumbled a hand through his hair. Why so nervous? He'd charmed plenty of people before. What was so different about this?

Jonathan and Regis, obviously.

Gods. He couldn't let himself think like that. They were just two normal people. Nothing special about this. He put a smile on his face and glanced in the mirror. Untucked a few strands of hair to give himself that just-got-fucked look. Ruffled his shirt and unlaced it. He poured half the whiskey out the window, then took a swig and swirled it around in his mouth, made sure it could be smelled on his breath. He would act drunk, hit on them both, and see what happened.

He headed out of the room. The front door stood ajar. Ten feet away, voices drifted in. "So what is this exactly? You just want to fuck him?" he heard Regis say, and Crow froze.

"I love you," Jonathan said.

Regis laughed.

"I mean it," Jonathan said. "Regis, I love you, not now but always, even when you're gone, even when we're fighting. You're my partner, my confidant, my best friend. Forty years from now, I want to die beside you."

Crow's throat closed up. He sank to the floor. The bottle was a thick weight in his grip.

"Jonathan," Regis murmured, "you don't need to…."

"It's not a matter of need," Jonathan said. "It's a matter of want. I want to stay with you, and I can only hope you want that as well. The rest of it doesn't matter. The kiss was a mistake. Not because of who it was, but because we agreed not to. From now on, we talk about these things first."

And then there was no sound at all, though Crow strained to listen. Only soft noises, things that could have been a kiss or a branch creaking, things that could have been movement or wind or Crow's imagination. Crow's imagination was everything then—it was their hands on each other, it was sighs and soft looks, it was a knife twisting in his gut.

His back stung. He remembered Jonathan's finger tracing one of the marks—the biggest mark. He remembered how Jonathan's arm felt around his shoulders. The weight of it, the warmth.

He pressed his hands to his ears and tried to shut those thoughts out. What was wrong with him? Jonathan belonged to Regis—Regis belonged to Jonathan—and he could not possibly allow himself to care about either of them. It was simply too dangerous. If he didn't look out for himself, who would?

What a horrible creature he was. He'd listened to a happy couple recommit to one another, and he felt jealousy. Was he really going to ruin their night with some tawdry proposition?

A bottle of whiskey and sex. What was wrong with him? Quiet as a cat, Crow got to his feet and left.

He left a short note on the bed, then slipped out through the bedroom window. No need to inconvenience anyone. Regis would get over it quickly. It wasn't like their friendship meant anything, anyway.

He considered turning into a bird. But the night was clear and cool, and the leaves crunched nicely under his feet, so instead he picked a direction and walked in it. He'd find somewhere to go. He always did. He wasn't sure how long he walked. The moon was at its peak.

He paused.

There was an odd feeling in the air, like ozone before a storm. Something snagged his foot. Crow ripped his foot away from the root, stumbling. Huh, he thought. Weird.

Then a force slammed him into the ground, dragging him to the middle of the clearing. Roots erupted around his body, pulling him taut, tightening around his wrists, his ankles.

A figure stepped over him.

"Out for a midnight stroll?" Septimus said.

Chapter FOURTEEN
Septimus

THE EMBERS of the fire were still warm. Cicadas buzzed around them. Jonathan lay with Regis in his arms, comfortable and lazy. Jonathan's mind was alight with the possibilities. Crow was right in the other room. It would be so easy to just... go get him.

"Look," Regis said. "I know I should be mad, but I'm not. Besides, you didn't kiss another man—you kissed Crow. That's completely different. That's like... like giving me a glass of wine with my steak and expecting me to be angry about it. I can try if you like, but honestly all I want to do is watch."

"So what are we doing? What are the rules?"

Regis immediately launched into a list. "I make a motion that we continue being exclusive. We will have sex with Crow once and only once, assuming he's interested. Once we've collected more information, we'll discuss this again reevaluate our position. Fair?"

"Fair," Jonathan said. They shook on it.

Regis scrambled upright. "I really want to watch you fuck him. Honestly. Just dying for it."

Jonathan groaned. "Can do."

"We should probably come up with a pregame plan. You know, coordinate what we want in order to optimize—"

Jonathan dragged him toward the door.

THE ROOM was empty. A breeze drifted through the window. The bed was undone, a whiskey bottle on the dresser. Regis picked up a note from the bed and read it aloud.

> *Sweet—*
> *Know, first and foremost, that I desire only your*
> *happiness.*

White—
I'm going to kill Myra the first chance I get. You
may check her tower for the body.

Regis ripped the note in half, set the pieces on fire, and then stepped on them. Jonathan collapsed onto the bed. Of course Crow had left. Crow was a contradictory bastard. The universe wouldn't let them have sex. Very clearly—and very calmly—Jonathan listed off every swear word he knew. "What a bastard," he said when he was done. "I mean, honestly, he couldn't even say good-bye?"

"No, of course not. That's what a reasonable man would do."

"He's a manipulative, cowardly, awful person."

"Just awful," Regis said. "The worst human being alive. I swear, I'm going to throttle him once we're done having sex with him." He hopped off the bed and leaned out the window. There were prints in the mud, and the mud wasn't dry. "He left recently. Maybe we can still catch him."

They looked at each other.

Regis deflated. He pulled himself away from the window. "There's no point."

Jonathan wanted to crawl out after Crow. He wanted to follow the footprints, find the man, pin him down and kiss him. Kiss him until neither of them could breathe. He forced himself to think rationally. "Yeah. He made his choice. We should... we should go to bed." He cracked a smile. "Besides. It seems like fate is determined to stop us. Even if we found him—and even if he was interested—lightning would strike us."

"A bear would attack."

"A flash flood, maybe."

"You know what? Fuck that. He doesn't get to run away this time. I'm going to find that son of a bitch. If he wants to leave, fine, but he's not going without a proper good-bye."

"You think we can find him?"

"I made him," Regis said. "I can always find him." He vaulted out the window.

"I CAN'T believe my daughter was stupid enough to go to her little safe house," Septimus said. "That blabbermouth couldn't keep a secret if her life depended on it. Two of my own servants knew." He stepped forward. His boots crunched in the dry leaves. "But you... you really take the cake. Leaving alone and unarmed in the middle of the night."

Septimus was dressed in grand clothing. Twigs tangled in the hem of his robes. He had a mage collar on his belt. Was he here for Regis? Crow wrenched against the roots. Solid and thick, and far stronger than him. They didn't budge, and he couldn't even gain any leverage. Fuck.

So he did the only thing he could think of.

He screamed.

Immediately, a thick root burst from the soil and pushed itself into his open mouth. The shriek became muffled, and Crow writhed, twisting his head and trying to force it out. It wound around his head. Dirt made him cough and choke.

"Oh, you poor thing," Septimus said. "You shouldn't have walked so far. They might have heard you." He crouched by Crow's head. "Stop struggling and listen. I'm not here to hurt you. I only want to talk."

He had knives in his boots. One coated with a paralytic, one with a sedative. If he could reach one, he could cut himself free. His hands were restrained at his hips. If he could somehow move his legs, or reach down....

"So you can think and reason," Septimus said, watching Crow's face carefully. "Fascinating. I've been trying to replicate your mother's work, but for some reason, the creatures I produce aren't like you. I mean, they look human, of course—that part's easy—but mentally, they're still animals. What did she do differently with you? Am I missing a journal? Could you tell me?"

If Septimus took the root out his mouth, maybe he could talk his way out of this. He met Septimus's eyes and nodded.

"Huh." Septimus folded his legs. "Well, I doubt you could give me a full understanding. You know, you're the first magical human to imitate humanity. It's almost like you're a real person." He touched Crow's face. Crow recoiled. He tried to, at least. The fingers were impossibly smooth and cold. Bile rose in his throat. "Hm. I suppose I don't need Regis. As long as I have you, I can figure out how you were made. It'll just require some tinkering. I'll keep you in my basement."

Crow fought again. Panic welled in his throat. Regis and Jonathan wouldn't notice his absence 'til morning, and even then, they'd assume he had abandoned them. He'd fucked up.

Septimus continued watching his face. "You know—" His voice was very quiet, very deadly. "I could have Regis hunted down and killed."

Crow glared at him.

"I could have both of them hunted down and killed," Septimus said. "They already destroyed some valuable city property. What if they knew who taught Regis?" He leaned closer. His breath teased Crow's lips. "What if I told everyone who really cursed the queen? They'd never stop looking for him. It would be a death sentence."

His throat felt raw from the root, dirt in his mouth. He shut his eyes.

"You could save him," Septimus said. "You could make all of this go away."

Crow opened his eyes in confusion.

"All you have to do is come with me," Septimus said. "Stay in my house willingly. Do whatever I ask." He rested his hand on Crow's lower abdomen, just above the hem of his pants, tracing a line down from Crow's navel. Crow shuddered at the unwanted contact. "Be my slave. And in return, I'll discourage the authorities from pursuing Regis, and I'll keep my mouth shut about his teacher. Deal?"

The root uncoiled from his mouth. Crow spat out dirt. He flexed his wrists. Still not budging. Damn.

"Come now," Septimus said. "This is what's best, don't you think? It's practically fate. You left without telling anyone where you went. Besides, he's happy without you. What do you say, Crow?"

Crow went limp against the ground. Regis didn't want him. Jonathan wanted him, and—

And in any other circumstance, Crow would have gladly had him. It was a relief to finally admit it to himself in the privacy of his own mind. He liked Jonathan. In quiet moments, he would allow himself the fantasy of being Jonathan's companion and traveling with him, fighting side-by-side, spending nights together. Maybe in a different world, they could have been friends. Maybe it would have led somewhere. They could've had fun, at least.

But Jonathan was with Regis. And Crow couldn't cross that line. Couldn't wreck what his only friend had.

It was meant to be like this, Crow realized. Even if he couldn't be with either of them, he could give himself up and save them both. They'd never know what happened to him. They would move on, both of them.

"I'll do it," Crow said.

Septimus took a tiny jar from his pocket. Colored paste. "Oh, good. Now, there's some oaths I want you to make."

The roots writhed around Crow. They pushed him onto his stomach and pushed up his shirt. Crow didn't even bother to struggle. There was no point in getting away. Even if Septimus unbound him now, he'd walk willingly into his prison.

Septimus drew a line of paste on his shoulder blade. "You will help me with my research in whatever way you can."

Crow gritted his teeth. The idea of taking oaths made him sick. The idea of being under a stranger's control, in general, made him sick. "I will help you with your research in whatever way I can."

The string of magic on his back. "You will never lie to me."

That was fine, Crow thought. He usually didn't outright lie, anyway. Lying was for amateurs. "I will never lie to you."

"You will do whatever I say."

Crow's body revolted at the idea. "No."

Septimus laughed. "You're going to do what I say regardless. If you don't, I'll ruin you, and I'll ruin Regis. This just makes it less complicated. You were made to serve, so why not embrace it?"

Crow took a shaking breath. He shoved his emotions aside, as he always had. He swallowed his pride. "I will do whatever you say."

More prickling lightning. Septimus's cold hand smoothed down his back. "Good boy."

Then a voice said, "Get your filthy hands off of Crow."

JONATHAN MADE his way through the underbrush after Regis. Regis stood ahead at the edge of a clearing, and he sounded pissed.

Jonathan could barely see in the dark. But he saw the light of flickering sparks in the grass, and when he pushed his way through the brush after Regis, he saw Septimus.

And he saw Crow.

Pinned to the earth. Thick tendrils—vines of some sort?—holding him down. Septimus had his hand on his back. Crow tilted his head and looked at them, blinking.

Septimus wiped paste off his finger, then stood, brushing himself off. "We were just finishing up. Crow, tell them you want to be here."

Crow's face went white. He bit the inside of his cheek. He seemed to be struggling against something. A pained look crossed his face, and at last he ground out, "I want to be here."

"See? He's fine. Tell them to go away, Crow."

"You two—should leave."

There were three tally marks on Crow's shoulder blade. Black paste. They sizzled and sank in, and Crow arched, hissing. The muscle of his back bunched. Regis stepped forward, and Jonathan stopped him. "Wait," Jonathan said in a low voice. "He's got Crow right next to him."

"It's okay," Crow said. He sounded pained. "We made a deal. Just… just go, okay? I'll be fine on my own."

"Your generous friend," Septimus said, "has fixed your mess. You and your paramour can leave. I don't see why we need to be enemies, son of mine. He'll be happier like this. He was created to be a slave. Why, with his mother missing, I bet he's been aching for a new master."

Crow pressed his face to the earth. He said nothing.

"Let me make this clear," Regis said. "I don't give a damn what you want. I don't give a damn what Crow says he wants, either. Smell that magic on him? On his skin, inside of him? That's mine. And if you don't let him go and get out of my sight within the next ten seconds, I'm going to rip out your throat and feed it to you." Septimus stared at him, openmouthed.

"Ten," Regis said. "Nine. Eight."

"I have thirty years on you," Septimus said.

"Seven. Six. Five."

Septimus rose to his feet. It was clear he was preparing for the end of the countdown. "Four. Three," Regis said, and without warning, he lashed out, a lightning bolt crackling from his palm.

"You said ten!" Septimus shrieked.

There were benefits to fighting as a couple. Regis stepped in front of Crow to defend him, and Jonathan knelt next to Crow. Septimus threw lightning. A silver shield flickered into existence between them, and the bolt slammed into it, scattering.

Priority one: release Crow. Prodigy or not, Regis was only twenty-one, and Septimus had decades of skill. Jonathan examined the roots. They were thick and woody. He fought to pull one from the ground, but it didn't budge. Jonathan began to pat Crow down for a weapon. "My boots," Crow hissed. "Left has a sedative. The right has a paralytic."

Jonathan groped downward. He drew the left knife and began to saw at the root.

"What are you doing?" Crow sounded exasperated. "Help Regis, you idiot."

"We're not going to win. We need to run." The knife wasn't cutting. He dropped it and pulled at the roots around Crow's ankle with all his strength. It came loose, and Jonathan fell back.

Crow kicked at him. "Then go!"

"Make me," Jonathan said.

Crow gave him a filthy look, then turned his attention toward Regis and Septimus. Jonathan grimaced; he gripped the root on Crow's other ankle. He didn't look up. It would only distract him.

He couldn't stop himself from hearing, though, nor stop himself from seeing the crackling flashes of light. A thump. A crash. A boom. A shriek, though the tone was wrong for Regis.

He fought to pull harder. His arms burned. When that didn't work, he dug into the earth with his nails.

Noises came from the fight nearby. The sound of earth moving and bark ripping as roots tore from the soil. Jonathan couldn't stop himself from looking up. Roots lashed out at Regis. Regis leapt out of the way just in time, but he stumbled and hit the ground. The roots barreled after him with pointed tips. Regis rolled, and the roots slammed into the ground beside him.

Regis threw out his hand and pulled. A tree next to Septimus groaned and began to topple. Septimus turned, horror on his face. He didn't have time to move. He disappeared into a crash of leaves and limbs. Regis pushed himself up and circled the tree warily. Without taking his eyes off it, he said to Jonathan, "Do you have him up yet?"

"The roots won't move."

Regis glanced down. He bent down to help.

The leaves of the fallen tree began to ripple. Like a swarm of flies, they came loose, then flew at Regis. One sliced his forehead, and blood dripped down the bridge of his nose. He raised his arms to shield his face.

Septimus stood up between the bare limbs. There was a bloody gash on his shoulder.

An invisible weight pinned Regis down. He strained to get up but couldn't rise to his feet. Instead of continuing to fight it, he struck the fallen tree with lightning, and the wood set aflame. Septimus leapt out from between the limbs. His clothes blazed. The weight released Regis, and he stood up.

Septimus made a motion as though he were dusting himself off. The flames rolled off his body and collected in the air, and he hurled the fire at Regis. Regis waved his hand, and a gust of wind blew the flames out.

Jonathan threw the knife at Septimus.

The knife fell ungainly into a bush. Probably because Jonathan had never thrown a knife before. "That wasn't a throwing knife!" Crow said.

"There are different kinds?"

Crow kicked the ground. "Of course there's different kinds! One's balanced for close combat, the other is—dammit, just grab the other one and fight him!"

The second ankle restraint came loose. He drew the remaining knife from Crow's right boot and dug at the dirt around Crow's wrists. He pried at the roots. More crashing. More light. More crying out. Jonathan didn't dare look. "I can't," Jonathan said. He fought back panic. "I know he needs help, all right? I know! I can't do anything. I don't know how to fight a sorcerer. But you—" The roots loosened. He took hold and wrenched. "You're good with those knives," he panted. "You could help him."

Crow's hands came free. He snatched up the paralytic knife.

He immediately went for Septimus. The movement drew Septimus's attention, and he sent roots spiraling after Crow. Crow vaulted over them, hitting the ground hard and rolling. He was on his feet again in a second.

Septimus moved to work more magic, but Crow was faster. He sank the blade into Septimus's shoulder.

Septimus gaped at Crow. He reached up, feebly touching the knife. He collapsed.

For a moment, they all stayed where they were. Regis stood, panting. He walked slowly to his father. He looked like an avenging god. Septimus tried to crawl away. He left a blood smear in the grass.

"So you brought a mage collar with you," Regis said. "How convenient. Planning to capture me and drag me back into your wretched manor? Give me the collar."

Septimus looked immensely relieved. He reached behind him and unhooked the collar from his belt. "You're going to collar me and let me go? Oh, praise the gods."

"Was that one of your coated knives?" Regis asked Crow.

"He'll be paralyzed in a minute."

"Good." Regis smashed the collar against a rock. The iron ring clattered to the ground. He held the opal in his fist.

"What are you doing?" Septimus's voice was slurred.

Regis laid the opal on Septimus's chest, then pressed his hand to Septimus's stomach.

"If I were you, I would hold very still. This is going to hurt."

Septimus's chest split open. The skin and tissue moved aside, revealing the sorcerer's beating heart. "Put the opal in," Regis said to Jonathan. "I can't touch while I'm working."

Jonathan did it.

Regis sealed the cavity shut. Septimus heaved for air. His eyes were wide. The whites were visible all the way around. He fought to speak, but all that came out was an angry gurgle. Regis knelt beside him and looked him in the face. "This will not kill you," he said quietly. "In fact, I expect you'll live a pretty normal life. Well, except for the fact that you'll never be able to use your magic again."

He yanked out the knife. A crackle of silver, and the wound shut. "Maybe you'll find someone skilled enough to take it out of you. Given the way you treat your competition, I doubt anyone strong enough will come to your rescue. Frankly, I don't care. But let me make this clear. If you bother me, my sister, my lover, or my friend again, I will kill you."

Septimus managed to croak, "I'll tell."

Regis kicked him in the ribs. "Tell people what? That I'm the apprentice of the Flesh Witch? Fine! So be it. I'll be bad. I'll be the very worst. Tell everyone I'm the most dangerous sorcerer in Tyria, and tell them that Jonathan White and Crow Belcane are mine."

Chapter FIFTEEN
Claim

MINE.

The word sank into Crow like a stone in a river. It felt—good. It felt right. He tried not to think about it that much. It probably said some uncomfortable things about him.

They blindfolded Septimus and dragged him a mile farther into the woods, then left. By the time they were done, Regis was stumbling over nothing, and he listed to the side. Crow supported him. Regis's body was warm, and he seemed thin. "I kind of want to go back and kick him some more," Regis muttered. "That bastard, treating you like an object. How badly did he hurt you?"

"I'm fine, sweet. Still spitting dirt, but fine."

Regis groaned. "We're officially outlaws now, aren't we?"

"Professional criminals," Jonathan suggested.

"I don't want to be any kind of criminal!"

"Really?" Crow said. "It sounds kind of fun to me. Besides, I think it kinds of suits us."

The other two looked at him, and Crow realized what he'd said. *Us.* He was supposed to leave with Athea, Chartreuse, and Peter in the morning. He'd already forgotten.

Jonathan broke into a grin. "You think so?"

Crow plowed on as if nothing had happened. "Well, yes. I mean, you were more or less a criminal before. Arresting people with no authority, breaking into private offices…. Jonathan, you beat a man up and hid him from the authorities in a trunk. I cut off his finger."

"You two have problems with authority," Regis sniffed.

"You demolished part of someone's house."

Regis gave Crow an injured look. "You were in trouble. I had to escape and find you."

"I know, sweet." He kissed the back of Regis's hand. "Thank you."

They lapsed into silence. When Crow became tired, he passed Regis to Jonathan. Between the two of them, they helped Regis back home safely.

Regis had forgiven him, apparently. That was enough for now.

Once they reached the cottage, Crow followed Jonathan and Regis into the second bedroom without thinking about it. The room was dark and warm. Regis snapped his fingers at a candle to light it.

Crow collapsed on the bed, stretched, and closed his eyes. He was so comfortable he nearly groaned.

A hand touched his navel. Crow's eyes flickered open. Jonathan looked down at him.

"What?" Crow said.

And then it hit him. The room was cool and sweet and smelled faintly of dust, and there was only one bed here. One bed—because this was Regis and Jonathan's room. "Oh," Crow said. "Sorry." He started to get up.

Regis shut the door and latched it.

Crow stilled. He didn't try to get up again. Jonathan hefted the bottle of whiskey. "Got started on this alone, I see," he said.

"Well, you know what they say. Liquid courage."

Regis kicked off his boots. "Liquid courage for what? Running off like a pansy?" He ran a hand through his hair. It caught in tangles immediately. "Dammit. Where's a knife? I'm sick of having long hair already."

Crow sat up. "No, no! Here, let me." He combed the tangles out of Regis's hair with his hands. He snapped his fingers at Jonathan. "Knife, please." Jonathan handed one over. Crow trimmed a few stray pieces, neatening the cut of it. He braided quickly. "There. That'll keep it out of your way."

He wanted them both. Badly. If he was going to make a move, this was obviously the time.

From an objective standpoint… he'd nearly slept with another man's lover. Now that he was forgiven, he was going to proposition them? No. There was no way for him to move forward from here.

He exhaled. He needed to back off. "I should go to bed." Quickly. Before he fucked up his friendship with Regis.

Something caught his foot for a second, and he stumbled. Was it magic? Regis steadied him. "So clumsy. You must be tired."

Jonathan caught his other arm.

Crow did not dare move an inch. He was half-hard and he had no idea why. Proximity to Jonathan, probably. Or maybe it was the way Regis was looking at him. He felt like he was being boxed in by wolves.

"You're sure you aren't hurt?" Regis said, sweetly concerned. "I should look at those oathspell marks on your back."

Crow tried to speak. His throat wouldn't work.

Regis leaned up, interlacing his fingers with Crow's black hair. He leaned in. "Take off your clothes," he said in Crow's ear.

Crow swallowed. Somehow it felt good to be cornered like this. To let someone else call the shots for once. To just... obey. Maybe Septimus was right about him. He peeled off the shirt, then let it drop. "Should I turn around?"

Instead of examining him, Regis simply flicked his hand. "Have at it," he said to Jonathan.

And then Jonathan crowded him against the wall and leaned over him. Jonathan's body was powerful, every inch hard and masculine. Jonathan leaned over him, and—very deliberately, giving Crow time to move away if he wanted—kissed him.

Slow, hot, and melting. Jonathan bit, then swept a tongue over the hurt. Teased inside. Crow was already half-hard; there was no disguising that. The kiss only heightened his arousal—against his will. There was no disguising how badly he wanted this. His erection was pressed between them, evidence. He couldn't hide it.

His hands fisted in Jonathan's clothes. Jonathan gripped his wrists and held him against the wall.

"Oh fuck," Crow choked out. It was all he was capable of at the moment.

Regis watched from the armchair. Idly, he picked up the whiskey bottle and began to work the cork loose. "He hasn't even touched your cock yet. Save the theatrics."

"Not theatrics. You—you want to—you want to watch—*oh fuck*."

"Well, this is unusual," Regis said. "Normally you have some idiotic remark to make."

Jonathan began to pull out the laces of Crow's pants. Crow clenched his hands. He started to reach up, but Regis made a gesture, and Crow's hands were held against the wall. Magical force again. "Mm," Regis said. "No, don't do that. Just hold still while he sucks you off."

Jonathan's hands stopping moving. His thumbs eased across the no-man's-land between Crow's pelvis and his dick. Crow pulled against the magical restraints, then gave up. He was in a room with one of the most powerful sorcerers in the world—and his very dominant partner. *Fuck*. He started struggling again. It felt good to fight, to know he couldn't win.

"Are you all right?" Jonathan murmured.

Crow couldn't answer. He wasn't sure. He was normally the aggressor during sex, but Jonathan put him off-balance, and Regis had changed during their two years apart.

"Here's the deal," Regis said. "I'm willing to let you have sex with Jonathan. Once. This is not blanket permission to fuck my lover whenever the urge strikes you. If you use this as an opportunity to manipulate either of us, you and I will no longer be friends. No more dishonesty. No more manipulation. If you stay, you give up control. Understood?"

Crow nodded. He felt as though he was going to burn up at any moment. "Do you want to leave?" Jonathan asked.

Wordlessly, Crow shook his head.

Jonathan kissed him again, more firmly this time, and Crow opened his mouth without even thinking about it. The kiss deepened. Briefly, he struggled, pulling at the force keeping his wrists together, but it was useless. He was caught.

Jonathan kissed his jaw, then his neck, his collarbone. His chest. Moving his way down. "Let us take care of you," he whispered. "You don't have to be in control all the time. Let go. Say you want it." He sank to his knees. He mouthed the bulge in the front of Crow's pants, lips parting sweetly around the curve of it.

Crow shut his eyes so he didn't have to look at the man kneeling between his legs. Despite all his experience, he was unused to this. Unaccustomed to being seduced. Unable to surrender. "I'm not—I'm not good at this."

"It's easy," Regis said. "Do you want him to suck your cock?"

"Gods, Regis. What kind of question is that?"

His voice was layered with cruelty. "If you want it, you're going to have to ask. Nicely."

And, gods, Crow thought maybe he could come just from the heat seeping through his pants. Just from being in this situation at all. He liked it when Regis ordered him around. Wasn't that a revelation.

He took a breath. He felt like he was stepping off a precipice. "I," he said, "I want—would you please—"

All he had to do was ask them to stop. He wanted it too badly. If he gave in, only bad things would happen. Was he a whore for affection? "Please," he begged. It was the best he could manage.

Jonathan squeezed his hand, then pulled aside the cloth. Crow had a split-second to feel cool air on his bare skin before Jonathan sucked him down.

The cottage was small. The walls were thin. Crow swallowed back curses and moans, gritted his teeth and tried to be silent. His whispers became frantic. "Fuck, Jonathan, please hurry up—"

Only that *please* seemed to provoke the opposite reaction. Jonathan slowed his pace, switched tactics, eased everything to a crawl. Crow's entire body arched—as much as it could, at least—and he tried to push in and speed up the pace. Whenever he did, however, Jonathan stopped completely and went with the motions, counteracting each one. It forced the already slow pace to become slower, and Crow found himself struggling for a climax he could not reach.

He didn't want to be sucked off. He wanted to be fucked. Was desperate just to grind against Jonathan's cock again. Were they going to get him off now, then again later? Or were they going to make him wait? He wasn't sure which was worse.

Creaking footsteps. Regis sidled between him and the wall and held him still. He kissed Crow's neck, and Crow threw his head back. Shudders went up his spine as Regis bit his neck hard, hard enough to bruise. The sharp pain was nearly enough to send him over the edge.

Jonathan reached up to cup Crow's balls, sliding a thumb across them, rolling them in his palm. Crow jerked, and this time Jonathan didn't move away. He sucked all the way down instead, swallowing. Everything overwhelmed Crow at once. The pressure, the heat, the slickness. The fact that the man sucking his cock was Jonathan—that Regis was watching them—the way his arms hurt from being restrained, the ache in his biceps as he pulled and writhed and fought—

A strangled shout tore from his throat. It echoed in the room. Regis clamped a hand over his mouth, stifling the rest of the noise. Crow gave in. The last of his self-control slipped away.

He came. He made tortured noises. All of them were muffled and barely audible. He sagged, panting through his nose. Regis didn't let go of his mouth.

Jonathan's throat moved as he swallowed, then let up. He glanced up, grinning, and licked his lips. "You good?" Jonathan asked.

Crow nodded weakly.

"Good," he said. And he took Crow in his mouth again.

Crow jerked, taking in a startled breath. Jonathan's tongue stroked his oversensitive skin. The touch was gentle and inviting. Crow hadn't even gotten all the way soft. Despite his discomfort, the stimulation slowly made him hard again. The sensitive feeling faded into pleasure. If Jonathan intended to make him come again, it was going to take a while. When Regis let go of his mouth, Crow whimpered. "Stop. No more." Jonathan kissed the head of Crow's dick, slick with saliva, then wiped his mouth. "Come to bed with us."

"Nngh," Crow said articulately.

They seemed to take it as agreement. Jonathan gripped his wrist, his hand fitting all the way around, just like a slave cuff. They pulled him onto the bed. "One more?" Regis said, stroking Crow's cock. Crow arched, pushing into the touch.

Yes, he thought desperately. *Please.*

He fought to speak in a normal tone of voice. "Well, if you want."

Regis laughed. He peeled off his shirt. "What do you say, Jonathan? We should get this out of our systems."

Crow inhaled through his nose. It felt like he couldn't breathe.

"Shouldn't we ask him first?" Jonathan asked.

"Yes," Crow choked out. *Yes, yes, yes. Own me.*

Regis stroked fingers in Crow's hair absentmindedly, making Crow shudder and relax. "Who gets him first?"

"You go ahead."

"Really? That's so sweet. You sure?"

"I'm enjoying myself just fine. Besides, I think Crow needs a break before I get a hold of him."

They were taking turns with him, tossing him around like a toy. He thought perhaps he ought to protest. When they were done with him, at least. "Come here," Regis said, dragging him over by the collar. Crow scrambled to keep up. "Clothes off."

"Are you bossing him around?" Jonathan sounded amused.

"I like bossing people around."

Regis really had become a lovely young man, though he didn't seem to know it. He looked deceptively pretty for someone who could throw tree trunks with a snap of his fingers. He began to unlace his breeches. Without being asked, Crow slid between Regis's legs and took his cock in his mouth. Regis's head lolled back. "Oh yes," he groaned, hips making small motions, little half thrusts.

He couldn't quite manage to fit the whole length of Regis's cock in his mouth. He reached up to use his hand, but Jonathan gripped his wrist and held him down against the coverlet. Unable to support himself, Crow choked.

Jonathan fisted a hand in his hair and held him down. Crow writhed. The hand let go, and he gasped for air around Regis's cock. The cruelty of it lit a fire in him, and he moaned.

Jonathan's added weight on his back took away what little power he had. He couldn't even draw all the way up and off. Neither of them would allow him enough room.

Jonathan let go of his head but kept a grip on his right wrist. He stroked Crow's back. The intimacy of it made Crow shudder—he hadn't had someone try to comfort him in a long time.

Regis's eyes glittered. He took hold of Crow's hair himself, then began to fuck Crow's mouth in long, languid strokes. "Touch him," he said to Jonathan. "I want to see how quickly we can make him come again."

There was a rustle behind him. Jonathan's weight eased off the bed. He came back a moment later. There was the sound of a bottle opening—then slick fingers gripped Crow's cock. Crow made a strangled noise around the dick in his mouth. The wetness from the oil made the grip feel unbearably good. He bucked into Jonathan's hand.

Jonathan held it still. Crow moved for him, fucking that tight, warm space. He kept sucking as he did. He wanted to come, but the friction wasn't enough. Just barely enough to make him desperate. He made a wordless begging noise. Regis laughed breathlessly. "You're really gagging for it, aren't you?"

Finally, Regis came, and Jonathan held Crow down until at last he swallowed every drop. Crow moaned weakly.

"My turn," Jonathan whispered in his ear.

He teased the rim of Crow's hole with two slick fingers. "Oh, please," Crow gasped, bucking. Only then did Jonathan slide his fingers in. After one orgasm and half a hand job, the sensation of something inside him was too much to bear. He crawled next to Regis, burying his face in Regis's shoulder. Regis held him and stroked his hair.

Jonathan took his time stretching him open. Maybe because he didn't want it to hurt. Maybe because he wanted to tease Crow. It had been a while since Crow had allowed someone inside him. In fact—

He hadn't allowed anyone to fuck him, not since he'd slept with Jonathan two years ago. He didn't enjoy it enough. Now he needed it so badly he thought he'd cry. "Do you need us to stop?" Regis whispered. Crow shook his head. He'd give them this, just for one night.

And—half-insane with need—Crow realized he liked this. The same way he'd enjoyed being tied down and whipped. He liked being toyed with, protected, loved, abused. The whipping had been frightening. But this—

This—

This moment felt different. Here in this room, at the mercy of the only two people in the world he trusted. Had he always had this submissive streak? He'd never allowed himself to feel it before. He'd never let his guard down long enough.

"You ready?" Jonathan asked.

No, never. "If you are," he managed.

The head of Jonathan's shaft pressed in, thick, and split him open. Jonathan bent over him, driving in and out. It was all Crow could do to lie there and breathe, clutching Regis like a lifeline. He muffled his moans into Regis's shoulder.

This was weakness. He loathed the part of himself that wanted to submit. He'd enjoy it for one night and get it out of his system, then leave with Athea in the morning. But now, he wanted it so desperately he could not bear to stop.

"More," he gasped. "Please. Harder."

Regis cradled his face and kissed him softly. He stroked Crow's cock. The leftover oil on Crow's skin made the fondling feel unbearably good. He bit back a scream, and he dug his fingers into the sheets. He shoved back in time with Jonathan's thrusts, pushing Jonathan inside as deep as he could. Gods, he needed to come, he needed to come again. Jonathan drew out nearly all the way with each thrust, and the ridge of his cockhead rubbed against Crow's prostate. It was ecstasy each time—a short burst of it, anyway. He needed more.

"It's okay," Regis whispered. "We've got you. Just let go."

He curled up, muffling a scream into the pillow beneath them. His second orgasm was more intense than the first. Pleasurable exhaustion radiated from every nerve. He went limp and let Jonathan finish. Now that he'd come, the sensation of being fucked was raw and overstimulating, but he gritted his teeth and bore it, squeezing around the cock in his ass.

Jonathan stopped long enough to push Crow on his back. Crow blinked at him hazily—Jonathan had a hungry look in his eyes. He looked at Crow like Crow looked at fine jewelry: a possessive need. He wiped a smear of seed from Crow's stomach, then pushed his finger into Crow's mouth, salt-bitter-tang.

Crow groaned. He couldn't get hard a third time. It wasn't physically possible. But his body made a valiant effort.

Jonathan started fucking him again, watching his face all the while. It was hard not to feel like an object—a piece of juicy steak or a particularly interesting piece of art. He felt like a valued object, though, which made it good somehow. Thrilling, even. Jonathan's rhythm became jagged. With a harsh gasp, he slowed, and his dick pulsed inside Crow. Crow let out a heartfelt moan. Feeling Jonathan come inside him was almost as good as an orgasm.

They were half-naked, soaked in sweat and come. In the morning, they'd be disgusting. Crow cared—he cared a great deal—but couldn't summon the energy to complain about it. Regis wiped off the come with a dry cloth. His erection nudged against Crow's stomach.

Crow laughed weakly. "Already?"

"You spent the last ten minutes humping my leg and moaning in my ear."

Jonathan collapsed between them. "I got it."

Crow was too exhausted to care. He shut his eyes. He fell asleep to the sound of Regis panting.

He woke, briefly, when they finished. He had the vague impression of being wiped off with something unpleasantly cold. He curled up around the body next to him—too large to be Regis—Jonathan?

They lay tangled in bed together. It felt just like falling asleep with Regis when they were younger. He couldn't extract himself from the pile, and he didn't want to.

All he saw that night was darkness. No dreams came.

THERE ARE many things in life that are both expected and willfully ignored.

It was for this reason that when Crow woke up and found himself sandwiched between two naked men, he felt an unsettling mixture of catharsis and surprise. He had known this was going to happen, but somehow it still came as a shock.

He carefully untangled himself and sat up, cracked his neck, and pushed back his hair. Leaned back on his palms and looked over at them, one then the other. Jonathan still slept like a corpse—if corpses snored, or kept a death grip on their bedmate, or looked quite so handsome. Regis twitched as he woke up and tucked the curls out of his face to blink at Crow.

"What's wrong?" Regis yawned.

Crow looked between the pair. Or not a pair; a trinity, now. He was one of them. They suited each other.

"What's wrong?" Regis asked again.

"Nothing, I suppose," Crow said, and he kissed them each. He snuggled with Regis and drifted off.

When he woke again, Jonathan was awake, and they were talking quietly. "…bounty hunters after us," Jonathan was saying.

"We need to get somewhere safe. After we kill Crow's mother, of course. We go snap her neck, and then we disappear for a while. Wait until things die down."

"The area where Crow and I used to live—you know, her tower—is pretty abandoned. There's a nearby town, but it's small. We could stay in the same region. I'm sure there's plenty of dirty peasants who need your help out there. Serial killers, cartels, bandits, people the queen hasn't cleaned up yet. You like that stuff, right?"

Jonathan stroked Regis's hair. "We could just take a vacation. I know you're sick of working all the time."

Crow shifted and blinked at them.

They both glanced at him. Regis flicked a strand of black hair out of his eyes. "Good morning, sunshine. Jonathan and I were just talking about you."

Crow yawned. "All good things, I hope."

"Jon says you left Belcane in a cage in her tower. Is that right?"

Crow nodded. "You gonna go kill her?"

"Yeah."

Dead silence.

Regis stared at him, face tight with some unidentifiable emotion. There was something building here. Was he supposed to go with it? Crow didn't want to ask, couldn't ask. Could not stand the idea of opening himself up to be rejected. Could not stand the idea they might not want him.

"You should come with us," Regis blurted out. Then he darted a glance at Jonathan. "He should come with us, right?" Jonathan nodded, and Regis focused on Crow again. "It's convenient, I mean."

"Convenient?"

"He's right," Jonathan said. "You can handle yourself. It's not like we'd have to look after you or anything. We can watch each other's backs."

"Right," Regis said. "Exactly. See? He agrees."

"It'll give Regis someone else to harass," Jonathan said.

"Me? You're the bully here."

"Yeah," Jonathan said without missing a beat. "C'mon, Crow. It'll give me someone else to harass."

Crow started to grin. "Am I to be carried off unwillingly, then? A captive?"

"I'll have Jonathan toss you over his shoulder."

"Like a sack of potatoes," Jonathan suggested, "or a demure maiden."

"Well, then," Crow said. He could not stop himself from smiling. "I suppose I'm trapped in the hands of two deadly criminals."

If you encountered EVELYN ELLIOTT, you'd see a small, soft-spoken woman wearing a sundress. At first she seems like a perfectly normal girl. Do not be deceived.

Her hobbies include watching grisly horror movies, torturing her characters, and tending to her flower garden. She enjoys long walks in the park and collecting the souls of small children. Whenever she reads a book, she always roots for the villain.

Avoid her at all costs. Absolutely do not chat with her on Twitter. Do not locate her on Facebook either.

If you dare, visit evelynelliott.com for short stories and deleted scenes.
Website: evelynelliott.com
Twitter: @ev_elliott
Facebook: www.facebook.com/profile.php?id=100011035004723

EVELYN ELLIOTT

BAD MAGIC

Spell Slave: Book One

Morality is relative. At least that's what young sorcerer Regis Teller convinces himself. He's done what he must to survive: working for a witch since he was nine, helping her throw the kingdom into anarchy, and taking his only comfort in her mysterious son, Crow. And soon, Regis is going to commit his first murder.

A do-gooder named Jonathan White has information the witch needs, and it's Regis's job to get that information and slit Jonathan's throat. But then Regis actually meets Jonathan. And Jonathan is perfect—a hero with a passion for justice and little regard for civility.

Lucky for Regis, Jonathan has a weakness for attractive men. Lucky for Jonathan, Regis is fast developing a conscience and a heart. But for Regis, keeping both of them alive at their adventure's end means breaking a magical oath and surviving his ruthless boss—all without telling Jonathan the truth. Falling in love is never easy, especially when everyone involved is lying through their teeth.

www.dreamspinnerpress.com

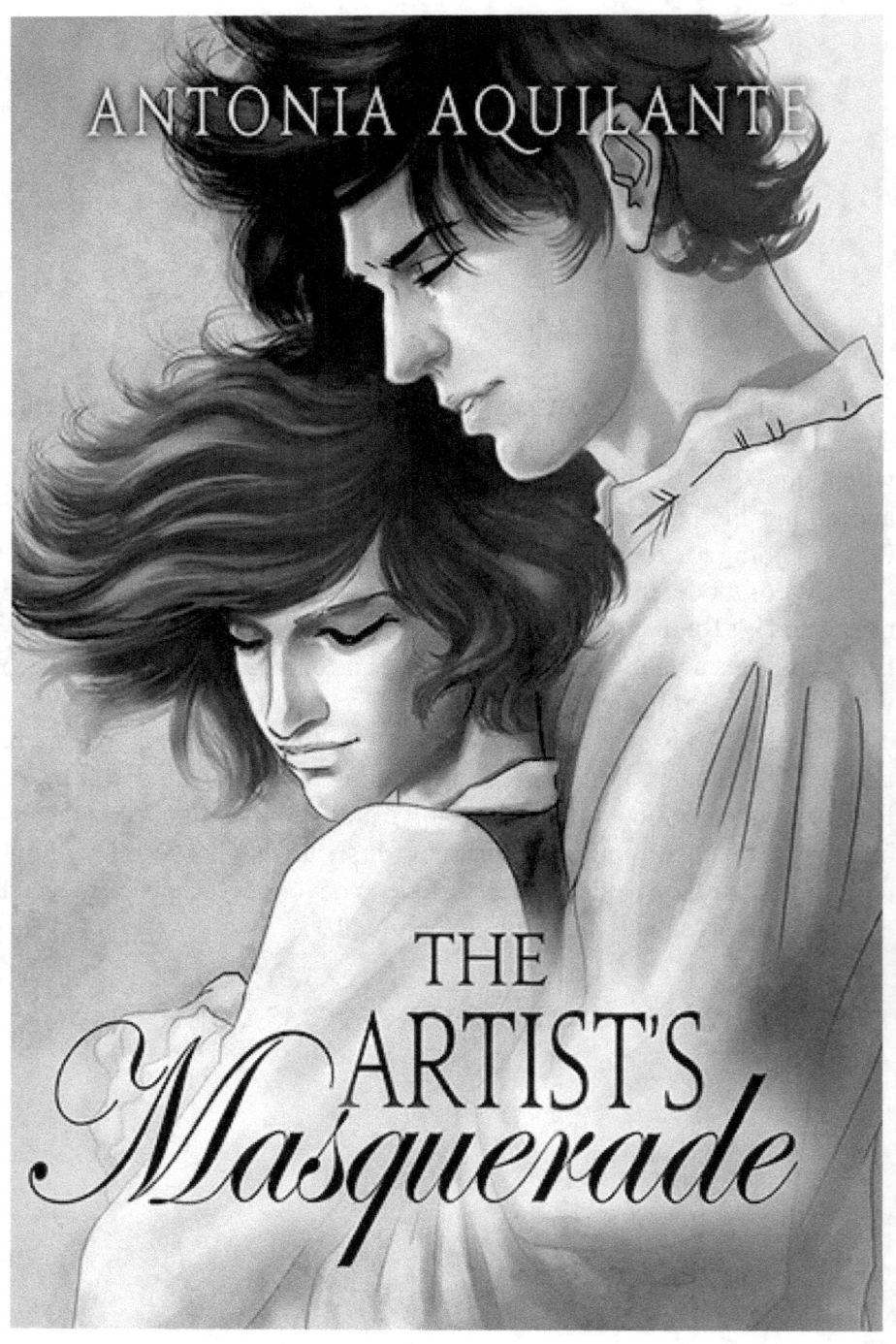

ANTONIA AQUILANTE

THE
ARTIST'S
Masquerade

Also from Dreamspinner Press